Channel Assault

Also by Kenneth Royce

Channel Assault

Kenneth Royce

McGraw-Hill Book Company

New York   St. Louis   San Francisco
Hamburg   Mexico

The author wishes to acknowledge the unstinting help provided by
the Imperial War Museum, London; and the following sources for
factual detail:

Foreign and Commonwealth Office, London
B + I Line, Dublin
The Alderney Museum
Herr Heinz Brocker
The Alderney Story 1939–49 by Michael St John Packe and Maurice Dreyfus
Operation Sea Lion by Peter Fleming
Gehlen by E. H. Cookridge
The Order of the Death's Head: Story of Hitler's SS by Heinz Hohne

And other sources who prefer to remain anonymous.

1 2 3 4 5 6 7 8 9 F G R F G R 8 7 6 5 4 3 2 1

ISBN 0-07-054172-8

LIBRARY OF CONGRESS CATALOGING IN PUBLICATION DATA

Royce, Kenneth.
  Channel assault.
  I. Title.
PR6068.098C4 1982   823'.914   82-7132
ISBN 0-07-054172-8   AACR2

AUTHOR'S NOTE

Nineteen forty-two produced the grimmest days of the war for the Allies. Twice during that year Winston Churchill was in danger of being deposed; that is a matter of record. This is the story of a third attempt to unseat him; a much more sinister and hitherto unpublished effort that could have changed the course of history. For there was another, outside, source of treachery that ran parallel to what was happening behind Churchill's back and which would have had the most devastating effect on Great Britain and the United States of America. Most of the sources of information are German and American. Most of the names are actual. As some of the participants are still alive, however, it has been necessary to make some name changes. There are representatives of both sides of the conspiracy still desperate to cover its traces, afraid of the repercussions that could expose them, even today.

K.R.

PROLOGUE

May 1940

The Hon. James Arden held his father's arm as he helped him along Pall Mall. It was the blackout, and the sky was thick with cloud, the darkness deep and threatening. Mid-May night had fallen early. They had reached the steps of the club and James pulled his father to a halt. 'We're here.'

Lord Arden peered around him. 'How the devil do you know?'

James smiled; his father was far from senile but his eyes had always been weak in the dark. It was a family trait that had somehow missed James, who could see the shadows of the steps and the pale form of the portico pillars rising above them. The two men stood by the railings outside the building.

'Are we alone, James?'

'Quite alone.'

'Are you sure?'

'Absolutely. Only you and I would be idiot enough to stand outside like this.'

'Then I'd better finish what I was saying before we go in.' Lord Arden found the railing and held on. The evening air was mild under the cloud layer. Arden lowered his voice. 'It's a pity Chamberlain has gone in the way that he did. After the Norwegian defeat and the invasion of the Netherlands he had no choice other than to resign. But now that Winston has taken over he'll take some shifting, believe me.'

'Perhaps he can win the war for us quickly.'

'We all hope that, but it would need a miracle.'

The two men lapsed into silence as footsteps approached and a shadowy form passed by.

Lord Arden continued in almost a whisper, 'We would all like a quick victory but it won't happen. Whatever its result it will drag on for years and it will be the economic ruin of this country. We will never recover from it in my lifetime, perhaps not even in yours. Even if we win we will be bankrupt.'

'That's a gloomy picture, Father.'

'It's a disastrous one, but I know what I'm saying.'

'We'd better go in. We're late already.'

'I know.' Lord Arden placed a hand on his son's arm, felt the rings on the uniform sleeve. 'When are they slinging you out?'

James laughed. 'It's not quite like that. They discovered I'm in a reserved occupation. I'll be out next week. Come on, I'll show you the steps.'

'A moment longer, please. And listen carefully. There will come a time during this war when an opportunity for peace will present itself; not surrender, but a real peace. There will come a time, too, when Winston's personal power will wane, when his blood and tears speech will take on new meaning, and the euphoria be left behind. We must be ready for that time.'

The older man paused.

'We cannot stand by and see the country begging for money and watch its standards slip into fatal decline. Meanwhile we must use the time, make our friends, discover our enemies within, and be very, very careful how we do it. But our day will come, believe me. And for the sake of Britain I hope to God it's not too far off. Now show me those damned steps.'

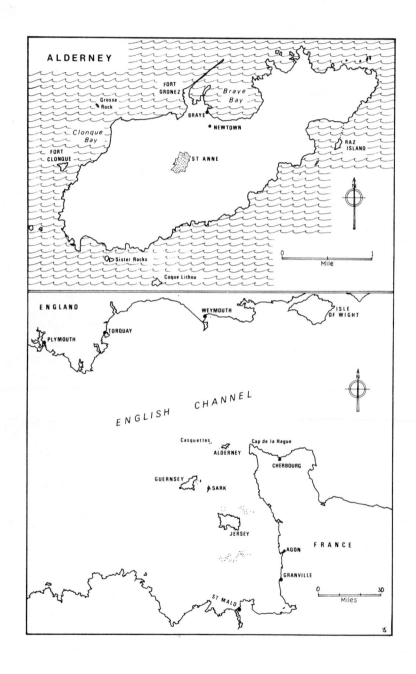

I

June 1940

She died as if she did not care. Fuller was never to forget her expression; it was almost as if she had welcomed death. It seemed that the whole country was fleeing. Refugees teemed towards them in two endless untidy columns, carrying their bundled belongings on backs, or heads, or handcarts, or donkeys. Most were walking; the luckier ones were crammed in trucks; all were heading south. There were tens of thousands of them on roads already jammed with army trucks and troops travelling both ways, some to battle, others wearily away from it. Red Cross ambulances polka-dotted the routes and added to the confusion. Horns blared, voices shouted and screamed, armoured vehicles clanked and poured fumes into the rising dust.

Fuller had never seen such mass despondency. Defeat was on every face. He dare not look at Claudie sitting in the car beside him; he felt her total despair as she watched her countrymen flee.

The Fokker had peeled off in a clear sky and had dived on the columns, screaming down, levelling above them, guns drumming. Donkeys jibbed, drivers swerved, and people screamed as they dived for cover. The plane soared upwards, the pilot giving the wings an arrogant twitch as he climbed away.

The old lady had heard the plane approach but she had stuck to her ground, continued to shuffle on, weighted by her bundle. The young truck driver behind her had not the same nerve; he veered towards her. She probably heard him too, but she was beyond caring. Just before the truck struck her Fuller thought he had glimpsed a fleeting change of expression on her seamed, defiant face, as if at the very last she wanted to live. But by then it was too late.

The truck stopped with the mangled body beneath it; the driver sat white-faced and rigid, unable to grasp what had

9

happened. Refugees on the back of the truck did not move for fear of losing their places. A woman wailed in anguish and rushed forward with others in an attempt to extricate the bleeding corpse.

Fuller pulled up and climbed out with his medical bag, appalled by the overall indifference of the mass. Tragedy had already struck them; what was one more, no matter how close? Some expressed their feeling by vainly shaking fists at the disappearing plane. What was left of the old lady was finally pulled to the roadside, together with her belongings. Her sobbing daughter cradled the dead woman in her arms, and the crowds moved on again.

So did Fuller and Claudie. They were heading into the heart of the human storm; forcing their way against its slow, unrelenting movement. But for this they would have taken as many passengers as the small Citroën would stand. Only nobody wanted to go back. The Germans were too near.

Claudie was deeply affected by the old lady's death. Knowing this, Fuller kept silent, concentrating on easing through, frequently having to pull aside to let army trucks go past. Progress was painfully slow.

'Don't say it,' she said at last.

He glanced over. The breeze was tugging gently at the hair escaping from her headband. She stared straight ahead.

'Say what?' he asked, raising his voice against the clatter.

She smiled faintly; he very well knew *what*, but he had this way of expressing naïvety when the opposite was true. He knew when to produce it and how to soothe her. She thanked God he was with her. 'That we should have left before,' she replied. 'You were right.'

'I'm always right,' he said with a grin, trying to break through her gloom.

She struck his leg, not meaning it. 'That was terrible back there.'

He did not reply. Claudie turned to him, not misled by his silence. She knew that George Fuller felt deeply about a lot of things. He had preferred to work in a small Paris hospital rather than tolerate the general stuffiness of his colleagues in his native London. She could not see him ever conforming; he simply did what he believed to be right, regardless of opinion. Her own presence with him was testimony to that. Her background would worry most men considerably but he seemed unaffected by it. She put her hand to his leg again, this time leaving it there. 'I love you,' she said simply.

'So you should. You've got good taste.'

She dug her fingers into his leg and he bawled out. He glanced up. There was no sign of the Fokker. He knew that he would have to turn off soon. Rommel had crossed the Seine and that was far too close for comfort.

They had set out from Paris that morning having first listened to the early radio news. They had picked up scraps of news en route; none of it good. The streams of evacuees were swelling, slowing them down even more. Again and again they had to pull in to let the military squeeze past, which meant edging into the ranks of the walking who cursed and shouted angrily at them. Every vehicle that could move seemed to be on the roads with hastily tied bundles on roof racks and sagging springs creaking. One could sense the enemy just ahead, and on impulse Fuller took the next turning to Versailles and when they branched off towards Rennes the exodus thinned noticeably. Fuller began to believe that they might be trapped. All he could do was to continue to drive towards the coast. Their only hope lay there. To head south was to be interned in France; it was impossible for him even to consider that possibility – he would sooner die.

Claudie lapsed into a deep depression, angry with herself for holding Fuller back. She had not wanted to leave Paris; but he had perceived the necessity of doing so if they were to remain free. She had placed him in danger by her stubbornness.

They continued with hardly a word passing between them, each preoccupied with their thoughts and fears. It was dark by the time they reached Rennes. Exhausted, dirty and dispirited they booked in at a small hotel.

In the packed bar they listened to the late bulletins coming over the radio every few minutes. Reports were confusing and conflicting; false assurances were misleading. The Germans were advancing. Nothing could stop them. Fuller hung on to that certainty and could think of nothing but escape.

Claudie and Fuller slept little that night. He would have preferred to drive on but there were problems of blackout and car lights were reduced to narrow slits.

They left early the next morning. Taking the St Malo road they branched east at Dol and headed north-west to Granville having rounded the Gulf of St Malo. They stopped at Granville for a break, and checked to find out if any boat might be leaving for England.

There was none available. No one would hire one out knowing there was no chance of it being returned, and willing crews for the highly dangerous double trip were impossible to find.

Fuller suggested to Claudie that they should continue north up the coast. She knew the dangers and sensed his fears but was adamant; 'Where you go, I go.'

'It could be suicidal, Claudie. Don't let me talk you into it if you're afraid.'

'Of course I'm afraid. For you, Englishman.'

They headed north. The roads had crowded up again and they were now driving directly against the stream. There were far more retreating military; haggard-faced troops, disillusioned and often unarmed. The congestion slowed them right down and Fuller had the gut feeling he should turn back. They could now hear the sound of guns and he glanced nervously at Claudie who sat tense and silent. Then suddenly the road was half empty as if the retreating military had come to an end. He seized the opportunity to increase speed and to gain what ground they could. For a while they were elated at their progress. Then, coming towards them, they saw an armoured column.

Fuller slowed. There was something too orderly about the column. What appeared to be two guns, one above the other, protruded from the centrally situated turret of the first tank. Two heads appeared through the hatch.

'Oh, Christ.' Fuller pulled off the road, stopping on its verge. From this angle he could just see the black and white cross below the turret. He felt helpless and bitterly angry with himself; he should have trusted his instinct and turned back. Claudie's hand gripped his on the steering wheel. As the column rumbled nearer the noise was almost deafening.

'The whole bloody German army. Sit tight.'

They waited because there was nothing else they could do. The thinned line of refugees had left the road to squat or lie at its verges, glowering as the massive column went past.

The tanks and troop carriers thundered by as if they would never end. Claudie could not bring herself to look up at the faces of the smiling and singing victors; Fuller could feel her nails digging into the back of his hand.

After the huge column had gone Claudie asked shakily. 'What shall we do?'

Fuller shook his head and sat silently for a moment. Then he started up the engine and turned to her. 'We follow our nose and hope to God that luck is on our side.'

They found a pension just north of Agon a little under fifty miles south of Cherbourg.

It was situated about a hundred yards from the sea. Troop movements could still be seen and the roar of field and tank guns was clear. Small arms fire was intermittent as isolated groups of patriots fought in pockets on the streets until they were wiped out or took cover.

In their small bedroom Fuller removed a Webley pistol from the bottom of his case. He loaded it carefully while Claudie watched in horror. 'They'll kill you if they find you with that.'

'Not if they're on the wrong end of it.' And because he realised that the gun was probably her first close-up of a lethal weapon he reassured her: 'Don't worry. It's for defence.'

He put the gun in the back of his waistband. 'It was my father's. He was a surgeon commander during the last war and spent eleven hours in the sea at the Dardanelles. Winston Churchill gave him a medal for it.' He smiled whimsically. 'They became quite good friends after the old man had told Churchill what he could do with his medal.'

'Is your father still alive? You haven't talked of him before.'

'He's still one of the best surgeons in England.' Fuller suddenly grinned. 'If you hadn't realised it before, I think you should know that, as a family, we must be among the most belligerent non-combatants around. We're an awkward lot.'

Her fear deepened as she saw the strength in his face and the quiet determination in the grey eyes. She was well aware of the reason for his banter. 'Don't do anything foolish. I would rather be dead than without you.'

He caught his breath, surprised at her tone. 'That was a *real* declaration of love.'

'Yes, I know.'

He was deeply touched. 'We've come so far?'

'After living together for eighteen months? After taking me from that place? For me it was a long time ago. I couldn't tell you before.'

'Why not?'

'You might not have recognised the truth. It might have been my stock in trade.'

'Claudie, Claudie. Never look back.'

'You do. You're still haunted by a failed marriage.'

'I'm no good at it,' he said almost brusquely. And then, 'If we don't get away soon it will be too late.' He did not add that it might already be.

The next few days were spent looking for a boat. Occupation was more evident by the day. On the 14th June, Paris fell. Fuller took Claudie out to a small bar and got her mildly drunk and they danced foolishly to old gramophone records.

On the 19th June, still having made no progress, Claudie's jewellery was stolen. It was all she had that was truly her own. Years of sordid living had provided her nest egg, never enough for the final escape, but all she had to show for the hard graft she had chosen. Fuller tried to comfort her but he realised that she was recalling the worst. A life he had not known suddenly showed itself on her face. 'I was going to give it to you. It's the only way we'll get a boat.'

'We'll find a boat. Trust me.' He now knew that his measures would have to be desperate; the risks were increasing every day. He was already surprised that their search had not reached the ears and eyes of the Germans.

By the 21st June they had still found nothing. The net was closing in. That day an armistice was signed at Compiègne to be effective at 1.35 a.m. on the 25th June. France had capitulated. Once under the jackboot the screws would be turned, life would become increasingly difficult. Registration. Identity papers. Obey or die.

Claudie and Fuller had often used the Citroën in their search but it had begun to attract attention and petrol was short. There was reason enough to be on the beaches and sometimes they swam, but now there were always Germans too close, too often.

They found a boat when they least expected it. About five

miles north of the town was a small inlet with a scrap of beach and rock clusters at its rear. Behind the rocks was a rising stretch of gorse and pebbles and beyond that the road which was often busy with troop movement.

The boat was wedged between two huge rocks which formed an open-ended cave, the small entrances of which had been covered with gorse. But for the steep banks rising immediately behind it the crude camouflage must surely have been noticed.

While Claudie sat on the pocket-sized beach to watch the road Fuller dragged some of the gorse away. Squeezing awkwardly between the rocks he found the boat almost wedged upright. He looked back through the gap to see Claudie sitting with her knees up, her skirt pulled high as if she was sunning her legs. It was a signal that someone was near; and it was also an effective distraction. Fuller remained still.

The sun was playing on Claudie's dark hair and her face, shadowing the hollows to display her bone structure. There was even a reflection on the dark lashes. It was a classic pose with her chin up, and he realised just how far she had come from the day of their first meeting in the subdued lights of the club. She pulled her skirt over her knees and he knew it was safe again.

The boat was old and built for inshore use; a small pleasure boat. The modest tank was full and there was a spare can of petrol but he did not know how many miles he might get out of her. Who owned her? Or had the Germans placed it there as a trap?

Fuller eased his way out again, checked with Claudie and carefully replaced the loose gorse. He helped her up and she brushed her skirt down. 'Well?'

'It wasn't made to cross the English Channel in a force eight gale.'

'Will it do?' she persisted.

He recognised the desperation behind the question; they were in no position to choose. 'In this weather, no problem.' He looked up at the road and wished it was further away. 'Let's get back and pack.'

Once in their room, Fuller produced a small atlas. The nearest British territory was the Channel Islands, the biggest of which, Jersey, was about twenty miles off the French coast. The most northerly of the islands was Alderney which lay some eight miles from France. The proximity of the Channel Islands made them vulnerable to German occupation. If they were to head direct for the English coast, which he calculated to be a distance of about a hundred and twelve miles away, they must pass through the gap between Alderney and the most westerly point of the Cherbourg peninsula, Cap de la Hague. To an experienced seaman this might be no problem but Fuller reasoned that he should time the passage through the gap at about dusk. Sufficient light to keep the boat away from rocks but hopefully insufficient to be seen from shore.

Without proper navigational aids he doubted that he could keep the boat central through the gap in complete darkness. There was also the question of engine noise. They had heard rumours that German patrol boats were most active at night, spotter planes performing the daylight patrols.

The risk of running out of fuel restricted their course. If they could reach the gap at dusk it would be dark by the time they reached the open Channel. Then if they headed north they must arrive somewhere near the south coast of England by dawn. It was all a matter of timing. And of luck.

Fuller realised the tremendous weaknesses of the scanty plan. The boat itself was an unknown factor. But he thought that Claudie knew the risks and, like himself, could not face the alternative.

Their faces were now familiar about town and Fuller had helped one of the local doctors with his clinic. But occupation produced both friend and foe; the very act of searching could not have been missed. Checking out of the small pension and settling the bill could be a danger. They could trust no one.

Faced with the actual escape they quickly saw the immediate problems. They would be seen putting their cases into the car, so they decided to leave them in the room. Fuller slipped what he considered to be a fair price for their stay under the lid of one of the cases. He kept the gun, and, being a warm evening, put it in his coat pocket which he placed over an arm. In his other hand he carried his medical bag; the locals were used to seeing that.

When they went to the Citroën they were glad they had taken

such precautions. There were people and troops about and it would have needed only one person to have grown suspicious for their whole plan to be put in jeopardy. They drove south out of town and turned north on to the main coast road as soon as they felt it safe to do so. The main road ran inland of Agon through Coutances, and four miles further on they took a minor road leading down to the coast.

Fuller eased the car off the road and down a scarp near the inlet. The rock tore off the rear section of the exhaust; with the silencer gone the noise was frighteningly loud. He switched off the engine and let her free-wheel. When the Citroën finally stopped, nose down at an acute angle, both he and Claudie knew that it would be impossible to get the car up to the road. There was no way back for them.

The car was now out of sight from the road. Fuller took an empty jerry can from the boot and siphoned off what was left from the tank. With the half-filled can and a container of water he walked the short distance to the hidden boat. Claudie adopted her casual position of sentry. He loaded the water and the petrol and went back for his jacket and medical bag, into which Claudie had crammed some sandwiches she had made in their room.

As he crossed towards the boat again he was aware of the weight of the gun in his jacket. He was still puzzled about the boat. There was no house or building in the immediate vicinity. For a moment he had a pang of conscience but they had gone too far to stop now. He looked up at the rocks and out to sea. The whole place was uncannily deserted and it made him uneasy.

He looked over to Claudie and could see that she was feeling the same. The elevation of the rocks hid the road as he neared them. He placed the bag in the boat, and draped his jacket over one of the seats. There was a locker under the rear seat by the outboard motor but he could not reach it in so confined a space.

He was examining the hull when he heard someone speaking German and he spun round. Claudie was sitting with skirt up to her thighs and arms round her knees. He should have checked sooner. She had signalled and he had missed it. A German soldier was standing by her with his back to Fuller; over one shoulder was a Bergmann submachine gun, the slits in the air-cooled outer casing clearly visible.

Claudie was trying to be helpful in French and she was using her charm. The soldier was quite happy to talk to her even without knowing what she was saying but he could not understand her lack of concern over the car; any fool could see that it was stranded, which meant she was too. He felt that something was wrong. He began to look about him. Inside the tiny cave Fuller reached for his jacket; Claudie was now trying too hard to hold the soldier's attention.

The soldier slowly pivoted, slipping the Bergmann from his shoulder as a matter of precaution. He was beginning to think he might have been ambushed. He saw the cave, the partly removed gorse, and he noticed a slight movement from inside. He brought the Bergmann to a firing position as Claudie kicked out against his legs. He staggered and a short burst from his gun chipped the rocks near the cave entrance. Then he stepped away and re-aligned his gun.

With heart in mouth Fuller fired his Webley, saw the soldier arch back before sinking to his knees and then keel over. Claudie stared, horrified, as she clambered up quickly. The soldier had almost fallen on top of her. She could not take her gaze from the contorted position of his body and the spreading stain on his jacket.

Fuller squeezed his way out, ran to the body, then glanced up towards the road. Had the shots been heard? There was a continual flow of traffic but nothing had stopped. Ignoring Claudie he dragged the body out of sight before checking that the soldier was dead; he was no more than a boy. Fuller looked back at Claudie to see her being sick. He went back for the Bergmann and put it in the boat.

He returned to Claudie, put an arm round her shoulders.

'I feel the same,' he said. 'But we must move.'

She was pale, and holding her mouth. 'Is he dead?'

Fuller nodded. 'If he wasn't, I would have had to finish him.' She must face new realities. For a moment she could not comprehend. She could still see the boy's face and was bewildered and afraid.

'You feel my job is to save lives? I've just saved ours. The rules have changed, Claudie. *C'est la guerre, ma cherie.*'

There was no time to waste. They removed the remaining gorse and heaved and sweated to get the boat from between the rocks. Once out, they pushed it down to the water's edge. There was no point now in looking back to the road. It was obvious what they were doing and they could no longer hide it.

Leaving Claudie by the boat Fuller went back to drag the soldier into the gap where the boat had been. He replaced the gorse and ran back to the boat. They took off their shoes and threw them aboard. When the boat was almost afloat Fuller told Claudie to climb in, gave a final push then followed her.

It took several attempts to get the outboard going and Fuller swore harshly but finally it fired and spluttered awkwardly before picking up. They moved out to sea, silently eyeing the crude tomb of the young soldier. If he had been on patrol he would soon be missed and the threat hung between them.

They were completely vulnerable now. The chug of the small engine was like a series of explosions in the summer air. Anyone watching could not fail to see them. Perhaps they would think they were joy-riding or fishing; who would be mad enough to attempt an escape in a cockleshell? The sea was blue and placid, and crazily it seemed that they had it to themselves.

With nothing to guide them they felt puny against ridiculous odds. Fuller headed for the low sun to get as far away as possible from the shore before turning north. He sat in the stern with one hand on the tiller and watched a sad-faced Claudie huddled on a seat amidships with her skirts up, drying her legs. She saw his glance and pulled her knees together as she flicked hair away from her eyes.

He said nothing but he was pleased at her little act of modesty. Claudie had gone full circle. He looked astern. They were close enough to get a good view of the shore activity; it seemed to have increased even in the short time since they had left. Somebody was bound to see them.

'They'll find him,' said Claudie, focusing on the rocks.

'Don't dwell on it.'

'You killed him with one shot.'

It was not something he wanted to brag about. 'It runs through the family. We're all good shots.' He did not want to explain and she accepted his reluctance; there was still much she had to learn about him.

'We are so alone.' She shivered.

He understood what she meant. It was unnatural. Their

horizon was limited because they were so low. But the skies were empty too, uncannily so, even for seven p.m., a time of natural truce between daylight and night-time air activity. Their progress seemed painfully slow and he began to think he had underestimated the time needed to reach Cap de la Hague. He swung north-west to cut time. It meant losing the shoreline more slowly, and he would have preferred to be out of sight of anyone before making their direction clear. But that was a risk he would have to take.

Saying nothing to Claudie he wondered if he had been so intent on getting away that he had failed to appreciate the real problems of arriving. He was trusting to luck and the odds were long. While he could accept that for himself he had no right to involve Claudie. Yet apart from escaping internment there was a deeper compulsion to go on which he could not explain. He was careful not to look her way.

'It's all right,' she called. 'I'm not a fool. I'd rather be with you and take my chances.'

'I may have miscalculated.'

'You could easily have done that eighteen months ago.'

'But I didn't did I? It's been good together. No regrets?'

'None.'

She lowered her eyes and retrieved the sandwiches from his medical bag. She handed him one and seeing the strain on his face she wished she had a drink to give him as well.

Once they heard planes but did not catch sight of them. They had seen no signs of fishing or of any other vessel. It was as though the whole sea was deserted.

Totally isolated now, land in any direction long since gone, they were all too aware of the increasing danger as they crept north. Now that Britain was out on her own they were heading into the centre of air and sea activity. Fuller had no idea how far out from the French coast they were nor how far from the Channel Islands on the port side.

They had finished their makeshift meal and a small bottle of brandy Fuller had found in the stern locker. He threw the empty bottle into the sea. It reflected like a mirror but it was too late to retrieve it, and they watched it drop behind them, still floating. They chugged on, the noise of the outboard becoming almost hypnotic. The sun disappeared and still there was nothing. The prolonged twilight was reaching its end when they heard the sound of a solitary aircraft. They looked up anxiously at the darkening sky. The aircraft had slowed down and was circling like an eagle. Fuller said grimly, 'It's a Junkers 87.'

Claudie was worried by his tone. 'That's bad?'

'A Stuka. Dive bomber. They have a special attachment which produces a dreadful scream . . .' He tailed off as the plane banked. It descended in an almost casual crablike glide.

'We've been seen.' It was difficult to understand why. The light was not good and they were such a small target. Had something reflected? 'Wave to him.' They both waved as the Stuka swooped low over them in a slow, friendly sort of way. It climbed away until it was almost a speck. Then it banked again and was returning.

Fuller reached for the Bergmann as Claudie stared in horror. The Stuka dipped and the shrill, frightening scream began as the plane made an almost vertical dive.

Fuller rose shakily. 'Over the side. Quick. *For God's sake go.*' The boat rocked violently as he grabbed her arm and thrust her over the side. He fired at the plane but he could not steady the boat and he knew his shots were wild. The scream was now deafening but through it came the rattle of guns. Fuller jumped into the sea and yelled at the top of his voice, '*Dive,*' as Claudie surfaced. He tried to grab her to take her down with him. She broke away and he was not sure what happened next.

He could not see; no light penetrated the water as he tried to gain depth. Something bumped against his legs. When he could hold his breath no longer he surfaced, gasping for air. Worried sick about Claudie, he called out with relief when he found her bobbing close by, shouting his name.

'I'm here,' he yelled and swam to her.

About a hundred feet from them flame and smoke far too big for the boat was erupting from the sea and debris was falling from the sky. For a moment they sank under again. When they surfaced, the boat was gone and light was too poor to pick up outlying traces. The pall of smoke was spiralling, flames gushing through it. There was a dreadful smell of burning oil and rubber.

'What in God's name has happened?' Claudie was treading

water beside Fuller and reached for his hand. 'You must have hit him.'

'No. He misjudged his dive. He was mad to try it in this light.'

'He sunk our boat.'

He was tortured by the despair in her voice. They were bobbing like corks, gulping in mouthfuls of salty water as they tried to talk to each other. 'If we go east we'll reach France? At least *that* we can be sure of . . .'

It was a test for him. 'If that's what you want?'

She clung to him and kissed him hard.

'I'll go where you go.'

'You know the odds?'

'They shorten with you.'

'Stay there.' Fuller broke into a crawl. He had seen something just clear of the flames. The heat was intense as he drew nearer. He made a grab at the floating bundle in front of him. The pilot, held in a pocket of air trapped in his clothes, had been thrown from his cockpit or had made a last second attempt to escape. His face was shattered, blistered by the nearby fire. Fuller did not need to check to know that he was dead.

He worked carefully, afraid to dislodge the air pocket. With some difficulty he finally removed the life jacket which the pilot had not had time to inflate. He then squeezed the flying jacket and the air hissed out and the pilot slipped down beneath the surface to his grave. There was no sign of a second body.

Fuller swam back to Claudie and helped her on with the life jacket. He found the air intake and the valve and turned the top and blew. The pockets of the jacket began to inflate. He closed the valve.

'It'll be awkward but it will keep you afloat.'

The fire had spread across the sea. Beyond it was a faint line on the horizon; so indistinct as to be almost a product of fancy. They struck out into the darkness towards it, leaving behind them the flaming ball that had been the Stuka.

They swam silently, hour after hour, treading water now and again for a few moments rest. The bitter cold began to take hold of their tired and aching limbs, depleting their strength still further. Fuller knew that Claudie was near exhaustion. She had learned to deflate the life jacket to swim and Fuller would inflate it again while they rested. He coaxed, cajoled and swore at her to keep her going while knowing that they could be heading for the open sea eventually to die. Periodically they heard the sound of high-flying aircraft.

Because of Claudie's nearness to exhaustion his own spirits flagged. They rested again and she refused to go on. She was numb with cold, her strength gone. She was lying back in the life jacket when he said, 'Listen. Listen to that.'

'It's no use, George. It won't work. I'm finished, cheri.'

'Listen, damn you.'

Above the soft movement of the sea there was another sound, also soft but rhythmic; sea suctioning on land. Claudie heard it then. It was south-east of them which meant they had passed the point from which it emanated.

Fuller turned towards the direction of the sound. He pulled Claudie with him. Some time later they struck land and struggled up a gently shelving beach. They climbed higher then collapsed, exhausted.

2

They lay on the shore shivering. Fuller cradled Claudie trying to warm her but they were soaked and the night air was crisp. After a while he made her walk up and down until she could take no more. She slept then and he kept watch over her until the sun started to shimmer over the sea. He now knew which side of the island they had landed. He aroused Claudie and she woke shaking with cold. They gazed around as the light increased. It was impossible to believe there was a war anywhere, it was so beautifully tranquil.

'Where are we?' she whispered.

'It must be Alderney. I think the hump at the end of the causeway is called Raz Island. British,' he added pointedly. To their left was a hill and ahead a road. There was a small collection of buildings but as yet no sign of life. To their right, on much higher ground, was an enormous castle some distance away.

The total silence of the island unsettled them; it was as though everyone was hiding. They set off, still wet and reached a road to find lying on it a dead emaciated cat. Claudie caught sight of a blue budgerigar on a bush. And then another.

'Cage birds? In the open?' They reached a smallholding. In a walled yard at the back four cows were lying down. Fuller noticed at once that they had neither food nor water nor had they been milked.

Two dogs lay dead in a pool of blood: an alsatian and a labrador. The farmhouse door was wide open and most windows were smashed. They called but no one answered. Inside, cupboards had been emptied, cans of food swept on to the floor, crockery shattered. They stepped carefully round the debris and squelched their way upstairs. The bed was unmade, sheets pulled back as if people had risen from it in haste. Chests of drawers were open, clothes hanging out and on the floor. Everything they saw filled them with a deep sadness. The place was deserted and ransacked. Outside again, Fuller freed the cattle to fend for themselves. On this clear June morning all they could feel was cold and desolation. There was something terrifying about the silence. Where was everyone?

Fuller said, 'Get out of those wet clothes and see what you can find upstairs.'

He went upstairs with her, made her strip and dry down; the whole time both had the feeling of being watched. Yet there was no one. She found underclothes, skirt and blouse that fitted reasonably well and she took a pair of sandals. He picked up a cardigan for her.

Fuller found socks that fitted and a pair of canvas shoes, but that was all.

They set off again, following the curve of the road, heading south-west. A pack of dogs was tearing a dead calf to shreds. The horror of it transfixed them. Domesticated dogs, a poodle, a collie, a fox terrier, an alsatian, three cross-breeds, all ripping chunks of meat from the carcass.

Everywhere were signs of devastation, wanton damage, desertion, dead and dying animals. They let loose some half starved chickens. Hastily dug shallow graves contained dead animals; one not quite dead when buried had succeeded in getting a paw out before finally dying, pathetic scrabble marks as evidence. Some owners had made time; rough crosses marking small graves. Part eaten meals had been left on tables, open suitcases dumped on beds or floors, bath water not drained off, towels and underwear scattered. In places the road was strewn with clothes.

During this shattering journey, the harrowing picture built up piece by stark piece. The islanders had fled at the drop of a hat. Why else would they leave home so dramatically, killing pets or setting them free, neglecting farm animals, leaving belongings, treasures and meals? *But who had done the vandalising?*

They called at several cottages, houses and farms and the despondency built up. The island was strewn with the flotsam of panic and abject heartbreak. They did not know what to say in this scene of grotesque, silent sadness. Fuller found clothes that fitted him but the physical comfort was nulled by mental numbness. The message the island had left for them was filled with terror.

By mid-day they were hungry but by then had found the quaint little town of St Anne. Claudie almost thought she was in Normandy as they went down the cobbled streets with their colour-washed houses. The devastation was here too, more marked in its compactness. Doors were smashed in or swinging open, shop windows shattered.

They wandered into a pub but the bottles behind the bar had been cleared out and some smashed in the rush. Every inside door was wide open. He searched the cellar. A few bottles remained and he took them back to the bar. Claudie called out from the kitchen and he went in with a bottle and glasses. He poured whisky liberally. 'Medicine,' he said. 'To shake out the damp.'

Claudie found some cans of food and she prepared a scratch meal. They ate in silence in the living room, uneasy and disturbed. They felt like intruders in a bizarre situation they were no part of. For the moment their own plight had diminished.

A whimper made them turn towards the door. A Jack Russell terrier had dragged himself from somewhere outside and collapsed in the doorway. Claudie leapt to her feet, her eyes opaque. Fuller could see the bullet hole from where he sat. He could also see the shallow flanks and the ribs protruding. The dog whimpered again and Fuller rose. He carefully lifted the wounded dog and took it to the bar. He laid it down on a barman's cloth and stroked the short, wiry coat. Large eyes swivelled up with effort and he saw the pain and bewilderment in them. He found another cloth, folded it, held it over the dog's mouth and nostrils.

'*No. No.*'

He swung round, startled by Claudie's scream.

'Go back, Claudie.'

'You're killing it.'

'The dog's in pain.'

'Don't, George. Oh God, please.' Tears were streaming from her, and she pulled at his hands, scratching them.

He took his hands away. Gently he said, 'Look at him,

Claudie. Make yourself. You want him to linger on like that?'

'*He's trusting you*. Please, George, cheri, can't you operate?'

He held his hands out in despair. 'With what? My bag went down with the boat. I need anaesthetics, probes. He must be put out of his misery.'

'*No*.' She pushed him aside and he did not stop her. 'He's lasted this long. He wants to live. Is the bullet still in him?'

The matter-of-fact question made him hesitate. He went to lift the dog but she stopped him, tears trickling down her face.

'I'll hold him, you look.'

The entry hole was clear. He had to bend down, look under the dog while she held it up. 'It might have gone straight through.'

'Can't you tell?'

'I'm not in the best of light. There are signs of rupture. It could have gone through. Small bore. Perhaps a two-two.' When he saw her look of satisfaction, he repeated, 'The dog's in pain, my darling. We don't know what internal damage there is.'

'I'll look after him. I'll nurse and feed him. Perhaps nature will cure him.' When the dog made a pathetic effort to lift its head she burst into tears again.

'All right. I'll help you.'

They found blankets, bandages, biscuits which Claudie crushed and milk and water which they fed into the little dog with an eardrop plunger they had discovered and cleaned out. Fuller bathed the wound and found some aspirin which he mixed with the dog's food.

Claudie gently stroked the smooth head and the liquid eyes showed gratitude.

'While you look after him I'll look around. We need more food and clothes.'

He went in and out of ransacked shops. All told the same desperate story of hurried departure. He reached the quay where the breakwater fingered out into the bay. A pathetic abandoned half circle of cars told the final story; bicycles, a motorcycle and another with sidecar. He could not know that over fourteen hundred islanders had been picked up on the 23rd June; that for three days from the 25th Guernsey boats had come and loaded the best of the cattle for safe keeping. Also that a French lifeboat had called; it was as well that he did not for it could have prompted an ugly answer to the question of damage and theft.

Anything in the way of a seaworthy boat had gone, some scuttled. He gazed down at the scene, thoughts of escape rising strongly again but now finding an obstacle. Could he subject Claudie to another terrifying experience? He knew how lucky they had been in the sea. He had not explained to her the tremendous braking power the sea has on the velocity of bullets. And then to strike this tiny island afterwards had been a miracle; it was only three and a half miles long.

He had acted impulsively, regardless of common sense and reason; it was almost as if they had been drawn here by some strange quirk of fate. He shuddered, yet it was warm. A deep feeling of foreboding spread through him and he held it there trying to understand it. He gazed inland without knowing why. The feeling was so strong that he could not understand why his reaction was not to seek escape immediately; instead it was acting as an anchor, as if, whatever it was, he must see it through.

He shook off the feeling with difficulty but a strange warning remained. The empty island was affecting him; he strode back to town but he could not completely get rid of the conviction that the island had yet to offer real terror.

He found the small jail and the islanders' weapons that had been locked inside. He discovered an old Colt .45 with some ammunition in a drawer which he stuffed into his pockets. He then climbed inland towards the cliffs in the south and located the tiny deserted airport. A few cows lay basking on the humped runway. The unnatural loneliness forced his thoughts inwards again, to the destruction, the unreality, the isolation. He was standing on what was no more than a large rock in the English Channel. He could see the faint smudge of the German-occupied French coastline less than nine miles away.

His gaze swept south to the abundance of sea campion, thrift and prostrate bloom that coloured the cliffs with so much life, but it failed to lift him. On the return walk he tried to close his mind to the death and neglect and the gusting breeze and to concentrate on what they should do.

The dog was sleeping and Claudie had gathered food and fuel, and found a primus on which she cooked eggs and warmed canned vegetables. Afterwards they moved into a house nearby, small and snug, carefully carrying the dog with them. Claudie changed sheets and pillowcases and when they were finally in bed they clung to each other as if for the first time; or perhaps the last. Everything, now, had quite a different meaning.

The next morning Fuller sounded Claudie out about leaving. She said she needed to hang on for a day or two to regain her nerve. He guessed that she really wanted to give the dog a chance but kept his silence. They continued to explore and Fuller kept an eye open for any craft big enough to reach England.

Claudie named the terrier Blanco for no reason she could think of except for its colour. That same day, Sunday, 30th June, two German aircraft flew south over Guernsey where the first one landed, before the second took a wide sweep over Alderney, circling the island slowly.

Fuller and Claudie watched it through a window. The engine noise was shattering after the silence. They now searched desperately for something seaworthy but it was increasingly clear that they were trapped. Claudie noticed that Fuller accepted the fact almost as if he had decided it was their destiny. It was not like him.

Finding an isolated house on high ground some distance from the little township they started to stock up with clothes, food, a cow, chickens, becoming reasonably self sufficient. Fuller took all the liquor he could find and began to drink heavily.

On the 2nd July, from the cover of bushes west of the airport, they watched the Luftwaffe land. They missed, however, the arrival of the seaborne reinforcement from Cherbourg.

That night George Fuller got drunk. When Claudie saw him load the Colt she thought he intended to take on the garrison by himself and pleaded with him to sober up. He reassured her, hung an old reefer jacket on the back of the dining-room door, placed a bottle and glasses on the table at the other end of the room and sat facing the door obliquely.

Claudie was sitting on a stool beside him not knowing what he intended to do. He poured drinks, and raised his glass to her.

An opened box of ammunition lay near the bottle of whisky. With feet up on the table, tilted back in his chair, he fired at the silver buttons on the jacket.

Claudie sat rigid, afraid to move, afraid to speak; *he was firing through the gap between his feet.* His eyes were screwed, his hand incredibly steady. The gun blasted out again and again, filling the room, echoing, the door splintering. It was the loudest noise the island had known for days. Speechless, she noticed that only one button remained. With great concentration, he broke the cylinder, shook the empty cartridge cases into his hand and reloaded slowly.

The last button was elusive; though he scythed it once it stuck to the jacket. He was still trying when the door burst open and two German soldiers pointed machine pistols at him. Claudie screamed.

3

June to October 1942

In a jubilant Berlin, not far from the Chancery, Admiral Wilhelm Canaris summoned his chief of staff and most trusted friend, Major General Hans Oster. Oster entered the office quietly, aware that his chief had just returned from a meeting with the Führer. He at once noticed the sober thoughtfulness of Canaris, a small complex man, but one he admired.

Oster well recognised that a lesser man than Canaris would have lost his position a long time ago. Hitler neither liked, nor really trusted him, and Himmler and Walter Schellenberg had been waiting for the right opportunity to oust Canaris from his position as head of the Abwehr for a long time; it was not until April 1945, on a cold dawn when Canaris, alongside Oster, was hanged naked at Flossenbürg Prison, that they finally succeeded.

Canaris glanced up from a memorandum, indicated a chair which informed Oster that his chief wanted to talk rather than simply pass on instructions. Canaris said carefully, 'I want you to go to Ireland.' Noticing Oster's surprise he smiled briefly. 'It has to be you, Hans. The Führer has made it clear that it must be someone totally reliable. You will meet an Englishman. Lord Arden.'

'The name means nothing to me. Should it?'

'No. His pedigree is long but he's a financier who has always remained in the shadows. He's in Debrett and that's about all we can find on him. He had interests in this country but always operated by proxy; competent minions. He's extremely wealthy and he's powerful. So we are informed.'

'Am I allowed to know why I'm meeting him?' Oster was the only man on Canaris's staff who could speak to him with such directness. But even he ensured that his tone was right; he knew that he was talking to one of the cleverest men in Germany;

31

anyone who could thwart Heinrich Himmler, supreme head of the Sicherheitsdienst, had to be.

'Peace,' replied Canaris, eyeing Oster closely for reaction. 'Peace with England.'

Oster stiffened, sitting almost to attention. Between Canaris and Hitler that word was an antithesis. Even Oster did not know the full facts, but he did know that Canaris was suspected of tipping off Britain about operation Sea Lion, the invasion of Britain. None of it could be proved.

But Canaris was walking a constant tightrope and as head of German intelligence he had many enemies. Even after the Gestapo had started the rumour of him being a homosexual he still remained in office and seemed outwardly unaffected. Canaris had always been aware that he was part of the old military aristocracy which Hitler was determined to weed out.

Canaris was also known to admire the English, but Hitler himself had a sneaking respect for them and provided they were considered the enemy it was tolerated. Oster knew all this and he suspected Canaris of keeping secret files should matters suddenly go against him.

'The Führer is putting out peace feelers? With the war going so well?'

'The *English* are putting out peace feelers.' Canaris sat back.

'Churchill?' Oster could not believe it.

'If Churchill knew about it we would not now be discussing it.'

Oster was slightly baffled. 'This is why I am to meet Lord Arden? What authority does he have?'

Canaris considered his words carefully. 'Discussions have been going on for some time. From last year in fact. Because of his knowledge of German and Germany, Lord Arden has been able to make tentative approaches through me. But it takes time and it is, of course, impossible to conduct a serious discussion without direct confrontation. The Führer has been kept informed and has finally decided that it should be looked at more closely.'

'Yet we know nothing about this man, Lord Arden?'

'We're not even sure of what he looks like. However, he is on the fringe of the SIS, that we know, and that made his contacting us somewhat easier.'

'The British Secret Intelligence Service? They use him?'
'Almost inevitably, I would say.'
'A traitor?'
'It would seem that he is a deep patriot. A thorough English-man. A great friend of Churchill himself, I believe.'

Oster took this in slowly. 'You are saying that an individual assessment of how England's interests can best be served is a patriotic viewpoint?'

Canaris shrugged. 'I wish I knew more about the man. These powerful backroom men are difficult to estimate. What I do know is that the Führer wants a follow through. I will arrange the meeting for you. You will then come back and report in detail direct to the Führer. This meeting may take a little time to arrange. One can appreciate Lord Arden's need for total secrecy.' As Canaris watched his friend's face he added, 'Don't try to work it out in advance, Hans. It will probably come to nothing.' And then, as Oster rose, 'I'll say it for you. The Führer well knows that I too would like peace with Britain. On our terms, of course. He knows that in our hands this particular issue will be well and thoroughly investigated.' He paused thoughtfully. 'What *we* don't know is what the Führer himself has in mind. It is probably far removed from anything Lord Arden has conceived. Watch your back, Hans and give the English lord a hint to do the same.'

Lord Arden stood by the Adam fireplace, above which hung one of Winston Churchill's paintings. He was very fond of the painting and gazed up at it now. He had seen Churchill only that day in this very room and had well understood his friend's disconsolance; a mood the great man would portray only in private.

There was nothing to uplift the nation on any major front. In North Africa Rommel had the British pinned back in pockets linked by minefields. Tobruk had not yet fallen but it was a miracle it still held. Since Pearl Harbor in December 1941 America had been reeling, and Britain had fared no better. Guam, the Philippines, Hong Kong, Singapore, Rangoon, Bataan, Malaya, Wake Island had all gone with others. Darwin had been bombed. The US Pacific Fleet on striking back in February against Wake and Marshall Islands had accomplished little but the action had at least raised the badly sagging morale, as had Midway.

For the Allies these were grim days. And the Germans rolled victoriously through Russia.

All this merely confirmed what Arden had always believed would happen. He felt no satisfaction at being right. But he was totally satisfied about what should be done, even if that meant going against old friends. Something had to be salvaged from the wreck; it might already be too late.

In Parliament powerful voices were baying at Churchill. There were many ill-pleased with the way he was handling matters and attempts had been made to oust him. Churchill was coping with the criticism and the political machinations behind the scenes and he was determined to hang on but he was at his weakest.

Lord Arden was a tall, thin, stooped man of some refinement. One of the common interests he shared with Churchill was art in most of its forms; the two families had been friends for generations. He was thin-faced to the point of gauntness, cheekbones, ankles, knuckles, all projected, yet he was steel hard. A man whose intelligence was never suspect and whose cold logic would at times be frighteningly accurate. His appraisals invariably left much food for thought. His weakness, though he saw it as a strength, was an almost total lack of emotion. He was a financial wizard and could wield vast influence. He was also a linguist of note and had been of some value to the Secret Intelligence Service.

In SIS circles he was known as a 'fringe bod', as many men of talent co-opted by them during the war were called. They served an undoubtedly useful purpose without sharing the real secrets. Arden knew the head of the SIS, Major General Sir Stewart Menzies, on a social basis though these days they rarely met. He also knew the head of MI5, Sir David Petrie, but even at Arden's eminent level he was being used without being an accepted part of the intelligence organisations. He both understood and approved, the arrangement.

It was not difficult for James to see that this evening his father was quite excited. There was no emotional sign, but he could judge by little mannerisms, like the way he tilted his sherry glass before sipping, and the way he said, 'I hate the mugginess in this room with those damned curtains drawn.' His father's mood had nothing to do with the curtains or the blackout.

The Honourable James Arden had his father's height without his stoop. Now twenty-five, it was more than two years since he had handed in his RAF uniform. He was exempt from national service because he was already a brilliant engineer, and possessed much of his father's financial genius; an almost unique combination.

There was something else they shared; both were self effacing in the extreme. Neither made speeches nor wanted fame or public image. Fundamentally they were incredibly shy, but both wanted power and knew how to get it quietly.

James was good looking, although with rather sharp, hard eyes, which feature he could counteract with an easy smile. Each only fully and completely trusted one man: the other. They concerned themselves with hard reality to a degree that amounted to a serious flaw.

James was relaxed in his chair, crossed legs stretched out; a false image of indolence. He observed shrewdly, 'It's cropped up again?'

'It was never dead. But communication has always been difficult. I think we're in business. I think we can make a peace treaty with Hitler attractive enough to depose Winston.'

James pulled himself upright and put his drink down; his father never jumped to conclusions. 'Obviously they've been in touch.'

'They want a meet in Eire.'

'Isn't that dangerous for you?'

'Not from the Irish. You mean this end? It will be noticed, of course, but I'll do it officially.' He smiled briefly. 'I'll apply to Stewart Menzies for an official travel warrant.' Arden noted his son's look of doubt. 'Much better than just pushing off to Ireland for MI5 to note or find out later. Winston's always wanted a listening device inside Hitler's head; I'll have to convince Menzies that I stand a good chance of providing one.'

James was still not convinced. 'Why should he believe you?'

'I have a list of top people our lot dealt with before the war. Some may have been interned but by no means all. He'll recognise the truth of that. It's best to do it openly.'

James could not recall when his father had not been right over really important matters.

Arden said carefully, 'I'm not being entirely devious. I would very much like to know what Hitler has in mind. Talking to his acolytes is not the same as knowing what he's really thinking. His problem is the people around him. They distrust everyone and each other. Yet without Hitler they would collapse. Winston has always been aware of this. He'd like to provoke *open* dissent at the top.'

'And wouldn't *we* collapse without Winston?'

Arden stared at his son coolly; he knew how the question was meant. 'Earlier this year our chiefs of staff formed a small inter-service committee to write an appraisal on what would most affect British morale. In essence, they reported that the elimination of Churchill would have a disastrous effect.' Arden put his glass down on the wide marble mantelshelf. 'An awful lot of murky water has passed under the bridge since that report. Storm clouds perpetually build up over his head. And there is a vast difference between elimination and discrediting.'

'Discredit a living God? An alternative offer to the people would have to be damned good.'

'We both know that. Winston recognises that at the moment he's at his weakest. That report is unlikely to stand up now.'

James rose to join his father by the empty fireplace. 'You still happy about your support?'

'You should know the answer to that. I've been careful in selection. And I've not been mean where money is a factor. We're talking about a hand-picked, highly influential, few.'

'It only needs one to get cold feet to ruin everything.'

Arden eyed his son suspiciously. 'Don't beat about the bush. You're talking of Barstrom.'

'I think he was glad about a stalemate. Now things are moving again he may prove to be a mistake.'

'It need not be a calamity. The others would close ranks. We're all experienced enough to do it effectively. Just now, this is not the only plot against Churchill.'

'It's the most ambitious; the most far reaching.'

'Barstrom worries you?'

'I think we'll have enough on our plates without the embarrassment of him.'

Arden was silent. From time to time he glanced at his son. 'We've never hedged with each other before, James.'

James took his time to reply. 'We've never before contemplated what we have at present in mind.'

Arden did not duck the issue.

'The whole future of the country is at stake. I hate what we have to do to Winston but we believe it's best for everyone else. The people are tired of war, tired of losing it, of living rough, of seeing no end to it. An honourable peace would solve all that.'

'Now it's you who's hedging, Father.'

'No. We both know it gives us power where we most think it should be. The aim is not dishonourable.'

'Barstrom.' James reminded his father.

'There is a war on, James. Casualties occur.'

They looked at each other quite squarely. 'Are we right, Father?'

'I believe implicitly in what we're doing. We either back out or continue on with all that implies.'

James nodded slowly. 'All right, I'll see to it.'

Arden laid a bony hand on his son's shoulder. 'I'm sorry you've been landed with it.'

'I don't intend to do it myself.'

'Then be very careful who you use.'

'It's not that I'm afraid to do it. I simply think I'd make a bloody mess of it.' James glanced at the buhl clock. 'Don't worry. I've had time to give it some thought.'

James Arden left the Sloane Street house to find himself in total darkness. He was used to this, as were all Londoners, and he quickly acquired his night vision. He walked to the Underground station at Sloane Square, skirting the roped off and ribboned heap of masonry where a bomb had exploded.

The Underground contained a mass of people, most of them uniformed. The smell was stale with the weight of human bodies. James felt conspicuous in civilian clothes but nobody gave him a second glance. Like his father, he possessed the capacity to become part of the backcloth of any scene. The train was crammed full when it came in and although he let it go the next was no better.

When he eventually reached Piccadilly Circus he picked his way carefully up Shaftesbury Avenue. It seemed ridiculous for so many people to be about so late at night and in a total blackout. The young were enjoying themselves before it was too late; the degree of camaraderie was high and the street girls were thriving. Hearing became an essential part of progress.

He turned left up Wardour Street and wound his way through to Greek Street. Being alone, he was accosted several times from the dense blackness of deep doorways. He walked on. It was not that he was against women or had high morals where they were concerned; he had simply inherited his father's singlemindedness. First things first.

He went down some steps to a sub-basement and opened a door. It was still dark inside but he groped forward, found the blackout drapes and went through them to another door. Light, noise and stale smoke immediately assailed him. The lights were subdued and barely penetrated the smoke pall which thickened like cloud near the dirty ceiling of the cellar. Tables and chairs were crammed in. Somewhere in the middle was a tiny dance floor, the heads of the dancers moving above the general mêlée. A small, but very active bar was in the far corner. The cellar was crowded; the music came from a gramophone near the bar. The laughter was standard, but the shouting and talking came in many tongues.

James squeezed his way through to the bar, waited his turn to get a drink from the overworked barmaids, and continued on to the opposite corner to stand against the wall. There was nowhere left to sit but it did not worry him. He had been here a few times before because he believed in being prepared.

The assortment of uniforms in the cellar, both male and female, interested him. The dark blue of the Royal Australian Air Force against the paler blue of the RAF. Shoulder flashes listed the sad history of present day Europe. Free Poles, Free Czechs, French, Belgians, Dutch, Norwegians, Danes, and Americans: they were all represented in this packed almost airless cellar. James began to pick out the regulars he had come to know. And they began to pick him out: he was an easy touch, always good for free liquor and he always bought liberally. They did not care that he was not in uniform; perhaps it was conscience money he lashed out, but he was never short of it.

The barmaids had quickly learned to overload his bill. James never complained.

He went through the routine as he had done before, slaps on the back, for he's a jolly good fellow. He weathered the amorous attentions of an ATS girl. His concentration was on one man, a slight, dark eyed sailor who one night had drawn a knife when a vicious brawl had broken out. The knife had been smothered by the sheer weight of numbers of those who jumped the man. James had never forgotten the look on his face, the frustrated evil quickly covered up as he realised the odds were against him. Since then the other regulars kept away from him and, for the most part, he would stand by the bar, drinking and eyeing the girls with increasing lust. He was a Free French naval rating.

Most of the Free French gathered in the York Minister, the French house, in Dean Street, which was actually run by a delightful and colourful Belgian named Berlimont. It was clear that the sailor was ostracised by his own compatriots.

Brawls were not uncommon in pubs and clubs where there were so many rivalries and uniforms. The police were rarely called in unless there was damage. And if they were the rival factions would close ranks in attitudes of total innocence to protect their comrades. Even from murder.

A few nights after the brawl James had witnessed, a Belgian soldier had been found stabbed in the back in Dean Street. His killer had not yet been found. James had remembered that it was a Belgian soldier that the French sailor had attacked in the club. It could mean nothing. But he had made a mental note.

He bought a drink for the sailor who told him his name was André. It might have been but it had been volunteered in an evasive way. James had the strong feeling that the sailor was Algerian French. They conversed in French. The fact that James had cornered André also helped drive away some of the hangers-on looking for free drinks.

James was careful not to leave with André but waited for him outside the club by arrangement. He let it be known that he wanted a favour and that money was involved. André knew that James had plenty.

They walked in the darkness, somehow avoiding others. André had drunk a lot but he was a hardened drinker and never seemed to pass beyond a certain stage of insobriety. He might become vicious with drink but he never staggered. They reached Shaftesbury Avenue. Crowded taxis with slits for lights fumbled past.

'How much do you charge for killing a man?' It was voiced in such a way that it could be taken as a joke or seriously. Either way, James's reading of André was that he would not be offended, and he was right.

André was silent for a while, a small dark shape exhaling liquor fumes close to James. He laughed a little. 'You serious?'

'I'm not short of cash. And I'm not talking about the little I carry with me.'

André knew that it was time to think more clearly.

'It depends how difficult it is.' No histrionics, no hedging. James knew that he had chosen well. This was not something new to André.

'It will never be easier. Name a fee.'

'I need to know who and where.' The statement was ice cold. No surprise. No qualms. Who and where. The voice of experience.

'Are your quarters far from here?'

'I'm in billets. I catch the tube. The last one is soon.'

'If you miss it I'll get you a cab and pay the fare. I don't want any mistakes.'

André did not reply to that. 'Half before. Half after.'

'You've got to name a figure.'

'I will when you tell me more.' Motive was not important, money was; it had to be thought out. Then a slight interest. 'You been watching me?'

'You appear to have the qualifications.'

'You're a good judge. You'd better keep it to yourself.'

'We'll both be guilty. After it's done we won't see each other again.'

'Okay. Now tell me.'

Sir Michael Barstrom sat beside James in the car. 'I don't know how you can drive like this. I can't see a damned thing.'

'Vitamin A. I eat a lot of carrots.' James had intended it to sound amusing to allay Barstrom but it fell flat.

'It's a damned inconvenient time. I hope it's justified.'

'Father will explain. He's made contact again. This time where it matters.'

Barstrom gave up trying to peer into the darkness; he could not see a thing and could not understand how James could. He sat back disgruntled. 'I thought it had died the death.'

'The conditions are right, wouldn't you say?'

'I don't think it's been thought through properly.'

'You did before.'

'I've given it a lot more thought since then. It amounts to treason.'

'Only if the chief authority of the state holds office with the will of the people. A matter of interpretation.'

Barstrom did not answer, feeling that he had said too much. But he was clearly unhappy. Then he said, 'Someone might talk y'know.'

Yes, you, you bastard, thought James. You are our one mistake. Over the last four nights he had constantly examined his doubt with regard to his passenger. Now he was satisfied, not with what must happen next for there would be no pleasure in it, but with the need for it to protect his father and his friends. 'Father will fill you in,' he said lightly. 'You can sort it out between you.'

'Are you sure this is the right way? It seems to be taking a hell of a time.'

'That's because of detours. There's still a lot of bomb damage around, streets closed off and some I'm not happy about. Don't worry, the petrol ration is too meagre to encourage one to go unduly out of one's way.'

For a while James himself thought he had lost direction. It was so difficult to find landmarks. Then he did and he breathed again. It was the second time this night that he had made the trip. He pulled up.

'Are we here?' Barstrom peered out of the side window, 'Can't see a thing.' He pushed up his glasses.

James climbed out, saw the shadow by the broken wall, and went round to open the door for Barstrom.

'Are you sure this is it? Doesn't look like Sloane Street to me. My God,' Barstrom turned to James, 'have you got us lost?'

He was never to speak again. As the knife went in his portly frame arched before his knees gave way. Even in the darkness

41

James could see the podgy face grimace in agony and the mouth open in a silent scream of excruciating pain. And then the knife was in and out again and Barstrom was dead, collapsing as if boneless.

James could not speak. André said, 'The money.'

James groped for it, handed it over with a shaking hand. He turned blindly to enter the car. André called sharply. 'You'll have to help me.' As he spoke he was removing Barstrom's wallet, ring and watch.

James gasped out, 'That's your job.'

'You must help me get him on to the wall. I'll see to the rest.'

They lifted the portly body with difficulty. When it was on the wall, André pushed and it fell into the deep rubble-strewn cavity of a bomb site. 'I'll see that he's well covered.' André climbed over the wall as James went back to his car. Before climbing in James was violently sick. He had not expected such a reaction. But then he had not expected to see Barstrom actually die.

The body was not discovered for another three years and then the remains took some time to identify. The tailor's labels on the clothes had decayed through constant damp, the rain penetrating the mounds of rubble that had covered the body until a mechanical digger shovelled it clear. The motive was assumed to be theft.

The disappearance of a top civil servant did not cause an immediate sensation; there was so much more important news. But the mystery gradually gained impetus as it remained unsolved, and then eventually disappeared from public speculation.

Two days later, aware of the shock his son had received, but passing no comment, Lord Arden decided to take his next step. He felt no sympathy for James; it was part of growing up. He knew of at least one suicide in which he himself had played a major part. Before the war a rival tycoon whose business he had eventually crushed had killed himself. Arden had felt no remorse nor acknowledged that he was to blame. The blame lay clearly in the weakness of the man himself; he had not been able to face defeat or the ruins about him.

He made an appointment to see Major General Sir Stewart

Menzies and met him in his club in Pall Mall. Over lunch Arden was quite open over his contact with Berlin and his need to go to Eire.

Menzies was one of the most astute and knowledgeable spymasters in the world. His contribution to the war had been enormous, his spy network the envy of every nation including Germany. He was held in awe by the Americans who had only recently set up the OSS.

Arden knew the risk he was taking but felt it would be a far greater one to operate clandestinely. When it came down to it he would be the only man on the spot and he had full confidence in his own nerve to carry the rest through. Arden's ability matched Menzies; it was simply different. What made it easier for him was that the two men had known each other for years. Arden's profound patriotism and interest in his own country was well known to Menzies.

'How do you rate your chances?' Menzies was toying with the meatless dish.

'I don't know. Hitler has his enemies within the hierarchy. It's a question of finding the most likely. I'm probably flying a kite.' He chewed reflectively. 'But it's worth a try.'

'Of course. Don't expect too much. If there is someone near enough to Hitler to keep us advised it would be of enormous help. Not easy to do. I've tried it. He plays one off against another so there's never a clear picture.'

'But you've succeeded, wouldn't you say? In another direction?'

Menzies did not bite. 'Communication will be your problem. I may be able to help if you establish a high level contact, but until then I won't risk my men.'

Arden acknowledged the warning. 'I simply wanted you to know. I want no crossed wires.'

Menzies nodded. 'I understand. You'll want a travel warrant then?'

'Only to keep the matter on record.' Arden smiled. 'I'm not short of the fare.'

Menzies smiled back. 'Neutral or not we have many friends in Ireland! I'll see if I can get them to keep out of your way. Let me know when.'

Menzies was thoughtful after Arden had left him. British

intelligence had broken the German codes, a fact Arden should not know, yet his lordship was in touch with the Germans, and Menzies had been advised of no messages relating to it. Menzies decided to check on intercepted coded German messages but his guess was that Arden was receiving information through one of the neutral London embassies, and that could mean by courier. If that were the case Arden was indeed flying high; high and dangerous and possibly via Madrid.

4

Fuller stared out of the window and watched the German troops. Claudie picked up Blanco and joined him, noting the tightness of his jaw. Two years of captivity had not eroded his bitterness; at times frustration had pushed him to the point of recklessness. Claudie was constantly worried about him. One day he would go too far and they would shoot him. From time to time she had warned him, playing on what would happen to her if he was not there. This would sober him for a while. But that was not her only fear. Ever since they had been there she had worried about the soldier Fuller had killed. The car must surely have been found and traced to him. Even now, after so long, it hung over her. They should have taken the body in the boat and dropped it in the sea. It was easy to be wise after the event.

When the Germans had first burst into their room Fuller had been saved by his own drunken state. Totally relaxed, he had gazed up at them blearily, nodded gravely, laid the gun on the table and had passed out.

For some time he was not the same man. He lost spirit as the odds built up against them. She stirred him up, upbraided him, called him a lousy Englishman and used her experience to rouse him sexually, anything to get his mind off defeat. It took months to get him back to near normal but she achieved it. And he was well aware of what he owed her.

The occupation had become progressively sinister. The Lloyds bank in Victoria Street, in the only town, St Annè, had become the island headquarters, the Feldkommandantur 515.

Seven elderly Britons had been found scattered round the island; they had decided to stay and to farm and they kept to themselves.

From the moment it was discovered that Fuller was a surgeon he had been put to work as a general practitioner. The garrison was originally too small to warrant a resident German army doctor. As the garrison grew, and Fuller still coped, there was appreciation from the German medicos who were being worked to capacity on the larger islands. The work helped him retain his sanity. Neither Jersey nor Guernsey had mass evacuated as Alderney had and British work parties were allowed in on a daily basis from the larger occupied island of Guernsey to help re-establish agriculture on Alderney. But these parties were now being drastically thinned out, and now there were some extremely disquieting developments.

Fuller learned from German military patients that in the previous October, 1941, Hitler had ordered the island to be converted into an impregnable fortress. It was difficult to understand why.

The initial benign administration had long since gone. The SS were now evident in large numbers. During this period, the spring and summer of 1942, Fuller had the strong feeling of something evil building up around him. He could find no other description for what he sensed. When he talked it over with Claudie he was not surprised to find that she felt it too. He recalled the sensation he had experienced shortly after they had first landed, the strong impression of terror that had so disturbed him.

This feeling persisted sufficiently for him to try to curb his sometimes openly defiant attitude to his captors. But it also filled him with the urge to find out what was going on. He knew that he was protected by his usefulness to them but as their numbers grew they would have to provide their own doctors. What would happen then?

Two men concerned him most; an SS captain named Heyden who made no pretence of his lust for Claudie, the only woman on an island of men, and Captain Carl Hoffman. Hoffman had been island commandant for a while but had been succeeded in February by Major Zuske. Hoffman had however remained as tactical specialist, a designation that was to become meaningless. At no stage did Fuller trust him.

An increasing shroud of secrecy covered the island like thickening fog. The whole pattern was changing. Civil affairs ceased, which was ominous, and now there was only the military. Information became increasingly difficult for Fuller to acquire and soon he realised he was receiving none. Because of his easy-going nature, his refusal to stand on his dignity, some of the lower ranks who had attended his clinics had grown to like him and had been useful in passing on scraps of news. All this changed almost overnight. Orders had been given; something which he could not find out about was going to happen.

The severe cut-back of the working parties from Guernsey coincided with a general tightening of security. It became clear that whatever was to happen on the island was knowledge to be kept within its shores. Fuller's patients not only clammed up when he gently probed for news but became clearly uneasy.

A different kind of cargo began to arrive at Braye Harbour, near St Anne's. Repeated shiploads of cement arrived, and with it the first batches of slave labour.

Fuller was sickened by what he saw. Officially he was no longer allowed near the harbour so he had to be extremely careful he was not caught spying on the influx of workers. The slave labour comprised mainly of French Jews and some German political prisoners. They were pitifully clad, some almost naked and barefooted. Many wore sacks, holes cut out for arms and legs. All were grossly undernourished.

Camps being built for them were not yet ready so, in Newtown and Braye, they were crammed into houses which had been wired in. Captain Carl Hoffman was promoted to major and took over the labour force. Under his auspices was placed another sinister arrival; the TODT Labour Organisation.

A frantic effort was now being injected into the start of the fortifications, which Fuller and Claudie discussed endlessly without arriving at a conclusion. If such an effort was being made along the French coast it would make sense. But why go to such enormous trouble for so tiny an island? It worried Fuller and he made repeated attempts to find out the reason for the island's fortification.

When Major Hoffman called at the house Fuller was both surprised and edgy. It took all his control not to throw the major out and, fleetingly, he was glad then that his Colt had been taken away. Observing Fuller's tension Claudie stuck close to him in the doorway.

The plumping Hoffman was correct in his approach, his expression behind his spectacles was almost pleasant. He saluted smartly in military style, shrewd enough not to present

Fuller with a stiff-armed 'Heil Hitler', and asked politely. 'May I come in, Herr Doctor?'

Claudie saw Fuller's anger rise and dug her fingers into his back.

'What is it you want?'

'Your help.'

'You can't seriously expect to get it?' Fuller was trying to contain himself. In two years his German had become almost perfect.

Hoffman was not put out. He knew all about Fuller; much more than Fuller realised and his instructions were strict. For reasons he did not understand but could not question, the doctor had suddenly become important; he must not upset him.

'We wish to construct a hospital.'

'Good. The poor devils at Newtown need one.'

'We need your help to design it.'

Fuller was caught off balance, halfway between contempt and professional interest. 'What's wrong with your own doctors?'

'You are to hand. There would be no point in bringing anyone over from Jersey or Guernsey. They are already overworked. You know local conditions and requirements. You are well esteemed here, Herr Doctor and your surgical knowledge will be invaluable.'

Fuller was interested now, in spite of Hoffman. Noticing the hesitancy Hoffman added, 'It will be a very special hospital. Completely up to date in every way for both military and civilians.'

Fuller saw an opportunity of helping those who needed it. 'Where will you build?'

'Here, Herr Doctor.'

'Here?'

'In your house.'

'You are mad, Major. The house isn't big enough.'

'You have a cellar, I believe.'

'For God's sake; it wouldn't take more than four beds.'

'Of course. The cellar would be the entrance only. You see, the hospital will be very secret, very special.' Hoffman smiled helpfully. 'We shall build it underground. The house will hide the entrance.'

Fuller was speechless. He felt Claudie's hand creep into his. A secret hospital underground on an island three and a half miles long? Why?

Lord Arden received the message through the Spanish embassy. Spain might be neutral but there was no doubt where her sympathies lay. She was Fascist neutral. Just as Portugal was Allied neutral.

The call had not come directly from the embassy, of course; without doubt Sir David Petrie would have MI5 maintain a careful scrutiny of the embassy, and the lines would be tapped. Someone had telephoned from outside giving a date and place, no more. The place was to be near Dundalk in Eire within easy reach of British territory. He now knew for an absolute certainty that he was being taken seriously.

Colonel von Schmettow, based in Jersey and German C-in-C of the Channel Islands, had complained in October 1941 that his troops had insufficient and outdated arms and equipment. At that time the occupation troops were second line and he had referred to them scathingly as 'Canada Commandos'. This derisory view of his own forces was due to the belief that the British could recapture the islands when they chose and his men would finish up in PoW camps in Canada.

Like all commanders he had exaggerated a situation in order to benefit his own forces. He had protested loud enough for Hitler to send his adjutant, General Schmundt, to visit the islands and to report the true position. Von Schmettow had evidently been convincing. By June 1942 there had been drastic change. Arms were still mixed but were now plentiful. The calibre of his troops had changed and their numbers had increased.

He would have enjoyed the justification of his earlier belief had he known that only that spring Winston Churchill had advocated the invasion of Alderney, the nearest of the group to England. The old bulldog was searching desperately for a morale booster, anything to lift the spirits of the people. After a long verbal battle he was eventually talked out of it by his chiefs of staff. If Alderney was taken, and there was no justifiable reason for the high toll on lives an invasion would entail, the generals knew that they could not hold it against the mass of German troops so readily available on the other islands and the main coast of France.

If this comforting fact was denied von Schmettow, another, to his immense annoyance, was evident: the unexpected return of General Schmundt on the Führer's instructions. What was more galling to him was that whereas Schmundt's visit to Jersey and Guernsey was almost perfunctory he spent a great deal of time on that deserted chunk of rock called Alderney. As C-in-C of all the islands von Schmettow resented the clear indication that certain matters concerning Alderney were being kept from him, especially since they had to be of immense importance for Hitler's personal adjutant to concern himself directly.

General Hans Oster was worried for his chief. Admiral Canaris was sometimes amused at his subordinate's insistence on searching the office from time to time. They both knew that Himmler had nominated Heydrich, chief of the Gestapo, to keep an eye on the Abwehr. Heydrich had been assassinated only a few weeks ago but this did not ease the situation.

Canaris was sure of himself, though, in spite of Oster's doubts. He glanced down at the top-secret memorandum. 'It originated from the Gestapo,' he said in answer to Oster's question.

Oster could not understand his chief's lack of wariness: or perhaps he was hiding it. 'Since when have the Gestapo passed information on to us?'

Canaris shrugged. 'They would have been told to do it.'

'By the Führer? Why would they inform him in the first place?'

'They may have regretted it had they not.' Canaris gazed thoughtfully at the memorandum. 'The apartment in Paris was left in a hurry. There was no attempt to cover tracks and plenty of evidence of who had lived there. Dr Fuller was living with a woman who had once worked as hostess in a Paris night club, a Claudie Grisons. He worked in a small hospital called St Marie. He had a car and, as a doctor, an extra petrol allowance. They obviously made an attempt to reach England.'

Oster sat quite still, closely watching his chief across the big desk. There was nothing so far to warrant the Abwehr being advised. Still less that this information should be passed on to the Führer by the Gestapo. So he waited patiently as Canaris turned a page. It was clear that his chief was dissecting the report as he went along.

'What obviously interested the Gestapo was the background to the man. Identity was easy to establish but there was, in a drawer, a framed Distinguished Service Order, with an inscription beneath it: "To the unsung heroes of the *Conquest*". On the back of this gallantry award was the name, Surgeon Commander S. FULLER. The Gestapo established that this was a Great War award. The *Conquest* had been sunk at the Dardanelles on the 18th March, 1915. There were only two survivors, Surgeon Commander Fuller was one of them. He is Doctor Fuller's father.'

'This is fascinating,' commented Oster drily. 'The Gestapo did well.'

Canaris smiled. 'If you think so little of them, why do you poke around this office? At the time this happened they were simply establishing facts, tidying up in general. The detail was passed through the machinery here in Berlin and might well have died there. It became something of an anecdote, a little bit of detection around the department. We Germans have always been fascinated by gallantry awards and here was a little mystery about one. What was the presumed son doing with his father's medal? What was an Englishman doing working in a French hospital anyway? Why take up with a tart? It was intriguing, something to talk about, and it was mentioned to Himmler over a luncheon. At the same luncheon was Ribbentrop, who overheard.'

Canaris glanced up at his friend and leaned back in his chair. 'And that, my dear Hans, was when the anecdote took another form. When Ribbentrop was our London ambassador he met the surgeon commander. He believes he is still alive. Samuel Fuller is apparently a very fine surgeon indeed. He is also a friend of Winston Churchill.'

Oster became interested.

'Just after receiving his medal at Buckingham Palace the elder Fuller ran into Churchill, who was then First Sea Lord. Churchill had apparently recommended the award. At the time he was trying to prop up the morale of his navy after the enormous losses at the Dardanelles, probably in much the same way as he must be trying to raise morale today. He lost his job shortly afterwards. His situation now may not be too different. Anyway, Fuller the elder is evidently a very outspoken man; he had seen his comrades die and told Churchill what he could do with his medal. Churchill persuaded him to keep the medal on behalf of the dead crew.

'This is a story Churchill himself told. The two men became friends. Both are blunt. But they live in different worlds. Fuller apparently hates politicians but he grew to admire Churchill who, in turn, always knew that he would get a straight viewpoint from the surgeon commander.

'Ribbentrop met Fuller only twice as he recalls. He learned of the son but never met him. What he is convinced of is that Fuller knew many of Churchill's friends outside the diplomatic circle. He attended some of Churchill's private, non-political gatherings. He believes that the son also attended some of them. Bear in mind that all this was at a time when Churchill was out of favour.'

'Is Ribbentrop sure of this?'

'As he wasn't invited to Churchill's private functions he cannot be sure. But it was part of his job at that time to note such things; where various people stood, what they might be doing.' Canaris looked up archly: 'He was provided with some assistance.'

Oster smiled. 'Indeed. So where are we now?'

'George Fuller, the son, is on Alderney with Claudie Grisons. Now note this: his car was found abandoned in a small cove on the French coast. That did not matter. What did was the soldier who was found shot dead and hidden in some rocks nearby.'

'*Fuller?*'

'The soldier was shot by a .45 pistol. Fuller had such a gun taken from him when our troops first landed on Alderney.'

'And the Gestapo let him live?'

'Fuller told them that he found the gun at the Alderney Police Station. But I'm sure the Gestapo intend that he will pay a terrible price for the crime. Eventually.'

'Herr Admiral, I'm confused. Of what use is Fuller to us? On Alderney of all places? And why the report now?'

'The timing of this report is ominous. That we should have

the background to Fuller is obviously considered to be of some importance by our Führer. I've no doubt that the detail took some considerable time to obtain and to correlate. It was a long time after taking Paris that the Gestapo went to work in minute detail, and longer still in the outlying areas.' Canaris glanced at the report. 'It was many months before the soldier was found. But I think this has been sat upon for a purpose. It has become time for us to know. Fuller, for the moment, is a protected person; we are requested to send out a liaison officer for him to make sure that he remains so.'

The two men eyed each other. 'Do you know why he rates so highly?' asked Oster. 'Because his father is a friend of Churchill's?'

Canaris did not answer. 'What I do know is that the directive to fortify the Channel Islands, sent out by the Führer himself, was delivered by hand by General Schmundt and was marked in pencil at the top, "VERSENGEN". It is something I am not supposed to know.'

'To be burned,' Oster remarked quietly. 'What are they hiding from us? And what possible use have they for Doctor Fuller?'

Some of the shoulder tabs bore a red shield with black and white bars in the top left quarter surmounted by the word 'Georgian' and the letters P.O.A. The initials were in the Russian Cyrillic alphabet. Translated they read R.O.A. Russiskaya Osvoboditelnaya Armiya. The Russian Liberation Army. Russians who preferred to fight for Hitler rather than Stalin. It was ironic that they arrived shortly before the first of the Russian slave labour.

A Gestapo office was now established under a diminutive man named Erich Kratz. To Fuller this was one more enigma in a growing chain. What could the Gestapo want here? Apart from himself there was no apparent enemy.

Fuller was torn between wanting the hospital built and his deep suspicion of the whole project. Professional need conflicted with human belief. Claudie, too, was appalled by the ill treatment of the half-starved work force, but, more practical than he, she accepted that there was nothing she could do about it; but she dreaded what he might have in mind.

She had dragged Fuller back when they saw Major Hoffman toss vegetable scraps to the stream of dust-coated slaves who came in and out of the old house. She felt sick as they grovelled and fought for the scraps but clung to Fuller like a limpet, knowing that he was close to killing Hoffman then.

She had finally managed to tear him away, scared of the consequences of his mounting anger. She did not know, because he would not tell her, that prior to this incident he had seen a group of labourers digging up dog entrails with their bare hands.

They went back to the new house which had been provided for them while the old one was gutted. And this worried Claudie, too. The house was reasonably furnished and comfortable and both she and Fuller had been placed on German officers' rations. Even a bottle of cognac had been provided. Why were they suddenly so solicitous to them when everyone knew what Fuller thought of the Germans? His advice over the hospital had already been given. She knew that Fuller was also worried about it.

She walked to the window as he said, 'We must get to England.' Through the glass came the intermittent sound of blasting beneath the old house. 'We must tell them what's happening here.'

She looked back over her shoulder, arms folded under her breasts. 'What chance have we now?'

Major General Sir Stewart Menzies read the brief report and smiled with pleasure. He had only once briefly met the man in the presence of the Prime Minister, but he had liked him on sight. It would be a pleasure to pass such news on to him.

To pacify the PM the generals had allowed themselves to be talked into a commando raid or two on the Channel Islands. They had been quite successful and had raised the morale of the islanders, without really achieving much. During the last raid on Guernsey two of the islanders had returned with the commandos. One of them had been on the agricultural working parties to Alderney, now apparently at a standstill.

Menzies already knew something about the fortifications

taking place on the islands as a whole; one of the profits from the raids. It seemed that Alderney was receiving an out-of-proportion attention although he knew nothing about the underground hospital being built there. What he had just learned, though, was that an English doctor named George Fuller was on the island and apparently alive and well.

Menzies made a note. Fuller's father would be delighted to hear for he had not been sure whether his son was alive or dead, or still in France. The advice would go through the usual channels which might delay it a little. But he was happy to send on such news. He thought that the PM would also be pleased for his friend. It crossed his mind that if the son was anything like his father it was a wonder that he had survived under occupation.

When General Schmundt returned to Alderney he had with him another man; a middle-aged captain wearing First World War medal ribbons and an Iron Cross 1st Class. His name was Joachim Brocker.

When General Schmundt left the island Captain Joachim Brocker stayed behind and later called on Fuller with a document case under his arm.

Fuller opened the door and pointedly filled the gap with his big frame, his young features coldly polite. The German smiled tolerantly. 'You would like to kill me, doctor?' The voice was cultured and soft.

Claudie was never far away when Fuller answered the door. She could not trust his reactions which seemed to be getting worse. She saw Brocker's quiet smile and before she could stop him, Fuller replied, 'All of you.'

Brocker nodded, eyes amused beneath the polished peak of his uniform cap. 'I'm sure I'd feel the same in your position. But before you kill me may I talk to you? Inside?'

No German had been inside this house since Fuller and Claudie had moved in. Fuller's hostility was a talking point among the troops; some were amused, some wanted him dead. Fuller noticed the row of ribbons on Brocker's chest. And the Iron Cross. He was reminded of his father, although he was not sure why. He found his anger waning; Brocker seemed a gentle person, somehow resigned and disillusioned. Brocker became the first German to enter.

Before sitting down Brocker produced a hip flask. 'Have you glasses?' Claudie fetched some tumblers. She put them on the table eyeing Brocker suspiciously. Brocker poured expertly, three even measures. He spoke colloquial English with ease. 'Schnapps,' he said. 'I believe whisky is your usual tipple but it's virtually impossible for us to get.'

'How do you know my usual tipple?' Fuller left his drink where it was.

Brocker smiled again. He had a pleasant, lined face that had seen the worst of everything yet had not abandoned humour.

'I've learned a good deal about you. You left a long and varied trail from Paris.'

Fuller went cold. He could feel Claudie concentrating on him yet he dare not look at her. The old apartment, the car, the soldier he had shot, flashed quickly through his mind. 'You're Gestapo?'

'God forbid.'

'Intelligence?'

'Nothing as grand. I'm a liaison officer.'

'There's nothing to liaise with me, Captain.'

'Someone evidently thinks that there is. The drink isn't poisoned, doctor.' Brocker placed his case on the table and opened it. 'I have something for you.' He produced the framed Distinguished Service Order with its caption. 'I believe this belongs to your father.'

Fuller was momentarily touched but was increasingly wary. 'That's very kind of you. My father never wanted it. Nor did he want to throw it away. So it finished up with me.' What else had they found? When he dared to glance across at Claudie he could see she was wondering the same.

'Your father would be a contemporary of mine. We shared the same war.'

'This war is very different, Captain.'

Brocker had his drink halfway to his lips. He stared blandly across the rim at Fuller. 'My superiors have an interest in what is happening here and in you. You have so far saved us from having to send a doctor here.'

'I have a regular monthly visit from one of your medicos on Guernsey. He keeps on eye on me.' Fuller paused. He had still not touched his drink. 'What is happening here,' he continued pointedly, 'is that the poor bastards out there are being treated far worse than animals. I'm not allowed to help them. If they're ill or injured they are simply left to die.'

'I've only just arrived, doctor.'

'You mean you can improve things?'

Brocker lowered his drink. 'I am only a captain. It would be misleading to imply that I could.'

'Then you're no better than Hoffman and the TODT and SS thugs.' Too late, Claudie had put her hand over Fuller's.

Brocker's fingers stiffened on the case. He had lost a little colour.

Claudie said quickly. 'You must try to understand my husband. He has seen so much brutality. He's not angry with you personally.'

Brocker said with cold politeness. 'My congratulations. I did not realise you had married since leaving France.'

It was the jolt that Fuller needed. If Brocker knew that much he might know everything. 'I'm sorry,' he said. 'But you'll see for yourself what is happening here.' And then, awkwardly, 'Claudie refers to us that way. It's convenient.'

Brocker rose. 'And perhaps keeps certain people at bay? You are a very attractive woman. The men must find that disturbing when they have only other men to look at.' He turned to Fuller. 'I will see if I can get dispensation for you to treat the worst of the labour force.'

'That will be a start.'

'But whether you like it or not, we are to work together. Your orders will come from me.' Brocker put on his cap, saluted both in military fashion, then left.

When he had gone Claudie raced to the window to watch Brocker disappear from sight. 'He knows,' she said without turning.

'He would have done something.' Fuller now reached for his drink.

'He knows,' she repeated fiercely. She turned to face Fuller. 'He knows you killed that soldier. What is he playing at?'

The labour force swelled enormously during July. More pitiful than before, the men worked in an almost permanent cloud of cement, bodies coated, lungs and eyes filled with dust. Bare and bleeding feet were commonplace. Their starvation diet comprised of thin cabbage or vegetable soup and black ersatz coffee. Milk, sugar and meat were never given to them.

Fuller was disgusted and found it almost impossible to remain passive. With the medical bag with which the Germans had supplied him and which he had found to be a useful entrée in many situations, he cycled south to the major excavations of an enormous naval battery emplacement.

That morning Fuller took a close look at what was happening. Human dignity was no longer even a memory for men who had developed into a separate species. Stretched flesh on visible bones, they were constantly beaten, often tied to barbed wire first; yet, somehow, most of them still carried on. Anyone who fell and could not rise was shot through the head. Some were pushed over the cliffs, often still alive and too weak to scream. One who fell twenty feet and broke both legs was left to die slowly and in agony. When Fuller approached another faller he was held back at gunpoint while the wreck that had once been a man was beaten to death. Sickened, Fuller turned away.

He cycled until he reached open country and sat behind a hedge, his stomach heaving. As a surgeon he had seen horrors that no ordinary man could have faced. This was quite different; there was no professional switch he could turn.

After a while he moved on. Excluding the hospital, he had counted over forty excavations and had learned new approaches which would take him out of his way. He memorised paths, tracks, open stretches he could negotiate to avoid the roads. In the two years here he had made a point of plotting every dwelling, farm, bolt hole that his memory could hold.

To try and rid his mind of the atrocities he had seen that morning he kept cycling, to find that he was heading towards Longy Bay where he and Claudie had first landed. Because it faced France only two resistance nests were being built there plus one on tiny Raz Island in the bay itself.

He stood above the beach looking at the placid sea, momentarily soothed by it and then he saw something humped near the rocks. He quickly checked about him. The work sites were some distance away but anyone looking in his direction would be able to see him. He laid the bicycle down carefully and casually walked down the slope on to the beach. It was a hot, cloudless day and he wore a short-sleeved, open-necked shirt.

He stopped when he realised that it was a body which he had seen. There were bodies near all the major sites, but they were located north and south-west and some in the lower centre of the island. In the hollow of the beach he was not so much on view except from Raz Island.

From where he now stood he could see fair hair spreading into the sand; that alone was different: the labourers were cropped to prevent lice. The body was slight, covered by some flimsy material, and then, with a start, he realised that it was a girl.

He tried not to make his direction too deliberate; he went over and crouched by the body, not at first touching it, making sure the rocks covered him from view. Spasms were passing through the girl's frame, her whole body juddering. She was lying face down. He put his hand out to touch her.

In spite of the sun her body was cold from exposure. She was in the shade of the rock and he guessed that she had been lying there all night. He felt her pulse, ran his hands carefully over her before turning her over. Her face was young, delicate and tear-stained, the runnels having dried in the sand adhering to her face. He must get her under cover.

Fuller knew where to go but the problem was to get her there without being seen. He turned his back to Raz Island and lifted her gently. She made no sign that she was aware of what he was doing. Holding her close he picked his way carefully north-east to a villa tucked in a fold.

The front door was missing, the windows smashed and the frames removed. The place was bereft of furniture. What had not been looted before the island had been occupied had been well looted since. Filth and litter covered the floor. Cobwebs screened down from the ceiling and rabbit pellets formed trodden pockets. Carpeting had long since been ripped from the stairs he now mounted, the boards creaked but seemed safe enough.

He took her into a south-facing room where she was the least likely to be seen if she went near one of the vandalised windows. Lying her in a corner he went back to his bicycle, collected his medical bag and now approached the house from the other side.

As he entered the room she was sitting up shivering, arms clutched round her slim body, eyes widening as he approached. Her lips trembled and she opened her mouth in terror.

'*Don't scream*,' he urged quickly in fluent French. 'Whatever you do, don't scream.'

She looked at him strangely, obviously frightened. 'I'm not German but English,' he assured her. He smiled. 'I suppose the accent foxed you.' It did not occur to him that she could be anything but French and he knew that she understood him. He held up the bag. 'I am also a doctor. It's important that we restore warmth and circulation.' He noted that although her dress was designed for a hot summer's day she must have travelled in it by night.

'You must exercise, touch your toes, swing your arms, anything. But stay away from the windows. The place is crawling with Germans. I'll bring you some food and blankets and some warmer clothes. It will be after dark. I have to be careful.'

She nodded and then suddenly burst into tears, her small hands covering her face. He made no attempt to stop her. When she was calmer she wiped her face and looked ashamed.

'It's all right,' he said. 'Did the boat go down?'

He thought she was about to cry again but she bit her lip, her head turning from side to side in anguish. 'We hit some rocks off the coast.'

'We?'

'Pierre went down with the boat.'

'Your husband?'

She shook her head and bit on a knuckle. 'My fiancé.' Everything she said was an effort as she relived a nightmare. He waited patiently and then she said. 'They shot my father. I don't know where my mother is.' Suddenly she steadied herself against the wall and stared at Fuller as if all the life had gone from her. 'I should have drowned with him.'

'You're far too young. Far too pretty.' Fuller rose. 'I must go. But I will be back. Don't give yourself up. Hold on. You understand?' She made no sign that she had heard or that she cared. She seemed to have gone within herself.

'What do I call you?' he asked. He thought she murmured, 'Jacqui'. There was nothing more he could do. 'Hang on,' he repeated. 'You'll be all right.' As he left he acknowledged to himself that the girl was a complication for which he had no solution.

5

Lord Arden took the Stranraer-Larne service to Ulster. The British and Irish Steam Packet Company services to Eire had been withdrawn at the outbreak of war. If Arden had any weakness at all then it was his fear of almost all forms of travel. He hated it, yet this was known only to himself; his iron will was such that he could effectively hide his fears.

He stood by the rails, jostled and unhappy, listening to the raucous behaviour of men returning to their units or joining new ones. And he reflected that nowhere was victory in sight. Tobruk had finally fallen. Churchill was under increasing pressure, and Arden knew that he must strike now; the time was ripe. He tried to keep his mind on what he must do, and away from the slight movement of the boat on a calm sea.

Arden disgorged with the mass; war was the great leveller. He picked up the hired car that had been arranged with difficulty; petrol was short everywhere.

He drove south to the border, suffered the inevitable hold up then continued through neutral Eire to Dundalk. The July weather still held good. Stopping at a hotel, he used their facilities to wash and to tidy himself and returned to the car. He climbed in almost without looking at the man now sitting in the front passenger seat, and removed the carefully folded copy of *The Times* from the top of the dashboard. He said drily, 'I hope you didn't have too bad a time of it; the boat was late, they always are now.' He smiled sparingly. 'The war, you know.'

General Hans Oster sighed in relief. 'I saw *The Times*. But one can never be sure.' He was wearing a rather old English-tailored suit; his tie was sober. 'You are Lord Arden?'

Arden nodded and drove off without another word. They went inland where the roads were empty. Eventually he pulled in. The high hedges either side of the empty road were full of yellow gorse. 'We can't go too far; a matter of fuel. May I compliment you on your English.'

Oster shrugged. 'It would not do for someone to be such an

62

obvious German, even in a neutral country.' He paused, then observed with a smile. 'A great number of these neutrals serve in your armed forces.'

Arden was checking the rear-view mirror. They were quite alone. 'We have our enemies here, too.' He pulled some folded papers from his inside breast pocket. 'This is our peace formula.'

Oster rifled through casually, not reading in detail. 'Isn't it dangerous for you to carry these around? They are not coded.'

'Our meeting here is dangerous. It cannot be avoided. I wrote the appraisal myself. I leave the coding to you.'

Oster said carefully, 'One of the big problems is that we know so little about you. We don't even know if you are who you claim to be. And even if you are whether you can be as influential as you insist.'

Arden reached for his wallet and Oster put out a restraining hand. 'Don't insult me, Lord Arden. An identity card would be meaningless.'

Arden let his wallet slip back into his pocket. 'Can you prove you are General Hans Oster?'

'All right. Let's take each other seriously.' Oster carefully put the papers in a special pocket of his jacket. 'I will read these later. Briefly, what have you in mind?'

'Disengagement. A simple peace treaty.'

Oster showed no surprise. He said quietly, 'I cannot think as the Führer thinks. Who can? I am only the messenger boy. But it might save time later if I try now to anticipate some of his objections. Please bear with me.'

'Of course. But don't take me for a fool. You would not be here at all if Hitler harboured serious objections.'

'Nor would I be here if it was considered that you are a fool.' Oster was half-turned towards Arden, his dissecting gaze fixed on the gaunt, uncompromising features. 'What is your motive for wanting peace? You don't strike me as a dove.'

'No, I'm not a dove. I would dearly like to see Germany lose the war. But I am a realist. If the war continues for much longer Britain may not recover; even if she were finally to win it. It is my belief that my country will never be the same again unless we stop it now. I want Britain to start her economic recovery before it's too late.'

'I can understand that, Lord Arden, but why should that interest us? We want Britain brought to her knees.'

Arden sat quietly as a battered car, caked in dried mud, rattled past. 'Don't under-rate the strength and wealth of the Americans. Britain has the guts to hang on and America has the money. Eventually they could bury you. My concern is that it will take too long and it will ruin us; certainly in my lifetime and most probably that of my son. What sort of victory would that be? The only thing likely to rise from the ashes is Bolshevism. And then we will have a war from within.'

Oster sat silently for a while. With something of a sigh he said, 'We are winning the war on all fronts. The Russians are running and the Japanese have ousted America from the Pacific Islands.'

'It may not remain like that, General. You are winning now but potentially the biggest threat to you is America's entry into the war. When Britain and America eventually get the bit between their teeth nothing will stop them.'

'A fool's dream, Lord Arden. All the signs point the other way.'

Arden turned awkwardly in his seat, his long legs catching under the dashboard. 'Do you realise what I'm actually offering you? Don't pretend that you're unconcerned by America's entry into the war. If Britain and Germany make peace with no strings, the American forces in Britain would have to go back home, General. And the various freedom fighters from the countries you have already over-run would be disbanded. In one stroke we would have taken the Western Alliance off your back. You could then concentrate your forces against Russia.' Arden gave a twisted smile. 'We might even surreptitiously supply you with arms to aid our recovery programme and to help you beat the Russians.'

'And you would be left free to concentrate on the Japanese.'

'We would leave that to the Americans. Once they are battle hardened they will be formidable. If we agree to a peace America will have a commitment to a European war she cannot possibly honour without the base of the United Kingdom. *She* would then be free to concentrate on the Japanese.'

'So you are offering us a release of troops for Russia and the Americans sent back home?'

64

'For an unconditional peace. There must be nothing in it that can be pointed to as any part surrender. I could never get it carried through. But a straightforward breaking off of hostilities, with the mood of the country as it is at present, would be very difficult to resist. Peace with honour. *That*, I am quite sure I can get adopted.' Arden hesitated. 'And the Channel Islands must be returned to us.'

Oster stiffened. He groped for a cigarette and Arden produced a case which he flipped open. 'Have one of these, General; they have tobacco in them.'

Oster raised an eyebrow, lit up, drew deeply and reflectively. 'The Führer, Lord Arden, is inordinately proud of his only British possessions. You have just asked the impossible.'

'They would be a stumbling block if you hold on to them. If you return them, there can be no effective argument against our peace treaty.'

Oster shook his head sadly. 'You don't realise what they mean to him. Our Führer had intended to visit them. His only reason for not having done so yet is that he does not like the sea. But eventually he will go there.'

'They can make all the difference between success and failure and it will show that Germans can be trusted.'

Oster said nothing to the insult. There was no point in false indignation. 'I will pass on this request.'

'Condition,' Arden corrected.

'I understood there were to be none,' rejoined Oster sharply.

'From you, General. You must trust me to know what is needed to achieve what will be best for both our countries.'

'I will pass it on,' Oster repeated.

'It's all written down for you. The moment is psychologically ripe. I want Britain to get her wealth back, not to suffer generations of near bankruptcy.'

'What we want might be quite different. But you will hear from us. Would you drive me back please?'

Oster was quiet on the drive back. He was digesting what Arden had told him; he did not think that the Führer would concur with the war so dramatically going his way. But he did know that his own life depended on him keeping secret what he had learned. He was to report direct to the Führer. Even Canaris must not know the detail. He was uncomfortably aware of the documents he carried on him and would feel better when he had painstakingly coded them and had burned the original. There would be no sleep for him that night.

When they arrived back at Dundalk Arden stopped the car near the hotel. The two men did not shake hands; their liaison remained quite impersonal. Just before Oster climbed out, Arden produced one of his thin, humourless smiles. 'That you don't know much about me does not say too much for your intelligence work, General Oster.'

'Or says much of your own ability to avoid publicity.'

'Perhaps. Your trouble is that you've failed to include me on one of your lists.'

'Lists?'

'The white list, and the black list.'

As work on the hospital continued at a feverish pace into August a strange liaison built up between Fuller and Captain Brocker. As labourers died off others took their places. When Brocker's guard was down Fuller detected the German's own disgust. It had an unexpectedly binding effect on them; they often talked together, careful to avoid brittle subjects. But Fuller took care to ration the time he was seen to spend with Brocker. He had not only his own safety to consider. Claudie had been starved of female company for over two years and he had seen the gradual effect on her. She was on an island of men, most of whom she detested. But for Fuller and the begrudging esteem afforded him she would have run into trouble a long time ago. Now they were being treated with a deference so unnatural that it worried him. He could get no reaction from Brocker about it and he believed the captain was just as puzzled.

He had insisted that Brocker accompany him on some of his medical rounds, always careful to avoid the derelict house which still held the escapee, Jacqui. They watched burials, three men to a coffin with a false bottom so that it could be pulled up and used again. They watched men who could take no more fall into the massive foundations of the gun emplacements to have concrete poured over them while they were still alive; fellow prisoners looking on without protest, or reaction, or hope, for they could be next. Sometimes a pathetic air bubble might pierce the surface concrete, sometimes a limb. Neither would be visible for long.

'What's it all about?' demanded Fuller when he could trust himself to speak. 'The fortifications are ludicrously out of proportion to the size of the island. What the hell is going on?'

'I know no more than you. And if I did you could not expect me to tell you.' But Brocker was also disturbed.

'But don't you think it's strange?' Fuller insisted. 'They're building an impenetrable fortress.' He was unaware that he had precisely echoed Hitler's directive to make Alderney *eine unangreifbare Festung*.

They strolled back in the direction of Fuller's house near the hospital. 'Doctor, I find it all inexplicable. Perhaps that is why I am still a captain. Time will tell for both of us.'

'Unpleasantly, no doubt.'

Brocker shrugged. 'We talk like this but I'm still a soldier, an old one perhaps who cannot change his habits. I like you, Doctor, and I respect you, but we are enemies. Do not forget that. Always remember whose side I am on. One day it might be crucial for you to remember that.' Brocker saluted and headed towards St Anne where his billet was.

Fuller watched him go, wondering if he had said too much. Then he shrugged; he was always saying too much but he felt strongly that Brocker was trying to warn him. He was convinced the captain knew more than he claimed.

Three officers shared the house Brocker lived in. They had a bedroom each, a wartime luxury, simply because the accommodation was available. He sat at a small folding table and rested his chin on his hands. He took his cap off, and the indentation it had made showed on his greying hair.

Brocker knew that he had closed his eyes too much. Sometimes he thought he was living on a different planet, that this small, silent island of terror had been ejected into outer space. What was happening here was alien to him. He had argued with both the commandant and Major Hoffman but nothing had changed. The slaves were expendable and there were plenty to fill the ever-increasing gaps. Somehow, only God could know how, they worked for twelve hours a day every day. They were literally worked and starved to death, except those who were killed in other ways; strangulation was becoming increasingly popular with the SS.

Was his wife, the aristocratic Jodie, closing her eyes too, as a matter of convenience? It was also happening in Germany. He considered the disappointment he must be to his wife, still only a captain at his age and with his length of service.

His son was already a captain at twenty-three. But Brocker did not care to think too much about Carl; he was on the Eastern Front. Victorious armies always suffered a high ratio of casualties. He was proud of his son but was not sure if the reverse was true. Was it possible that his wife, son, and his daughter – now with the Strength Through Joy movement – had a sneaking contempt for him? His wife's letters arrived monthly, the same precise content, pride in the children, concern for them, but never for him, no matter how he read between the lines. They were the standard letters of a dutiful wife but not of a loving one.

Brocker heard one of his colleagues moving about downstairs. He went to the window and looked out across the sea towards England. Out there somewhere was a nation fighting against hopeless odds. Even Fuller admitted that his country was doing badly but he still carried the crazy notion that the British would somehow survive. Even in the event of him being right, he was convinced that Fuller would not live to find out; the doctor was being fattened for the kill.

Brocker stared out of the window sadly. Fuller would die as soon as his usefulness was over and that usefulness was something much more important than medicine.

Brocker went back to his chair and reflected on what he himself had to look forward to. Not much more than Fuller. He did not relish returning to the house outside Frankfurt, to a dutiful wife and a family whom he doubted he would really know anymore.

Fuller knew that he was heading for trouble by protecting the French girl. For two weeks now he had visited her, taken her food and blankets. His visits were spasmodic, sometimes as much as three days apart, but he had tried to build up a little food stock for her and had provided utensils and a can opener.

Claudie was frightened for him. These days her intuitive

fears were growing stronger and more difficult to live with because she could not pinpoint their base. Then she felt deep sorrow for the girl. How could any young girl survive for two weeks in hostile territory, on her own in a derelict house? Her nerves must be at breaking point. And if she cracked Fuller would be dragged down with her.

Claudie would have been far more perturbed had she known that Fuller's thoughts were turning to more dangerous channels than she could imagine. With the whole atmosphere of the island changed and the new secrecy that now blanketed virtually all comment on what was happening, yet was clear to see, problems began to develop under the heavy-handed system. There were instances among the troops where human nature reacted against rigid discipline. Fuller was not at all sure where exploiting these minute cracks would lead him, but he had always followed his impulses.

He followed one now as he went up the bare, scrubbed wooden stairs of an NCO's billet on the fringe of St Anne. He entered a room on the second floor and crossed the floor to the occupied bed.

He gazed down at Sergeant Max Kremple, his fingers groping for the pulse. As he held the strong wrist he noticed the sergeant averted his gaze. There were three other beds in the room but Kremple's colleagues were on duty, just as he should be. The sergeant was lying flat, hair very dark against the pillows, although his complexion was fair, his eyes grey.

'How's the pain?' He spoke in German.

'No better, Doctor.'

'Tell me again where it is.'

Kremple indicated the opposite side to his appendix. 'It's there all the time. Sometimes worse, sometimes not so bad.'

Fuller pulled up a chair, looked round the room. 'Is there anyone else in the house?'

'They are all out. They won't be back until one.'

'So you can talk freely?'

'Talk?'

'I should release you for duty. You know that, Sergeant.'

'For duty?' Kremple struggled up against the pillows. 'I am not fit for duty.'

'You always have been. From the time I first called on you.'

'I'm not lying, Doctor.' Anxiety touched Kremple's eyes. Sweat beads formed just below the hairline. Hands fidgeted.

'I know you're not. The pain is real. But you are not physically sick.'

Kremple was puzzled and worried. Fuller softened his tone. 'I am a surgeon. Your problem is not surgical. I sent you to Guernsey for X-rays and other doctors examined you. They found nothing wrong. You have been returned to me because you are my patient. I, too, can find nothing wrong.'

'Doctor, I swear I'm in pain.'

'Nevertheless I shall advise your officer that you must be returned to duty.'

'No.' Kremple showed his fear. '*No*. I'm not fit. I will tell my commanding officer that you are trying to kill me by making me return.'

'If you do that I will have to explain to him why you are sick.'

Kremple lost colour.

'Relax, Sergeant. I believe your pains are psychosomatic. They are real to you but induced by a mental state. What is it that worries you?'

Kremple pushed himself further up. 'Nothing worries me.'

'Are you worried about home? Wife? Children?'

'I'm not married. My parents are both well.'

'Is there anything here that upsets you?'

'It is boring. It would be nice to be on the mainland.'

'But that wish would not give you pains. Why don't you want to return to duty?'

The eyes flickered. 'Because I am sick. In pain.'

'Is it because of what you have seen?'

'I don't understand you.'

Fuller noted the alarm. 'Then let me tell you what I have seen.' He related what he had witnessed that morning and of the callous beatings and murders he had seen previously. 'Does that sort of thing worry you?'

'It's none of your business. You are a prisoner here.'

'Then there's nothing I can do for you. I'll send in my report.' Fuller rose, pushed the chair back against the wall. Kremple was shaking his head in torment.

'Don't put in the report, Doctor. Please.'

'I can't help you. I'm sorry.' Fuller walked towards the door, not looking back.

'Doctor. *Please. Don't send me back on duty.*'

Fuller turned. 'We've been over it, Sergeant. There's no point in doing it again.'

'I can't go back on duty. *I can't.*'

'Why?'

Kremple fell back against the cheap headboard, sweating freely now. 'I can't face it.'

'In this I am not your enemy. Are you ashamed?'

Kremple fought for composure. 'Of being a soldier? No. I am ashamed that we tolerate those pigs in the TODT. They should all be put on the Eastern Front; they would mess themselves and cry for mercy as those poor bastards here do.'

Fuller came back into the room, stood over the bed.

'What did you see?'

Kremple tried to wriggle out of committing himself, but when he finally met Fuller's gaze he accepted that there was no way back. 'I've seen them die where they drop, beaten, fall over the cliffs. I've seen them fight over potato peelings, over soup not fit for pigs. I've seen them too weak to cry out in pain. I've seen them plead to be put out of their misery.'

'I've seen these things, too, Sergeant. Are you sure that's all?'

Kremple squirmed again. He looked everywhere but at the doctor. 'Some are *pushed* over the cliff. I can still hear the screams of those who had the strength left. But the worst was when I saw them dropped into the fortification walls. There are dozens, perhaps hundreds of them in there.' His eyes closed. 'They were dropped into the wet concrete and walled in.' His voice sank as he continued. '*I could see their limbs moving as the cement closed over them.*'

Fuller pulled the chair out again, sat down. He said nothing as he watched Kremple's struggle. The sergeant was reliving the scene. He lay back, panting, staring sightlessly at the ceiling before he turned his head towards Fuller. 'I'm afraid to go to sleep because then it all comes back. And the pain is worse.'

'How is it now?'

The question took Kremple by surprise. His hand flew to the

area of torment. 'It's . . . I don't know. It seems to have shifted.'

'Shifted or gone?'

'I don't know. I don't know. Doctor, what am I to do? I can't go back. I would puke as I did then.'

'Is it something you can confide in a senior officer?'

'It would be considered a weakness. To protest at treatment of the Jews with the Gestapo and the SS here is to put in a transfer request to join them.'

'What do you think you should do?'

Kremple shook his head in despair. 'I sometimes feel like stepping off the cliff myself.'

'I can't protect you much longer.'

'I need help, Doctor.'

Fuller weighed it carefully. 'You could desert.'

Kremple steadied immediately. The thought frightened him considerably. Fuller added, 'Obviously if you can stomach going back you would not need to think of it.'

'Desert?' Kremple grimaced; the thought mind-shattering. 'How can anyone desert on this island?'

Fuller shrugged. 'I'm merely putting to you an alternative to going back. I dare say there are places on the island where one could hide.'

'For how long? It's impossible.'

'Until you can escape to England.'

'That's escape? To become a PoW?'

'Wouldn't it be better than seeing live, emaciated bodies sink slowly as they struggle in wet concrete?'

Kremple could not answer. He stared at Fuller, his mind working, his thoughts passing over his face. Would he be exchanging one nightmare for another? Which could he live with? 'They would search the island for me. The Gestapo would take their revenge, make me an example.'

'That's possible. Unless they thought you were dead and buried.'

'Buried?'

'A substitute body. There are plenty lying around. Braye Bay is full of them. I've repeatedly warned your people of the health hazard.'

Kremple was silent. The idea was bizarre. 'They would need

72

to identify me, see the body.'

'That can be safely left to me. There's no one here capable of contradicting me.'

Kremple was no coward, he simply could not stomach what he had seen: the idea was sudden and strange to him, against everything he had been taught.

'I'm not trying to corrupt you, Sergeant, but to save you. Either way your secret will be safe with me.' Fuller rose again. 'Don't let me push you into it. Think about it. If you want to go ahead send one of your colleagues to me to say the pain is worse. I'll know what to do.'

'What about food? How would I live?'

'We'd have to steal it. Who knows better than you where supplies are? Anyway, I must be off.' He hesitated at the foot of the bed. 'If you find the decision difficult just bear in mind that you're between the devil and the deep blue sea so what difference does it make?'

'I cannot tell you,' remarked General Oster uneasily. Admiral Canaris looked up in surprise. 'My dear Hans, I haven't asked you.'

Oster was gazing down into the street; he could just see the Brandenburg Gate. It was pouring with rain. 'August,' he said. 'Who would believe it?' He turned away from the window to face his chief; he appeared apologetic and guilty. 'I know that you haven't, Herr Admiral. The fact is I would much prefer to tell you but when I reported to the Führer he made it all too clear that I must tell nobody.'

Canaris was going through some reports. He waved a hand. 'I know what's happening anyway.'

'Of course. But the detail of Lord Arden's request was for the Führer's ears only.'

'And yours, Hans. Do sit down, you're distracting me.'

'I wish I did not know,' Oster said with feeling.

Canaris was amused. 'I'll tell you something else you'll wish you did not know.' He clasped his small hands across the desk. 'I'm to arrange another meeting with Lord Arden.'

'With me?'

'No. You've done your part . . . The preliminaries are over.'

'I'm surprised the Führer is going so far. I . . .'

Canaris held up a warning hand. 'Be careful or you'll be telling me what you say you must not. Anyway, I don't want to know, although it's not difficult to guess.'

'Who will go this time?'

'My guess is Ribbentrop. My job is to see that Lord Arden knows where and when.'

'Where?'

Canaris gazed steadily at his friend. 'Alderney.'

Oster was not sure whether he was surprised or not. 'That name keeps cropping up. Is there a particular reason?'

'I can perceive more than one.'

'It's one thing to give Lord Arden a time and place, but how will he get there?'

'Perhaps the Führer, in his wisdom, is presenting his lordship with an opportunity to show whether his contacts are as good as he claims them to be. There will be other reasons.'

Oster nodded slowly in agreement. 'It's easier to see now why the English doctor has survived the Gestapo there. I don't much like it.'

'It means,' observed Canaris quietly, 'that the good doctor has been protected by the Führer directly, or at least by Himmler. I hope that when they've finished with him they kill him cleanly.'

'Is that all? You seem to be . . .'

Canaris gestured impatiently. 'You ask me why Alderney; with the massive fortifications going on there it becomes even stranger. Why fortify so frantically when a peace deal is in the offing? And I believe the Führer is now eager for such a peace. Why choose Alderney for the talks unless our leader is showing one of his bouts of warped, vindictive humour? Why are all vital communications regarding the island hand-delivered?'

Oster stared, transfixed.

Canaris smiled bitterly. 'I see the penny has dropped. When Britain has her peace, and the last American has gone home and the British Army is disbanding, we will invade. Don't you think?'

'*And Alderney will be invasion headquarters?*' asked Oster breathlessly.

6

Jacqui was careful how she approached the window. She had learned how to cross obliquely to it; to crouch so that she could peer from a lower corner of the frame; and had taught herself to cross the room well away from the windows so that there was no chance of her being seen from outside. She had learned how her shadow was cast if it was sunny and at certain times of day. She had trained herself to stop and to listen at the merest suggestion of external noise. Her life was one of total solitude and unnatural behaviour. Most of her daytime movements were crouched, like an animal.

She had no one to talk to but herself. And she had all the time in the world to recapture the terrible moments when her father had been so bloodily cut down. There was nothing to distract her from recalling the frantic struggle when the boat had struck and Pierre had disappeared from her life forever.

The English doctor had been marvellous. And now she had met another French woman not much older than herself and it had been unbelievably reassuring. But Claudie had gone and the trauma returned. Claudie was not confined and she had her man to help her. She was not an isolated, shivering, scared prisoner with only horrifying memories for company and terrifying prospects beyond these weather-battered and crumbling walls.

It was dreadful to be alone like this. Even with the occasional visit of friends. The mere sight of a German uniform could reduce her to a trembling wreck. There were moments when she thought her head would burst open; moments when she mumbled to herself, or cried, or stared out to sea in the dark towards the point where Pierre had disappeared. And there were moments when she wanted to dash from the house and scream, and scream, and scream, all the way into the sea until it closed over her.

Major Carl Hoffman stood stiffly to attention and saluted, 'Heil Hitler.'

'Heil Hitler.' Lieutenant Colonel Helke, Alderney's present commandant, nodded briefly to a chair in front of his cluttered desk. 'Sit down, Major.' He held up a document marked, 'MOST SECRET'. 'Read that in my presence. When you've read it, sign it at the base of the last appendix on page four.'

Hoffman adjusted his glasses and after reading only the first paragraph said, 'This directive is itself an appendix to the original directive from the Führer, Obersturmbannführer.'

'Just read it, Major. It's for our eyes only.'

Colonel Helke sat straight and quite expressionless while Hoffman read. Helke was perturbed. He was getting instructions but no clarifications. And he was aware that he had better not refer back for explanation. He strongly suspected that Major Hoffman knew far more than he about what was going on and why. Although the major kept his place, was always correct, the colonel was left with the feeling that Hoffman wielded more power than he did. It was nothing he could really put his finger on although he was convinced that Hoffman had received some of his orders direct from Berlin; he had noticed the high-ranking officers who had, from time to time, come over from Cherbourg for the sole purpose of seeing Hoffman. He was sure that these officers were no more than couriers and that they delivered sealed orders for Hoffman.

Colonel Helke did not like certain matters passing him by but he had the intuitive sense to keep his counsel. At least Hoffman had not made it difficult for him. There had been one particular time during General Schmundt's last visit when Helke had himself received an instruction. Schmundt represented Hitler. Helke had been ordered to let Hoffman get on with the building of the hospital unimpeded; Hoffman was to have direct control over the project, to an extent that no other officer was to be allowed there.

German architects, with advice from the English doctor, had drawn up the plans but every worker had been supplied by the TODT organisation. Not only had slave labour been used exclusively but they had been kept in a separate compound so that they could not talk to others; among them were carefully selected builders and engineers. Those working on the hospital had been granted special rations to keep them alive.

Helke had learned to close his eyes to a project which even he was not permitted to inspect. He strongly suspected that the document Hoffman was now studying had only been delivered to him personally because it was of a largely military nature and, as commandant, he was certain to find out its contents anyway. His inclusion, he felt, was a harmless sop.

Hoffman finished reading and handed the document back to Helke very politely.

'Your signature, Major.' Helke flipped the pages over, held them down on the desk as Hoffman bent over to sign. It was only during pinpricks of authority like this that Helke felt he could effectively use his rank against Hoffman. 'What do you think, Major?'

Hoffman was careful. He had been instructed not to offend the colonel in any way. Internal conflict was the last thing he wanted. 'Very impressive, Obersturmbannführer.'

'Have you any idea why? Don't you think it disproportionate? On an island this size?'

'Perhaps we under-rate its importance, sir. Its position is too near to France. We don't want to encourage the British to try to re-capture it.'

Helke gave Hoffman a look of disbelief. 'Are they likely to try?' He flipped through the pages again. 'These are in *addition* to the original directive 16.' He glanced down. 'Three more naval coastal batteries. To the west by the Griffoine four 15 cm guns, to the north-east by Saye Bay, four 10.5 cm guns. To the east of that three 17 cm guns and middle south the naval artillery HQ. Plus the additional army artillery.'

Helke looked up for reaction and, seeing none on the moon face, read from the document again. 'Booby-trapping, wiring and mining of all the cliffs and beaches. *Thirty-seven thousand* mines in all. And overhead anti-airborne landing charges.' Helke appeared exasperated. 'Can the island take all this without everyone blowing themselves to bits?'

'I'm sure that it can, Obersturmbannführer.'

Helke glanced down again and commented non-committally, 'I see that we're warned that the navy is to increase the number and area of sea mines.' And because he was floundering while Hoffman remained impassive, he added. 'How is the rest progressing?'

'The network of storage tunnels for food and ammunition

magazines is well advanced. The one under Essex Hill is several hundred yards long. I think you saw it recently, sir.'

Helke nodded. 'I see the airport is to remain unusable.'

'A simple matter of cluttering it. It can be cleared at a moment's notice.'

Helke rose and put the documents in a smallish safe which had been concreted to the floor. 'I suppose the answers will come eventually. We should be in Moscow before the end of autumn.' Helke remained standing.

Hoffman accepted the implied dismissal, gave an assurance that the work would be carried out and saluted once again. Before he reached the office door Helke called out, 'How is the hospital progressing?'

'It's almost finished, Herr Colonel.'

Helke was surprised. 'That's remarkable going.'

'We've been working round the clock.'

Helke did not ask how many men had died in the process.

He was cowering against the back door, eyes upturned and pleading like a dog. Claudie had gone out to the dustbin and had been careless with the light. She jumped back, terrified, dropping a bucket. The wretch silently implored her not to be afraid but her fear remained. She could not move: the smell was obnoxious. He crouched like a beggar, hands out in supplication, eyes enormous against the shrunken skin. He had not the strength to harm anyone. The realisation steadied her. She was suddenly aware of the light. It would bring the Germans. She called back into the house, *'George. Quickly.'*

Fuller came hurrying out and took one look. 'I'll get him in, you close the door.' He held the thin arms, so brittle he was afraid of breaking them. Supporting him was no problem, there was little weight. He spoke in German, 'Can you walk?'

The man nodded, his head grotesque on the spindly neck. His bare feet left blood smears as Fuller helped him in. Claudie closed the back door quickly and wiped away the bloodstains. Fuller called back to her. 'Get some food and milk.' Their rations were now stretched beyond the limit with the supplements they provided to Jacqui but they still had a cow.

He half-carried the man up the stairs, propped him on a chair and ran the bath. He sponged him down. It took three fills of the bath and a good deal of tightly rationed soap to remove the cement dust caked into the skin. Claudie standing by with bread and milk, handed them to Fuller. The man, still naked, fell upon the food before Fuller could move. Fuller turned away and put the milk down on the glass shelf. He had been about to warn the man to eat slowly but realised he would be wasting his time. He picked up the filthy sack with the cut-out sleeves and dropped it on the landing. He took Claudie into their own room.

She closed the door behind them. 'George, he can't stay here.' She was pleading with him.

'Do we hand him back?'

'They'll shoot us for harbouring a slave.'

'To send him back would be murder.'

'What about food?'

'I might find an answer.'

'Oh, God. Life is bad enough without this.'

'And Jacqui? Do we hand her over too?'

'I know. I'm afraid. I grow more afraid by the day.'

'There's a spare bed in the other room.'

'We are crucifying ourselves.'

'We've survived.' He gave her a boyish smile. 'We're still together.'

When he spoke like that she could not resist him. 'But for how long?' She avoided his gaze. 'I'll clean the bath down.' And then, 'Get him into the spare room. If I see him like that again I'll be sick.'

Inside the bathroom the escapee stared hungrily at the empty plate from which he had licked the last crumb. He backed like a cornered animal as Fuller approached.

'You can sleep here tonight. Put these on.' Fuller helped him put on old pyjamas. 'You've escaped from Sylt?' It was the name of the first concentration camp on British soil.

'From the tunnel.' The reply was an effort.

Fuller was curious. 'Which tunnel?'

The big eyes stared, uncomprehending.

'You mean the hospital?'

The gaunt head swivelled slowly. He made an effort: 'They've killed all those who worked on the tunnel.'

'*On the hospital tunnel?*' insisted Fuller.

The man swayed and Fuller steadied him. A skeletal finger pointed down. 'Hospital? The Tunnel.' A finger pointed again. The escapee did not seem to know about the hospital.

Fuller could see he was pushing him too fast too soon. He had to leave it for the moment but he was deeply puzzled. 'What's your name?' Fuller could see the mind groping. Names had long since ceased to exist.

'Vassily Gorkov.' So soft that Fuller had to ask him again.

A Russian but his German was good. 'I might be able to spare you a little more food later. Too much too soon could kill you.'

'It would be dying in paradise.'

'No, it would not. You can sleep in this room here.' Fuller opened the door and they went in. He then pulled blankets out from the cupboard, threw them on the bed. 'You must be quiet. We won't betray you.'

They had been speaking in a dark room, the only light filtering from the landing. The house was one of the comparative few with electricity. Fuller turned as he was about to leave. Gorkov crouched on the bed, his emaciated form was only a faint suggestion in the dark. Fuller closed the door and heard Claudie cleaning the bath. He picked up the stinking sack Gorkov had been wearing and went downstairs with it. He could not burn the sack on a warm September evening without attracting attention but neither could he bear to keep it in the house. He pushed it into the dustbin. When Claudie came down he was washing his hands.

She wiped her forehead with the back of her hand and he noted again the charm she could get into so small a gesture. 'They'll come looking for him, George. It scares me.'

'I doubt that they'll miss him, they have so many.' But Fuller was thinking of what Gorkov had said about killing the men who had worked on the tunnel. Which tunnel?

'Hoffman counts them. I've seen him.'

He was about to pacify her when someone knocked loudly at the front door. They stared at each other without moving. Fuller motioned to Claudie to stay still. He was thinking rapidly; the sack was in the bin outside. There was a long gap and then the hammering started again, prolonged, urgent.

'I'll have to go. Sit there reading something.'

He delayed as much as he dared then went to the front door. Two armed soldiers stood before him, one behind the other.

Admiral Canaris stayed at his desk long into the night. In spite of the size of the room there was a claustrophobic feel to the place with the heavy blackout curtains drawn. Although he preferred to work in this office, the main files were secreted under the building where there were bomb-proof rooms to retreat to in the event of an air raid.

There were others staying as late as he; all his staff were under pressure of work. Tonight, though, he wanted his solitude. He had to think and for once he preferred not to confer with the one man he knew he could trust. He had sent General Oster home.

Canaris had been informed that the full peace talks to take place on Alderney with Lord Arden would be in late September, and told the names of the two men nominated to represent the Führer. The choice of Joachim von Ribbentrop came as no surprise. The ex-ambassador to London was a skilled negotiator. However, the second choice was puzzling. Walter Schellenberg was a protégé of Himmler's in the SS. The combination of the two men was itself unlikely. It also meant that Schellenberg was to be the Führer's confidant in this, the man to keep an eye on Ribbentrop.

As Canaris sat back in the solitude of his darkened office he tried to work out Hitler's reasoning. He could understand his own involvement in the affair. He was better placed than anyone to set up clandestine meetings on neutral soil, better placed to communicate on enemy territory. But why Walter Schellenberg, a non-diplomat, a man who Canaris was well aware had the backing of Himmler to replace Canaris himself at the Abwehr? Their scheming had not worked and the admiral was convinced that it never would. And Ribbentrop would not be pleased with the choice of Schellenberg. Having a high official of the SS breathing down one's neck was hardly conducive to efficient negotiation. Or had Hitler reasoned that it was?

The perplexing aspect to Canaris was that Schellenberg should now be so highly rated. It was a warning worth having. He would have to watch his back more keenly than ever. But it also indicated that his assessment of Hitler's real use for

Alderney seemed to be accurate, and that worried him considerably.

Fuller kept his nerve. He noted the insignia. They were not SS.

There was a noise upstairs and he moved to block the doorway completely, hoping that Gorkov would not panic. He noticed the nervousness of the soldiers as the first one spoke.

'Herr Doctor, Sergeant Kremple is very ill. The pains are much worse. He insisted that we call you.'

Fuller concealed his relief. 'I'll get my bag.' He closed the door before grabbing his jacket and making a brief explanation to Claudie. He joined the soldiers outside and they hurried on foot to the troops' billets. It was a long walk and he was sweating by the time they entered the house. The soldiers slept in the same room as Kremple but he bade them wait downstairs while he went up. Kremple was alone in the room and Fuller closed the door behind him.

Kremple was groaning softly and clutching his stomach as he rolled on the bed.

'All right, Sergeant, we are alone.'

Kremple opened an eye. 'Did they believe me?'

'I am here at their call.'

'Where are they?'

'Downstairs. But keep your voice down.'

Kremple was uneasy. It was now or never.

Fuller said, 'I'm going to isolate you. Let me get this blanket wrapped round you.' When he had finished only part of Kremple's face was visible. 'Lie absolutely still and leave the rest to me.'

He went downstairs to the rest room where the two soldiers waited. He noticed that both were corporals. In a concerned tone he said, 'I must get the sergeant over to my house. There's a shed in the yard where he can be isolated. I've given him a pain-killing injection but I think you should call the medical orderlies. We need a stretcher and the ambulance.'

One of them ran off while Fuller kept the other talking. From the number of beds upstairs he knew there was another soldier somewhere. 'Is it possible to move your beds out?'

The corporal had not considered it. 'I suppose we could bring them down here. Why, Herr Doctor?'

'I believe the sergeant has a rare disease. If I'm right then it's contagious. I must do some tests. The bedroom upstairs must be fumigated in any event. The medical orderlies can deal with that. Meanwhile, touch nothing of Kremple's.'

'Yes, Herr Doctor.'

When the ambulance arrived Fuller explained the position to the orderlies and advised them to wear gloves when moving Kremple and burn them afterwards. They brought the sergeant downstairs on the stretcher and his lack of movement gave an impression that death might already have struck. They loaded him into the small ambulance which was a converted van. The best medical aids were on the bigger islands.

Fuller travelled in front with the two orderlies. It was extremely cramped but he made it clear that he would not travel in the back with Kremple. They reached his house, the slits of light barely picking the way and Kremple was offloaded while Fuller unlatched the yard gate that Gorkov must have used that same evening.

The shed was a rickety lean-to with broken slates and the panes missing in the only window. It stored buckets, garden tools and odd bits and pieces that Fuller and Claudie sometimes used. The cow grew restless as they fumbled with the shed door. One of the orderlies fetched a torch from the ambulance and used it guardedly while Fuller cleared a space on the floor.

By this time the orderlies could not get rid of Kremple fast enough. Fuller closed the shed door and slipped the piece of stiff wire through the haft of the lock which was all that stopped the door from blowing open. He walked back to the ambulance with the others. 'It's not ideal in the shed but I can't risk having him in the house.'

They understood perfectly, and considered him reckless even in having Kremple near the house. 'Don't forget to fumigate the room,' he told them. 'The ambulance as well.'

They already had it in mind. When the ambulance pulled away Fuller leaned against the wall exhausted, wondering why he should endanger himself for a German sergeant. He went in by the front door to explain to Claudie, dreading her reaction.

She sank slowly to a chair, gazed up unbelievingly. 'What are you doing to us? Jacqui, this wreck Gorkov. *And now a German sergeant*? You have gone mad? Don't destroy, us George. Don't let us lose what we've found.'

'I can't leave him there, Claudie.' He saw her sag. 'I know that you're afraid. But do we sell our souls to these people? Stand by, let it all happen?'

'We have for two years and more.'

'Things changed in the spring. You know that. Neither of us knows what is happening but there's a stench to it.'

'I know I can't change you. Nor should I try. But I can't stop fearing for you.'

He had difficulty in meeting her gaze. 'I'll be away some time.'

She scooped up Blanco and held him like a child, burying her face in his fur so that she could not see Fuller leave.

Sergeant Kremple was standing nervously as Fuller unlatched the shed door.

'We have to find a replacement for you.' Fuller tossed a pair of makeshift sandals at the dark, stocky figure. 'Braye Bay should be the easiest.'

Kremple, realising that he was now totally committed, pointed out the risks. 'Gun emplacements are being constructed there. There'll be guards.'

'If we make for the middle of the bay, then use the beach, there should be a reasonable chance.'

'There are excavations in between.'

'The whole bloody island is full of excavations. You'd better bring the stretcher.'

Kremple reminded himself about why he had deserted, the horrors he had faced. He said, 'I won't let you down. I know you've placed yourself in danger.'

'Let's get moving, this could take most of the night.'

The journey was difficult from the start. Although they both knew the island intimately it was impossible to recall each pitfall, every single working. There was no light. Most of the time they advanced in a crouched position carrying the rolled stretcher awkwardly. There were areas which had been developed agriculturally. To avoid leaving a trail through the crops they were forced to make constant detours.

The island was now peppered with resistance nests, heavy

and light flak sites, infantry strongpoints and the massive underground work for the big gun emplacements. None of these were complete but much of the work was now well advanced. The dogs were barking at Sylt concentration camp but the two men were moving away from it on a course north-east through the rough centre of the island. The wind was biting as they slowly progressed over higher ground; it helped cover the sound of their own approach but it also cut out the possible noise of sentries. The sky was overcast and it was pitch dark.

They had to stop frequently. The wind dropped for a few minutes and the silence was torturous. There was no sound of any kind. They were struck by the sudden uncanny quietness. Not even the sea murmured. Then at last the wind sprang up again.

As Fuller and Kremple drew near to the harbour they took a rest, lying flat behind gorse, trying to get their bearings.

Kremple saw the faint suggestion of vaporised breath on the crisp air and wondered why Fuller was taking such risks for him. Fuller touched him lightly on the arm. It was time to move on.

As they reached roughly the centre of the bay, they were aware of sentry posts each end of the beach. The sea stirred against the breakwater out in the harbour. Straight ahead lay England.

They kept to the rear of the beach, picking their way through gorse and over sand dunes and shallow gulleys. Keeping low they could see the outline of workings on the high ground to the north-east.

With the guards so alert along the coast, movement was exceedingly slow. The sand covered the sound of their approach but was often treacherous under foot.

They carried the stretcher between them. Fuller, leading, scanning the ground for a corpse. A sentry coughed above them. Kremple tugged on his end of the stretcher to warn Fuller who lowered his staves and signalled Kremple to stay where he was.

Fuller went on alone, pace by pace, taking his time, searching the comparatively pale stretch of sand. He tripped and fell with a thump. Bruised, mouth half-filled with sand, he lay there afraid to move, working the sand out of his mouth with his tongue.

He rolled over slowly; it seemed that he had not been heard. Groping, he discovered what had tripped him; a naked foot, partly covered by gorse which hid the rest of the body. With great care he lifted the body and picked his way back to Kremple.

Fuller lowered the body on to the canvas and Kremple led the way back along the beach to their agreed exit point. Eventually reaching the house they lowered the stretcher. Kremple could contain himself no longer. 'If you put him in a coffin no one will believe it's me; there's no weight.' He looked down at the patch of skin and bone as if accusing it directly.

Fuller was unperturbed. 'Let's get into the house.' He opened the door and they carried the body into the surgery, lowering the stretcher on to the examination couch. 'Stay here and don't make a sound.' Fuller disappeared and Kremple was left alone with the corpse. He forced himself to look at it. The skin was almost transparent, with a slightly luminous quality. Every bone was visible. The eyes were completely out of proportion to the rest of the body and stared out of a head that was huge and gaunt. He felt sick. Fuller returned with a bucket of water.

The Englishman took his jacket off. 'I'd advise you to do the same.' As Kremple removed his pyjama top Fuller closed the eyes of the corpse. He was matter of fact, knowing what was going through Kremple's mind. The sergeant seemed to be on the point of vomiting. 'Max, you'll find packets of plaster of Paris in the floor cupboard. Get them out.' He turned briskly. 'You help me prepare it but I'll put it on.'

They worked silently, and Kremple was relieved to be active again. Fuller was deft. There was no need for finesse but expertise was built into him. It was some time before the corpse was mummified in plaster; he looked gruesome. Fuller rinsed his hands in what was now the remnants of the second bucket of water and said, 'It's still wet but lift it.'

Kremple had difficulty, 'Now, perhaps it's too heavy.'

'No. It's fine.' Fuller left the room again and returned with Kremple's blanket and a large needle and thread. With Kremple's help he stitched the blanket up round the corpse. He stepped back. 'I think I've got the right height, don't you?'

Kremple did not know how Fuller could be so detached and businesslike. He studied the form that was supposed to be himself and agreed that it was about right. But it was a crazy idea; they'd never get away with it. Fuller had to speak to him a second time before he grasped what was being said. 'You'll have to share a room tonight. Tomorrow we'll try to sort something out.'

There was nothing Kremple could do but agree with everything Fuller said. Belatedly he realised, with a sense of shock, that he was completely in Fuller's hands. He would not survive without the doctor's help.

'Let's get him into the shed. He can dry off there.'

Using the stretcher they went out by the back door. Afterwards they returned to the surgery to tidy up. When they had finished Fuller said, 'Your room mate is an escapee from Sylt.'

Kremple recoiled. 'He'll kill me in my sleep.'

'He won't know who you are and he'll do what I tell him.'

Kremple shivered. 'Can't I sleep down here?'

'No. Your officers are also my patients. I want no one on the ground floor. Anyway, the night has almost gone. Don't wake my wife.'

He led the way up the stairs, wondering if Claudie was listening. Blanco growled as they reached the landing and Fuller fetched blankets from the cupboard. He opened the spare room door and heard scuttling. He switched on the light. Vassily Gorkov was cowering in a corner, his crazed eyes peering over the blanket pulled up to his mouth.

Kremple stopped at the door and said, 'I'm not sleeping with him.' Gorkov reminded him too much of the poor wretch they had just encased.

'Yes you will.'

'Then we'll leave the light on.'

'If you wish.' Fuller crossed to the window to make sure there were no chinks in the drawn curtains.

Kremple took the blankets and went to the corner opposite Gorkov. They sat staring at each other, the bed unoccupied.

Fuller said, 'I want no trouble from either of you or we're all dead.' He looked from one to the other. Gorkov was glaring malevolently at Kremple. They had to get used to each other or die. After another warning Fuller closed the door and left them to it.

Kremple fixed his blankets; he was hard on the floor but he had suffered worse. He faced Gorkov all the time. He slipped off the sandals made from worn car tyres and tucked the blankets round him. Gorkov was shivering but his eyes were wide, unblinking, their rims the pale pink of anaemia. Kremple said, 'I deserted because of what they are doing to you.'

Gorkov continued to stare. For some time now he had lived on lies, false promises, meaningless reassurances. He had seen men and women leave the camps with hope etched on their faces because they had been fed sadistic lies. They had never returned. He made no attempt to analyse what Kremple had said. The German was a soldier, he didn't need to wear a uniform for Gorkov to know that. He would recognise a soldier out of uniform for as long as he lived. What he could not separate in his tormented mind was the ordinary soldier from the TODT officials or the SS who were hand in hand with them.

The two men remained in their separate corners, staring, each fearful of the other. Gorkov had no strength but such was the intensity of his stare that Kremple began to believe he was holding a weapon under the blanket. He dared not fall asleep. He had propped himself in the corner, much as Gorkov had done, when the light bulb gave out. At first there was total silence, even their breath was held. Then a scurrying sound started in Gorkov's corner and Kremple tried to pierce the darkness. He could smell death in the room.

7

Major General Sir Stewart Menzies was tired. He was suffering the pressures that go with a country at war. Although his intelligence network was better and more effective than that of his opponent, Admiral Canaris, the strain on him and his men was the greater. Because the Allies were doing so badly they were all the more reliant on accurate intelligence reports to help stem the enemy. Menzies looked as if he had not slept for days, but his eyes were bright, ever observing, and they focused steadily on the man sitting opposite him.

Lord Arden was conciliatory; he had enormous respect for Menzies but recognised that there was no chance of getting him on his side. 'It's good of you to see me. I hope it will be worth your time.'

Menzies rubbed his eyes wearily. He turned on the swivel chair. 'They've contacted you?'

'In the usual way. I think it's dreadfully slack.'

Menzies smiled faintly. 'Only if MI5 find out. Go ahead.'

'It's tricky. They want me to be in Alderney by 25th September.'

Menzies showed his surprise. 'Alderney? To rub it in? How can you justify being there? Assuming that you can get there at all.'

'That's where I'll need your help.

'To get you to Alderney?'

'Oh, no. They will arrange that. Partly at any rate. My contact wants a meeting set up there to discuss an exchange of sick prisoners.'

'Ah!' Menzies toyed with a pencil but his gaze was still on Arden. 'You would like me to forge your way into the International Red Cross?'

'That would turn a covert operation ostensibly into an overt one.'

'Quite. But these meetings are usually on neutral ground.'

'I realise that. But as they've far more prisoners of ours than we have of theirs, they could be, as you suggest, trying to rub it in. I'm not in a position to argue. And as there will be no bona fide members of the IRC present, I assume that nobody else will object.'

'I hope your contact knows what he's doing. You could be walking into a trap.'

'That occurred to me, Stewart, but really, what the hell would they want me for? What secrets of yours do I hold, or of David Petrie? And what military knowledge have I? I hardly know a tank from a tandem.'

'You're more than qualified to give an accurate appraisal of how things stand here.'

'Well they wouldn't get one out of me and I can't see them going to all this trouble for that.'

Menzies tapped the base of the pencil. 'You're happy about this?'

'I don't know. I started the probe for a willing voice that end and can hardly complain about present development. I'm not happy about Alderney. At first it seemed an odd choice until I learned part of the reason.' Arden was very conscious of the scrutiny from across the desk but he was playing the game which his huge financial interests had taught him to play so often. His gaze held Menzies quite comfortably.

'Hitler is sending his personal photographer to the islands to take back an artistic record of progress for the maniac to gloat over.'

'*Henrich Hoffman?*' Menzies stiffened. 'Are you sure?'

'That is my information. The bogus Red Cross meeting has specifically been arranged while he is there.'

'But Hoffman and Hitler are cronies.'

'You gave me the impression that your own ear is so close to the ground that any contact of mine would be superfluous.' Arden knew, as he spoke, that he had delivered a good stroke.

'Don't be silly, Charles. There are only two other men Hitler is likely to confide in; that damned Hungarian astrologer of his and Max Amann.'

'Max Amann?'

'There's no secret about it. Amann served with Hitler in the Great War. He was a runner in the 16th Bavarian Reserve Infantry. He rose to corporal and won two Iron Crosses. Now

90

he runs the Nazi Party's printing presses. But even he is not so constant a companion to Hitler as Heinrich Hoffman who goes everywhere with him.'

Arden was impressed by Menzies' memory for detail. 'I don't suppose he will be travelling alone. But he will be there.' Arden was studying Menzies' reaction, but it was difficult to define. 'I don't have to remind you that Rudolph Hess was also a very close crony of Hitler's. And he finished up here.'

Menzies did not respond. 'Am I to understand that there will actually be a discussion on the exchange of prisoners?'

'There will have to be. Local eyes must be satisfied. Canaris has set it up. He will have been thorough and no doubt will have selected his men for the Red Cross.'

'Canaris has been exceedingly helpful, wouldn't you say?'

Arden sensed he was on dangerous ground. 'Hasn't he been before? You will know that far better than I.'

Again Menzies skirted the issue. 'I hope you're not walking into trouble. If Heinrich Hoffman is your man he's a prize worth having.' Menzies frowned and there was clearly something troubling him. 'You do realise that Hoffman may not be your man at all and if he's not whoever contacts you will have to be extremely careful with Hoffman there.'

'I have considered that. All I can do is to go and see what happens. I will be protected by the umbrella of the International Red Cross.'

Menzies grunted. 'For what it's worth.' He turned his chair again to view Arden from a different angle. 'Who was your contact in Ireland?'

'Do I have to tell you?' Arden was playing out his hand.

'No. But I can't think of anyone safer who you can tell.'

'Hans Oster.'

'You've been flying high, Charles. Congratulations. At this rate I shall be surprised if the Old Fox and Oster last out the war.' Menzies could not know just how prophetic was his observation. He asked slowly, 'So how will you get there?'

'Fly to Lisbon and they'll take care of the rest.'

'I wish you all possible luck.'

'I'll see what I can spot on Alderney while I'm there.'

'They won't let you see much.' Menzies straightened his chair. 'Do you know Samuel Fuller?'

Arden braced for the next question, was taken by surprise. 'The surgeon? Winston's friend? Yes, of course.'

'Have you met his son?'

'Two or three times. Not for some time, though. Rather like his father. Both brilliant surgeons but non-conformists. Why do you ask?'

'The son is on Alderney. See if you can look him up while you are there. Old Sam would be delighted to have news of him.'

'I'll be glad to. I'm sure they'll let me.'

Menzies sat still for some time after Arden had gone.

Weariness had left him and he concentrated on his slowly moving pencil. He made another note to remind him to get his documentation department to arrange an International Red Cross identity card, then he slowly reached for the green scrambler. 'Prime Minister, I would like to see you if you can spare the time.'

James Arden was concerned. He had complete confidence in his father but they were beginning to walk a narrower plank. He poured two whiskies and took one over to his father who was standing by the window. 'You don't think he suspects anything?'

Arden took the drink. 'I've no way of telling. He referred to Canaris as the Old Fox; a name Menzies could well qualify for himself.'

'He doesn't seem to worry you. It's not like you to under-rate anyone.'

'Oh, I don't under-rate him.' Arden raised his drink. 'But what can he do? The need for immediate peace may be a desire of some influential politicians but the only people this side of the English Channel who have taken positive steps towards it are you and me. There's nothing he can do without sound evidence.'

'He can refuse your IRC identity card.'

'He won't do that. If he's suspicious he'll want to see where it all leads.' Arden sipped slowly. 'I wonder what name and nationality he'll give me.'

'It's a pity you went through him.'

'There was no alternative. I can't suddenly disappear without comment; that *would* arouse suspicion. There'd be a record of my flight to Lisbon and we have enough people there to watch where I went next. No, I've done it openly, and what I've told him I've done is well within the brief granted to me by the SIS.' Arden could see that his son was still worried so he added, 'If Menzies has any suspicions at all my guess is that they're directed at the Germans playing me for a fool, rather than at me personally.'

'I hope you're right, Father.'

'James, listen to me. What difference does it make? In the event Alderney is a good choice if a surprising one. It's an island populated by Germans. Even Menzies would be hard pushed to penetrate there. When I return I can claim failure, agree that I was deliberately misled and that they hoped for something from me. But if I come back with a signed treaty of intent from Hitler then that will be placed in the appropriate hands here. Our part, for a short while, will be over. And that document will be a political bombshell.'

James caught some of his father's fervour. 'When you put it like that I must agree.'

Arden gave a wintry smile and then asked, 'You remember young George Fuller?'

'I haven't seen him for years. Not since before the war. I remember his father better.'

'George is on Alderney.'

'Really? A prisoner?'

'Not a very amicable one if he's anything like he used to be. Like father like son.' Arden paused.

'I think Menzies is hoping that George can feed me with what is happening on the island. That alone should give substance to my going, wouldn't you think?'

The Office of Strategic Services, the American wartime intelligence organisation, suffered much criticism from its own countrymen during its formative years. Directed by the short, dynamic, close-cropped, grey-headed General William S. Donovan, it worked well and closely with British intelligence agencies. 'Wild Bill' Donovan rode the early barbs from the diehards in G2 who initially referred to the new organisation as Oh So Stupid, or Oh So Slow. As the OSS progressed and collected some of the American college blue-bloods, this appellation was changed for a new form of derision: Oh So Social and Oh So Sexy.

That this offensive appraisal came from his own compatriots, albeit, those at base, did not deter 'Wild Bill' for one moment. His thinking was ahead of theirs and time was to prove him right. General Donovan became a legend and came to Britain as early as 1940 to check out the gloomy and inaccurate forecasts of Joseph Kennedy, American ambassador to London.

It was to be ironic that the man destined to be head of the OSS in Britain was, years later, to become US Ambassador to the Court of St James during the Presidential reign of Joseph Kennedy's son Jack. But during September 1942 it was extremely unlikely that David Bruce's mind was on politics at all.

Because, at that time, American experience was of necessity limited, David Bruce was rather surprised to find someone as illustrious, in intelligence terms, as Major General Sir Stewart Menzies calling on him in his basement office under the US London embassy. It was particularly surprising because the identities of the heads of the British Secret Service were kept very secret indeed, certainly to anyone outside their realm.

While Menzies asked him how things were going Bruce was wondering what really was in the general's mind. Menzies was at the top of the tree; the unexpected visit had to have purpose. And an important one.

Menzies did not take long to reach his point. 'I want to borrow a man from you. German speaking.'

Bruce was surprised. He did not believe that Menzies was so short of German-speaking operatives. Moreover, established SIS agents were extremely experienced and the wartime additions had two years training in hand over their American counterparts. He was suspicious.

'Do I get him back?'

Menzies did not hedge. 'Possibly not.'

'Highly expendable then? Suicidal?'

'It could turn out to be. But then all these missions are.'

Bruce became slightly annoyed. 'You wouldn't want one of my men because you don't want to lose one of your own?'

Menzies was bland. 'Would I do a thing like that?'

'I don't know you well enough to answer. Your reputation

came to me well cloaked but considerable. I'd feel happier with an answer.'

Menzies nodded in consent. 'Of course. There are sound reasons unconnected with risk why I don't want to use any of my own people.'

'That's part answer. You mean, you've been infiltrated?'

'No. Not to my knowledge. But there are certain ears that have access to a great many important people. I am not sure of their range. It may be that I am being deceived by someone unnamed and I would hesitate to specify the depth of that person's contacts. I could find out but it would take too long. If I am being over-cautious, then my request would be wasted.'

'And a man could die unnecessarily?'

'I'm afraid so.'

Bruce was both intrigued and flattered. His common sense told him that Menzies would make no idle request. 'You have a conviction and you would like our help?'

'If I was utterly convinced, I would know what to do without troubling you. I'm convinced only that I should follow through a line of enquiry for which I need a man who is not employed by any department of mine.'

'This unnamed person must have a lot of access.'

'He has. Just how much I don't know. And that's the crux. I'm sorry I can't be more specific.'

Bruce smiled. 'You were hoping I'd be only too glad to supply you with someone.'

'It was naïve of me. But I like the way you protect your men.'

'I guess that's something I'm still doing, Sir Stewart. I'd like to know what you want him for.'

'To go to Alderney and make contact with someone there.'

'Alderney? That's one of your Channel Islands near France?'

'The nearest to France and also the nearest to England. About a hundred and sixty miles south of Weymouth.'

Bruce searched his memory. 'The only German-occupied British soil? Isn't Alderney the one which was completely evacuated?'

'That's the one. There's an English surgeon on the island named Fuller. My information from a source on one of the other islands is that he tried to escape from France way back in '40

95

and his boat was dive-bombed by a Stuka. There's a French girl with him named Claudie Grison.'

'This the man you want contacted?'

'Yes. If the information still holds good we know where he is.'

Bruce said, 'Is this guy safe? I mean if we send a man we don't want him betrayed as soon as he gets there.'

Menzies laughed. 'If he's anything like his father, and I understand that he is, you've nothing to worry about.'

'Do you get my man there?'

'Naturally. I'll tell you where and when he's to report. We'll get him to within a mile or so of the coast and he can continue by dinghy. The currents can be treacherous around that coast. We'll have to choose our time carefully or he won't make land.'

'When would you like him to be available?'

'I gather you agree to help?'

'You've helped us enough.'

'Then as soon as you can get a man. Well before the month is up.'

'That gives little enough time. Equipment?'

'If he's to stand any chance at all he had better be dressed as a German officer. I'll see what we've got on the units over there. We can arm him with a German submachine gun and a German radio.'

'If this island is swarming with Krauts he'll be lucky to be able to use a radio.'

'It's the only way we'll know when he wants to get out.'

'Or to pass on what you want to know before they find him?'

'Either way. You're being very helpful.'

'Why not?' said Bruce easily. 'All you want is a man who can pass as a German officer, make his way through completely hostile territory, carrying a high-powered radio; and is expert enough to find an English doctor on unfamiliar soil and obtain for you whatever it is you want to know. At the same time it's probable that we won't get him back anyway. No trouble at all, Sir Stewart. We've got stacks of them.'

'But you'll see to it?'

'I'll see to it.'

Fuller took the food up to spare Claudie. Gorkov and Kremple were facing each other from opposite corners of the room just as he had left them, their heads and eyes were drooping but somehow they had kept awake. Observing their distrust of each other he said brutally, 'Get used to each other or go back.' It was necessary. And then more gently, 'Work out how we can steal some rations.' He turned to Kremple. 'I'm off to arrange your funeral. That should please Gorkov.'

He went into St Anne's to the medical centre. The two orderlies were on duty, attending a clinic full of men with minor cuts and bruises. Anything more serious they sent on to Fuller whose surgery started at ten. He signalled them to join him in the dispensing room and closed the door behind him. He kept his voice low.

'Sergeant Kremple died in the night. I am convinced that he died of a contagious disease with similar symptoms to kala-azar which I encountered in India. Has he ever been to the tropics?'

Neither man knew. Both were tired through fumigating everything in sight and they had not gone to bed until the early hours.

Fuller went on, 'I've encased him in plaster and stitched him in a blanket. I burned the one he used in the ambulance. If you'll take my advice you'll bury him at sea. As far out as you can. Today. I believe there are some dinghies at Fort Clonque.'

'Doctor Spiedel is due in two days time. What shall we tell him?'

Fuller was well aware that the visiting doctor was due. 'If you tell him the truth it will mean that he'll turn the whole island upside down. You'll be working day and night on useless inoculations. The labour force can't be ignored; they'd be considered a prime danger. You know how thorough Doctor Spiedel is. It would take days. Otherwise,' he added persuasively, 'you can tell him that Sergeant Kremple believed he was dying and requested to be buried at sea.'

'You would back us up, Herr Doctor?'

'You know I would.'

Fuller still saw the dregs of doubt. 'It's my firm opinion that there is now no danger to anyone on this island resulting from

Sergeant Kremple's illness and death. I'm far too experienced to say such a thing lightly.'

They had great respect for Fuller.

'That's good enough for us, Doctor.'

'Get rid of him quickly. He's in my shed. Kremple was X-rayed on Guernsey but what he had would not show on a plate so don't worry about Doctor Spiedel. I'll deal with him.' He noted their relief. 'One more thing,' Fuller stopped by the door. They waited expectantly, hanging on every word. 'I'm a non-combatant like yourselves. Kremple was a soldier, my enemy perhaps, but a good soldier. Full military honours, gentlemen. Good day.'

They sat on high ground near Essex Castle looking out towards Raz Island. South-west of them three massive gun emplacements were being excavated. Overhead, the birds were restless, wheeling on eddies of air; a strong wind had whipped up the sea and ripped the clouds to shreds. It was wild and peaceful. Blanco was running in and out of grass clumps, sniffing happily for rabbits.

'We've got to get off this bloody island and warn Churchill of what's going on here?'

Claudie squeezed Fuller's hand. In the early autumn chill they both wore jackets. She was still sick with worry over what he had done for Kremple and Gorkov. And she knew that the Germans could make sure that they would never leave the island.

'Why should anyone want to seal off Alderney?' Fuller continued. 'Gorkov said the workers on the tunnel were killed. But I don't think he means the hospital tunnel. I want to find out. Why is there this urgency, and why so massive a scale?' The sound of blasting came as an unwanted endorsement. Claudie could find no words to answer him.

They took the usual circuitous route to visit Jacqui to drop off what they could spare. The continued solitary confinement was having a terrible effect on the girl. Only terror of the alternative held her together.

Squatting against the walls below window level as they always did, Fuller said, 'We're still trying to find you another place.'

'You mean change one prison for another?' The comment was biting and unjust.

Fuller said gently, 'Jacqui, the whole island is a prison. But you can stretch your legs at night.'

'Very little now. They've been mining the beach.'

Before anyone could stop her Claudie rushed out of the house. As she raced towards the beach she could see Blanco paddling along the sea edge.

She tried to keep the panic from her voice as she called out, *Viens ici. Maintenent, cheri*. Come.'

Blanco raised his head at an angle. Claudie's voice was the sweetest sound he knew. But his mood was mischievous. He wagged his stump of tail and Claudie could see he was going to play up. 'Blanco. *Mon petit, cheri*. Please. Come.' She crouched and held out her arms. She had saved him. She couldn't bear to lose him now. As if she needed it, she suddenly saw, just feet away, a notice post, each warning below another. HALT! STOIJL! ALTON! MINEN! MIJNNEN! MINES!

'Walk away. He will follow.' Fuller had come up behind her.

'I can't.'

With difficulty Fuller said, 'It might be better if you don't watch him come back.' They could see where the sand had been raked over all the way along the shore. Claudie glanced at Fuller with frightened eyes; there was nothing either of them could do.

Blanco ran into the sea then back again as a roller engulfed him. He stood on the wet sand shaking himself before coming towards them in a mood of happy defiance.

The dog did not approach in a straight line. He stopped now and then, sniffed about, then started scratching in the sand. Fuller and Claudie found the strain unbearable. Blanco lifted something in his jaws; it looked like seaweed. He ran round in wide circles with the weed hanging from his mouth like a streamer, as if he was performing laps of honour.

Claudie buried her head in Fuller's shoulder, unable to watch. And then Blanco was bringing his prize towards them.

As Blanco drew nearer he picked up Claudie's distress, dropped the weed, and came full speed towards her, his little legs moving incredibly fast, sand flying. Fuller tried to swallow. So near now. The terrier leapt at Claudie, landed in her willing arms and, squirming, tried to force her head back so that he

99

could lick her. She clasped him as if she would crush him, and tears of relief gushed from her. 'Oh, Blanco, Blanco.' The wiry white body wriggled in her arms but there was no risk that she would let go.

It was a long time afterwards when Fuller said to her.

'Don't ever do that again. Not ever.'

Claudie was startled and hurt. 'What did I do?'

'Rushing out as you did could have put Jacqui at risk. It needed just one German soldier to be curious.'

'But Blanco . . .'

'He must take his chance.' Fuller had his arm round her shoulders. 'You must face the fact that there are much bigger issues here than Blanco.'

'But I love Blanco.'

He did not say anything. He understood.

'I don't know how he got away with it.' She shuddered.

'His weight. A bigger dog would have been blown to bits.'

Still cradling the terrier Claudie said, 'Whatever you say, Jacqui is a far greater danger to us than Blanco. She can destroy us all.'

The double concrete paths leading up to the house must look from the air like a normal driveway. The convincing metal facade that had replaced the front of the house swung on huge hinges and pulleys. When it was lowered the house appeared intact.

The false wall was pulled up for Fuller and Captain Brocker to enter. They were now on first name terms and their friendship had developed, always though, with reservation. They were very formal in the presence of their sole guide, Major Carl Hoffman.

The underground approach was arched for strength, the incline sharp. The walls were roughly finished brick but as the network opened up Fuller noticed that some chambers were plastered. Ventilation ducts had been bored through and it was obviously bomb-proof.

The tunnel curved to the left, leading to a series of rooms. There were four fair-sized wards on one side. Opposite was a large operating theatre, an X-ray room, an administrative office which would take several desks, a rest room, and, at the end, toilets and store rooms and a dispensing room. The first two rooms on each side of the tunnel were for examination and casualty cases, each with two cubicles.

Fuller was pleased with what he saw, but he kept asking himself the same question again and again. *WHY?* Why was it here? And for how long would they allow him to run a hospital like this? If it was used to capacity German doctors would have to be brought in and when that happened his usefulness would be over. Someone must have that in mind. But when?

For something blasted and mined so quickly it was impressive. Hoffman told him that the first batch of equipment would arrive the next day. They walked back slowly and had reached the beginning of the incline when Fuller saw a smaller tunnel branching off and wondered why he had not noticed it on the way in. Was this the tunnel Gorkov had meant? But Gorkov had pointed down as though it was vertical. Fuller turned into it and Hoffman called out, 'That is not the hospital, Herr Doctor. Your tour is finished.'

This extension had not been part of his design. 'What is it then, Major?' Fuller felt the anxious pressure of Brocker's fingers on his arm as he spoke.

Given his own way, Hoffman would have got rid of Fuller a long time ago. Fuller had been skating on very thin ice which surely could support him little longer. That Fuller enjoyed protection merely increased the depth of his hatred. The smaller wing held a secret the doctor must not be permitted to see.

Ignoring Brocker, Fuller continued down the narrow tributary on his own and Hoffman hesitated. He had not been specifically instructed to stop Fuller going there but his instinct told him that this was a blunder. He had to weigh that against his unexplained instructions to be tolerant of Fuller's attitude. But since he realised that the real secret would still be hidden from Fuller's eyes, he decided not to block his way.

Hoffman followed Fuller while Brocker remained at the junction of the two tunnels. Hoffman felt a contempt of his compatriot whom he considered was too friendly with the Englishman. It was all storing up in his mind.

Fuller was intrigued by the tributary complex. At the end of the corridor a central metal door opened into a very large room.

It was empty except for a huge, glass-fronted shallow map frame covering an area of the rear wall.

Before reaching this room there were several smaller rooms on either side of the corridor. They were small only by comparison; still big enough to take four beds each. Water and electricity pipes had been connected. All the rooms were well finished and there were adequate drainage outlets, wash basins and shower cubicles. In one room a naval commander was reclining in a chair reading a newspaper; he got up and closed the door quickly as Fuller drew level. It flashed through Fuller's mind that a U-boat had arrived at Braye the previous evening.

On the way back to the surface Fuller tried to hide his qualms; it was far from easy, but instinct warned him that to display any kind of suspicion in front of Hoffman would be folly. This was confirmed by Captain Brocker when the two men were eventually alone together and walking towards Fuller's house.

'You were foolish to antagonise Hoffman: the major would dearly like to shoot you, given the least excuse.'

'Since when has Hoffman needed an excuse?' Fuller snapped back. 'He's obviously been ordered to lay off me.'

'Just as obviously as I was sent to liaise with you. It's time you considered the reason.'

They stopped at the front door and Fuller turned to face the older man. 'Do you imagine I haven't? Do you think it doesn't worry me? You could tell me but you won't.'

Brocker removed his cap and gazed down at its polished peak. 'No, I couldn't. I wish I could. Perhaps only Hoffman knows.'

'Then I'll have to find out some other way.'

'Be very, very careful George.' Brocker gazed pointedly at the door then lifted his cap. 'Do I put this back on or are you asking me in?'

Fuller thought of Kremple and Gorkov upstairs. There was nothing he could do but invite Brocker in. He opened the door and called out to Claudie to warn her that Brocker was with him.

The two men entered the small living room. They had developed the habit of selecting particular chairs and as Brocker sat down Fuller realised just how close he and Brocker had become. They looked at each other uneasily as Fuller said bluntly, 'There's a big room at the end of the tunnel, it looked like a briefing room.'

'Have you ever seen a briefing room?'

'No. But it bloody well looked like one. There's a wall map case.'

'George, you are reminding me that we are on opposite sides and that is a pity.'

'I'd like a closer look at that bunker.' Fuller had used the word without thinking.

Brocker stiffened, his expression suddenly thoughtful. Then he gazed at the ceiling. 'What was that?'

Fuller had heard a scuffle, too. 'What was what?'

'Movement. Who's in the bedroom?'

'That'll be Claudie after Blanco.'

As Fuller spoke the door behind Brocker opened and Claudie started to come in, the sound above still audible. For a moment Fuller could not move as he watched Brocker's face.

8

Lieutenant Rod Schroder studied the map again. It had been carefully drawn, but there was still an immense amount of detail missing. The light in the room was weak and he moved to the edge of the single bed in an effort to get more directly under the naked bulb.

The billet was spartan and initially Schroder had shared it with a fellow officer who had been moved from the moment that David Bruce had sent for Schroder. There had been other briefings since then and all of them had been personally handled by Bruce. Even so Schroder had an increasing impression that everything he had been told was second hand and that Bruce had someone looking over his shoulder.

It did not matter. The mission was suicidal and the moment Bruce had put it to him that he would not force Schroder to go and would accept him only as a volunteer Schroder had known that he was not expected to return. In the first place he was to wear a German officer's uniform and to carry German army issue equipment. For that alone he could be shot as a spy.

He had been told of the large number of gun sites being built, but information as to location was scanty. Britons from Guernsey, the nearest island to Alderney, who had commuted there to work had tried to get information but most of it had been unreliable guesswork and, anyway, the work parties had been stopped before they could see too much.

The only person on Alderney likely to have updated and accurate knowledge was trapped on the island. Schroder wondered about George Fuller and whether he would ever be able to make contact.

Rod Schroder came from Philadelphia but was in England at Oxford University on a post-graduate course when war broke out. Probably due to his father's wide range of business contacts in Britain and his numerous friends there he had always been an Anglophile, which was part reason why he had decided to stay on. Many other Americans had done the same and had joined the British forces.

As his name implied Schroder's ancestry was Germanic and the language had passed down the line. But over a hundred years had elapsed since the first Schroder had emigrated to the United States. In spite of inter-marriage Schroder's blond, Saxon ancestry was unmistakable. He was tall and well built with blue eyes and a firm face, and he was fortunately blessed with the sense of humour necessary to withstand the sometimes merciless leg-pulling that his name and appearance induced from his colleagues.

At the moment he was glad that he was alone because he could openly show his fears. He was not a soldier and recognised that he could never be one. Because he spoke German so well he had at first been used for interrogation purposes and for a short time had been seconded to Colonel Pinto's staff. Then Schroder had undergone field training with the commandos and had enjoyed their company, if not their ruthless professional ability.

When America had entered the war and her forces had come to Britain, it had been with mixed feelings that he had transferred over to them. When the OSS was formed he was a natural to join their initially small numbers. But he had come to think he had done the right thing. Until now.

He was puzzled, as David Bruce had also been, as to why an American was being used on what, ostensibly, should be a British operation. No explanation had been given to him when he had raised the matter.

If knowledge of the gun sites and the general disposition of German troops was scanty, general information about the island was plentiful. Someone had taken great pains to correlate detail from some of the fourteen hundred evacuees from Alderney. Whoever had done it had considered it important enough to provide a mass of detail for Schroder to examine.

There was really too much but aided by the plan he soon detailed the information he really needed. The first thing he had to do was to find the doctor. The rest would follow from that. He had long since memorised what he was to tell Fuller, if he was lucky enough to reach him, and that in itself was puzzling and surprisingly minute. Secrecy on all aspects of the mission had been stressed but it was a warning that was not needed. Schroder was fully aware that his life was at stake; secrecy was built in to the need for self-preservation. He studied the map again and again.

The next day he went for a walk in the crowded West End of London, past the dismantled statue of Eros and the protective boarding that covered the island structure in busy Piccadilly. He loved it here. But the air raids had taken their toll; he watched as tired people went past rubble and roped-off areas as if it had always been like this. The lights never came on now and traffic was sparse.

After the walk round and a light lunch he returned to his billet and unlocked the door. His few things were packed including the Oberleutnant's Pioneers uniform. The car called for him mid-afternoon. The ATS driver gave him a bright smile and he climbed in the back as he had been instructed to do. The presence of the ATS girl confirmed to him what he had already suspected; this really was a British operation. And they considered it sufficiently important to provide him with a car and chauffeuse when he could have travelled to Weymouth by train.

Schroder slung his grip on to the seat beside him, observing the set glances the girl gave him through the rear-view mirror. He wanted to talk to her but found that he could not. It seemed, too, that she had been briefed to leave him alone. He thought back to the information he had been given and which he had burned before leaving. He still had the map and pulled it from a pocket to look at again.

It was still light when they reached Weymouth and the girl drove him straight down to the docks where he was met by a British naval commander whose face was still tinged by the ruddiness of youth. But his face belied his experience. Schroder did not know that the commander was a pre-war submariner and had already survived a depth-charged submarine during which he had lost most of his crew.

Schroder felt shabby in his creased civilian clothes as the two men shook hands. 'Smith,' said the commander. 'Glad to have you aboard.'

'Jones,' returned Schroder. 'If this is aboard I'm all for it.'

They grinned at each other and the trust was instant and mutual.

'Nobody told me you would be American.' Smith led the way along the quay and they stopped at a collection of wooden huts, recently erected and lying well back.

'I'm not,' rejoined Schroder. 'I'm disguising my accent.'

'That's the stuff, old boy. Knew that you were. No true American could be so atrociously nasal.'

Schroder warmed to the commander as they quietly laughed together. Smith opened the door to one of the huts. Inside, a single window looked out to sea. There was a plain table and some chairs and running along the short window wall, a crude sloping desk had been fixed high enough to stand behind.

The two men stood at the desk and Smith produced an Admiralty chart which he held down with drawing pins. 'Now we've learned so much about each other let's get down to it.' He stabbed at the chart using his forefinger as a pointer. 'There's a lighthouse here at Casquettes to the north-west of the island. Currents are a bit tricky but the weather forecast is good.' He glanced sideways at Schroder. 'I can see the physical reason why you're going. You look like a bloody Kraut.'

Schroder smiled wryly. 'It's been said before. This is roughly where I want to get to.' He pointed out the spot.

'I'm going to run between Guernsey and Alderney and then bear north. Come up behind it as it were.'

Schroder looked at the chart. 'Isn't that risky? These are shallows aren't they?'

'They are and we'll be too bloody near France. But our risk is nothing to yours so we'll do the best we can for you. They're least likely to expect anyone that side and it gets you nearer to where you want to go. Okay?'

'Fine.'

The commander folded the chart. 'I'm not all sweetness and light. There are likely to be fewer mines on the south side.' He smiled. 'They'd hardly expect an invasion from France, what?' Then more seriously, 'I'll pinpoint it as accurately as I can and give you your position before you leave us. Any questions?'

'Where's my gun and radio?'

'On board.' Smith eyed Schroder's grip. 'There's more room here to change but it's not dark yet and it might look a bit odd if the locals see a Royal Navy officer taking a walk with a German army officer. Change on board. Cramped but necessary.'

107

'Sure.'

'You all right?'

'Nothing I can't come to terms with.'

Smith laid a hand on Schroder's shoulder who could now see that the commander was older than he had at first looked. 'Never cease to marvel at you chaps. Send us a message and we'll get you back. We'll check frequencies on board. We'd better go.'

As they left the hut which Smith locked, Schroder asked, 'Are we under water all the way?'

'Good Lord, no. It's a good distance for the time we've got. And we've got to get back. I'll take her down when it's necessary.'

As Schroder changed he understood what Smith had meant about being cramped. The submarine was vibrating as it powered through the water and in spite of the fact that the commander had lent Schroder his own quarters there seemed precious little room to move. Using the edge of the bunk to steady himself he pulled on the uniform and the jackboots and adjusted the hat in front of the small mirror. Then he checked the radio which he would have to strap to his back.

He picked up the SMG with which he was already familiar; it was a machine pistol MP-38, 9MM. Everyone called it a Schmeisser, and everyone was wrong. This was a weapon for a fast-moving mechanised army and it weighed 9 lbs. With a muzzle velocity of 1250 fps it fired 500 rounds per minute. It was a good gun but Schroder hoped that he would never have to use it.

He left the gun and the radio in the cabin and lurched along the alleyway. The submarine seemed to be a mass of pipes and narrow alleys and protrusions designed to catch his head. The commander was in the tower so the crew were free with their smiles and badinage as Schroder appeared. One crewman threw him a 'Sieg Heil', and Schroder was glad of the light relief. He climbed the ladder to the conning tower.

Joining the small group in the tower Schroder was startled by the nearness of the sea. It was dark but he could both hear and see the water swilling over the bows. He preferred it to the constant hum of machinery below but it also brought him up with a jolt, remembering just where he was and why. Above them the wind was making a strange whine as it passed over the 'Jumping Wire'.

Suddenly everything was for real. London, his billet, the briefings were all gone. In spite of rigorous training he realised that in the field he was totally inexperienced. They all had to start somewhere; there had to be a first time. It occurred to him that for his first time his superiors had picked a real plum. Perhaps that was exactly why he had been chosen; an experienced field operative would be too valuable to lose. Resentment built up in him and then resignation. Many men had already died; he could claim no special privileges.

The commander noticed his thoughtful silence. 'The sea's running well, Mr Jones. It's in your favour.'

Schroder looked down at the dark wash which lightened as it broke against the hull. 'I'm glad you told me,' he replied drily. 'For a while there I was fooled.'

'There's some rum in my cabin. It's for you. And then have a sleep. We'll call you well in time.'

Schroder gazed out into the night. The empty sea gave him an uncanny feeling. It was dark and open and went on forever and they were all standing just on top of it as if it was the most natural thing to do. 'Thank you,' he said. 'I'll do just that.'

There was no engine noise. Nothing. Even the sea had quietened unless he had got used to the sound of it. A few miles away was occupied France. And ahead, unseen, was Alderney, also over-run by the enemy.

'I've got as close in as I dare,' whispered the commander. 'Follow a compass bearing dead north. You're just over a mile away. Good luck.'

They shook hands as ratings helped with the rubber dinghy. The sea seemed calm until he tried to grip the oars. The submarine now appeared immense, towering over him like a massive whale. As he pulled away he feared he would capsize but he kept going and gradually gained confidence. As he started rowing he was facing the submarine, but all too soon it had disappeared. Now he was alone in silence and darkness and the sea.

His arms ached but he was careful to put the oars in cleanly so that he made no noise; the rowlocks were padded. Progress was slow and he did not know how long it would take him to reach shore. From time to time he glanced at the compass which he had placed between his feet. The gun and the radio were wedged at the other end of the dinghy and had been covered with a blanket supplied by the submarine crew so that there was as little effect as possible on the compass from the metal of the equipment.

He rowed for so long that he began to believe he had missed the island but the phosphorous-tipped compass needle still pointed north. He kept going, his loneliness increasing with the rising swell and the strengthening breeze. His lack of preparation began to show. It had all been too rushed. What had seemed possible on land no longer did so out here.

Schroder then heard the same sound that George Fuller had been comforted by some two years earlier; the breaking of surf on shore. He kept rowing with total concentration. A mental layout of the island came to mind and he realised with horror that he still had the map on him; he should have destroyed it before leaving the submarine. He groped in his pocket, found the map, tore it in shreds and scattered it in the sea.

There were cliffs on the south-west end of the island and behind him he could pick up the heavier sound of the surf on rocks. He made a correction of direction and continued to row, ears alert for the slightest sound. There was the throb of an engine but it seemed miles away. Suddenly the breaking of surf was louder and he glanced round. He was too near to rocks and the dinghy was suddenly bucking and almost out of control. He tried to change direction again but the tide swept him on.

And then he struck something and nearly fell overboard. He grabbed at a passing shape and his fingers scraped painfully down a rock. Visibility was virtually nil. The only thing he could see with certainty was the spreading white surf as it crashed down on the shore.

There was no time to think things out. He snatched up the gun and managed to sling it around him. When he reached for the radio the dinghy almost stood on end and the radio slid towards him and he managed to grab it and scoop up the compass.

As he fought to stay aboard he somehow pulled the radio

harness over one shoulder but he was badly balanced. He grabbed at the nearest rock and clung on with all his strength. The sea swirled furiously round him as he tried to peer inland and the radio kept swinging out and bumping against the rocks. There were barely discernible shapes ahead of him and behind them he thought the shadows were more regular. The dinghy kept trying to go its own way but he managed to hold it with his feet. Easing his way round the rock he found a more sheltered area where the dinghy steadied a little but was still see-sawing under him. Finding a good handhold on the rock he crouched down and released one of the air valves on the dinghy. Half the dinghy began to submerge as he groped for the other valve. Now grasping the rock with both hands he pushed down with his feet until the dinghy disappeared. Clinging there, the gun and radio falling awkwardly across his back, Schroder struggled to pull himself out of the sea.

At last clear of the water, he was panting and sweating and soaked from the waist down as he lay painfully on the jagged rock layer. He considered that the miracle was not so much that he had survived but that his cap had remained lodged on his head; it had been padded to hold it tight but it was amazing that it had held firm.

Working his way across the uneven barrier was difficult and exhausting. He waded through static pools between rocks and finally reached a small beach at the foot of a cliff. He had hoped to avoid the cliffs but as far as he could see this one appeared not to be sheer, although too dangerous to tackle at night.

He squatted on the beach, unhappy and wet and listened to the sea while he recovered and began to pick out the shapes around him. Something glinted at the foot of the cliff and there was a terrible smell nearby. Just ahead of him something was moving. As he crawled towards a rock cluster, the smell got stronger. He put out a hand towards a pale shape and recoiled sharply. A skeletal form was wedged between the rocks, half in the water, half out. A painfully thin arm was sweeping backwards and forwards with the sea. The smell was so strong that it made him feel sick and Schroder realised that the body was in an advanced state of decomposition. He withdrew quickly.

He could now see that the glint of light came from an empty beer bottle; he could smell the residue of beer when he sniffed its top. He held the bottle thoughtfully. Unless it had been thrown from the cliff top it suggested that the small beach had been used. And if it had there must be a path leading up the cliff or one leading off from the beach.

To remain immobile in wet clothes would mean shivering his way through the rest of the night. He had no torch with him and it would have been folly to use one anyway. Relying on touch and limited sight he explored the beach, squelching his way ponderously over the sand as quietly as he could. Eventually he found the base of the path.

Even in daylight the path must have been difficult to climb. At times it was almost perpendicular and because of its acute angle it snaked considerably, repeatedly hairpinning. Schroder followed its dangerous course upwards mostly on all fours and with the MP-38 and the radio strapped firmly to him. He kept going, wondering what might be waiting for him at the top and occasionally reflecting on how many more dead bodies were wasting away below.

Fuller was not at all certain that he had fooled Joachim Brocker. When Claudie started to enter the room, Fuller, after the initial shock of seeing Brocker's obvious suspicion, went to the door and once past Brocker, who had his back to it, mouthed at Claudie to retreat. After silently forcing her out he urgently signalled to her to go upstairs and to keep the escapees quiet. Fuller then called up the stairs as if she was already there. But on returning to Brocker he was dismayed to find Blanco on the captain's lap.

From that point Brocker seemed in a hurry to go. He refused the offer of coffee and it was unusual for him not to pay his respects to Claudie. There was nothing Fuller could do and he knew it would be a mistake to make further excuses about the sound in the bedroom above them.

It was then still early morning; the visit to the hospital had been soon after dawn. With time on his hands Fuller escorted Brocker most of the way to the captain's billet but there was uneasiness between them and when he turned back he was worried. He trusted Brocker as a man but dare he trust him as a German officer? Yet at the moment there was nowhere else he could hide Kremple and Gorkov. He had to find some place for them, and there was Jacqui to consider too. He knew better than anyone that the young French girl was very close to breaking point.

Fuller deliberately took his time. He wanted to sort things out in his mind before being confronted with Claudie again. He had placed her at risk and he must find a solution before it was too late, if it was not already.

As he neared the house his worries intensified. He varied his route yet again in the hope of finding a place where Jacqui, Kremple and Gorkov could hide under one roof. The sight of a German officer talking to Claudie at his front door brought his mind back sharply to immediate dangers. Claudie seemed to be having trouble.

As Fuller drew nearer he noticed salt marks on the man's jackboots and his breeches were water-stained; nor could he miss the SMG and the radio. 'What's the problem?'

As the officer pivoted round Claudie said quickly, 'He keeps asking if Doctor Fuller lives here.'

Fuller thought quickly; everyone on the island knew that he lived here. He eyed the officer curiously, noted the blue eyes and fair hair and noticed too his unit tags. 'I'm Fuller, what do you want?'

The officer looked around to make sure no one was watching; 'I've been sent from England to find you.' Schroder spoke in English.

Fuller could not believe it; the man had an American accent. All the time now he was looking for traps and he wondered if this was one. He noted the water marks again and said, 'Get in quick.'

They went into the living room. Schroder unhooked his SMG and radio and laid them on a chair. He turned to Claudie, 'I'm sorry I scared you, ma'am.'

Fuller did not ask Schroder to sit down, he was still suspicious.

'You've come from England?'

'Last night.'

'How?'

'Submarine, and dinghy for the last bit.'

'Where's the dinghy now?'

'I sank her.'

'And you took all this trouble to find me?'

Seeing Fuller's continued suspicion Schroder said, 'I've been holed up all night in a gully on the cliff top. It was too dangerous to try to reach you in the dark.'

Claudie said, 'I'll get you a hot drink,' and went into the kitchen.

'And how did you find me this morning?'

'I memorised a plan but in the end I had to ask a soldier.'

'*You what?*'

Schroder became angry. 'Look, feller, I've stuck my neck out to find you. I can do without criticism.'

Fuller tried to calm down. 'You must forgive my incredulity.' He indicated the boots. 'You've been in the sea, your breeches are still wet. The unit whose tags you wear left the island months ago. You were also carrying a radio which officers here wouldn't deign to do. Everyone here knows me and where I live yet you stop a German soldier to ask the way.'

'Goddam it, I'm not that stupid,' snapped Schroder. 'I called out to him from a distance. I made sure I went near no one.'

'You've been very lucky. You must have picked the right soldier. Perhaps it was too early in the morning. Please sit down. Get your boots off, we'll try to put some polish back on them.'

Claudie came in and placed a cup of coffee in front of Schroder, who noticed her glance. 'Ma'am, I know what you're thinking. I was chosen just because I look like a German. I'm Lieutenant Rod Schroder.' He turned back to Fuller. 'And I was instructed to tell you that your father is alive and well.'

Fuller smiled and his face changed. 'A bloody American,' he said, unbelievingly. 'Well, I never.'

Claudie had placed herself between Schroder and the gun, a move that both men noticed. 'Claudie is more difficult to convince,' Fuller pointed out. 'You have to satisfy her. You must understand our position here.'

Schroder looked over at Claudie. 'You're very lovely ma'am.' He smiled slightly. 'I guess that should confirm the brass neck of an American. But I do mean it.' He sipped the coffee and wrinkled his nose. 'I don't know why they've used an American. Nobody would tell me. But I did find you, lucky or not.'

Fuller said cautiously, 'Your job was *specifically* to find me?'

and before Schroder could reply he added, 'From the way they prepared you it almost seems that someone wants to get rid of you.'

'That's not too fair. They're working on scanty information over there. And they were in a hurry.'

'So precisely *who* sent you?'

'My boss sent me. That's as far as I'll go. Someone considered it important enough to get me over here to tell you that a guy called Ardense will be visiting the island, that you know him, and they want you to find out what he gets up to.'

Fuller was immediately suspicious. 'I don't know anyone of that name.'

'I'm told you do. Maybe he's using another name.'

'You sure you got the name right?'

'No. I made it up.'

'Okay, I asked for that. And you don't know why an American was sent?'

'I've no idea.'

Fuller sat on the edge of the table. 'All right. Someone arrives, somebody I know. Somehow. I find out why he's here. And then what?'

'We radio for a pick up. I understand that someone will be listening in twenty-four hours a day, every day. That's how important it is. I tell them where to go for the pick up in a simple code I've memorised. If help doesn't come we radio what we know and then you're stuck with me.'

Fuller heaved the radio on to the table. 'It's big and it's heavy.'

'It has to be; it's long range. What's the danger of monitoring?'

'Very little here. Apart from us they have only themselves to contend with. The bigger islands might be different.' Fuller was examining the set. 'Have you seen the back of this?'

'I've been too busy hunking it.'

'You'd better look.'

Schroder rose as Fuller turned the set round. 'Jesus Christ.' The back of the set had a huge dent. 'That must have happened on the rocks. Have you got a screwdriver?'

Claudie went out to get one. When she returned with it she could see that Schroder was worried. The American took the back off with difficulty. When he peered inside the case he shook his head in anguish. 'The valves have gone. Can we get it repaired?'

'Only by the Germans.'

'Shit! Ma'am, I'm sorry, really sorry.'

'I've heard worse from George,' said Claudie drily.

Fuller glanced at his watch. 'We'll have to work something out, but I must get back to the hospital.' He straightened to eye Schroder critically, then he gestured helplessly. 'You're a brave man. It's a great pity about the radio, though.'

'If I had landed on the south-eastern beach as I should have done it wouldn't have happened. I don't know what to say.'

'If you'd have landed there you'd have blown yourself to bits; the beach is mined.

'You sound as though you'd have preferred that.'

Fuller reached the door. 'After the risks you've taken I've no right to give you that impression. I'm sorry. But without the radio it will have been in vain. You've risked your neck for nothing and now we have to decide what to do with you. For us, it's one more problem.'

Claudie, always practical, said, 'Isn't it time Jacqui had company?'

Fuller nodded thoughtfully. 'Look after him, love. Tidy up his uniform and I'll take him over there later. Meanwhile get the gun and radio out of sight.

Fuller led Schroder to Longy Bay. 'Stick by me and you'll be safe. No one is likely to stop us. I'll see that they don't get close enough to see too much of you.'

They continued openly across the southern stretch of the island, giving gun sites a wide berth. It was much easier to reach the house in daylight but far more troops were about.

'What's going on here?' asked Schroder.

'A good question. When I've met this strange person whom I'm supposed to know and when I've discovered what he wants, I might have some answers.'

They were nearing the house now. Fuller enjoyed a feeling of security with Schroder beside him. Provided watching eyes were sufficiently distant he need not apply too much stealth in his approach. He slowed the pace and did not make their final direction too obvious but he knew that with the illusion of a German Oberleutnant by his side, few would take notice.

They reached the derelict house in the gulley. At the front door he stopped. 'Wait here. And remember what I told you.'

Fuller called softly to Jacqui as he went up the stairs. She was crouched in a corner as she always was when he arrived. 'The man I'm about to bring in is dressed as a German officer. He's not German but an American sent over from England. He will stay with you. Don't be alarmed at his appearance.'

Jacqui swivelled her wide eyes up at him and something about her reminded him of Gorkov. She was deteriorating rapidly, her pretty face beginning to hollow.

'He won't molest you and he'll be good company.' Fuller smiled down at her. 'And he has some chocolate he brought over.'

Fuller called softly down the stairs for Schroder to come up. Schroder entered the room and, even prepared for it, was startled to see a fair-haired slip of a girl cowering in the corner. She was pretty, though he could see at a glance that she had suffered. And she seemed so vulnerable. He gave her a wide smile.

'Do you speak French?' asked Fuller. 'I forgot to ask.'

'Schoolboy French,' Schroder replied.

'This is your chance to improve it. Rod, meet Jacqui. He's come to help us.' Fuller avoided Schroder's look of surprise.

9

Admiral Canaris looked out towards the Brandenburg Gate with mixed feelings. He wanted peace with Britain and so did the Führer. Their reasons and conditions were quite different. But there was another reason now why Hitler was drawn towards the Lord Arden proposals. There were problems on the Russian front. It was imperative to take Moscow before the winter snows set in, and it was already early autumn.

The German advance had ground to a halt and the generals were sounding their usual infuriating warnings. General Kleist had tried to push south from Mozdok in a series of surprise attacks but had been stopped each time. The position had stabilised but it was not good enough.

While the Allies at present were too scattered and too disorganised to contemplate an invasion, it was still necessary to tie down divisions in France, Holland and Belgium as a precautionary measure. The Russian front could well do with the backing of further divisions to settle the issue quickly; it should by now have been over.

Yet in spite of these problems the build up in the Channel Islands continued, a fact that satisfied the admiral that his interpretation of the Führer's intentions was correct. If Lord Arden betrayed Churchill, Canaris was convinced that Hitler would then betray Arden.

There was another matter of concern for the Führer. Joachim von Ribbentrop had a virus which had put him to bed. Hitler was furious at the unwelcome timing of the unfortunate Ribbentrop's illness. Klaus Wendel, Ribbentrop's deputy, would now be going to Alderney. With him would go Himmler's crony and Canaris's enemy, Walter Schellenberg, head of the SS foreign intelligence department, RSHA VI. Canaris was well aware of the irony of having to arrange the clandestine meeting himself.

So the Arden meeting was definitely on. Or at least the final discussions were to take place. Canaris returned to his chair deep in thought. He understood the importance of ascertaining Lord Arden's credentials. It must be established that he was who he said he was and that he carried the power he claimed. Canaris had dealt with self-effacing, shadowy characters before. Some of them were empty shells. Others wielded far more power than Chancellors or Prime Ministers yet were unknown to the man in the street. His instinct told him that Arden fitted into the latter category and he wondered if Arden's need for peace was sufficiently strong to verge on the fanatical, and to obscure issues that might be detrimental to the very aims he was seeking. Time would tell. British intelligence might be playing a cunning game.

But as Canaris sat quietly reviewing matters he realised that he lacked sufficient detail to make a final judgment. Which was why Hitler had asked him to send Hans Oster to meet Lord Arden. Hitler knew that Canaris and Oster were close friends. So close that neither would consciously put the other at risk. Whatever the temptation Canaris could not ask Oster for the details of the Arden proposals. And without them, interpretation or not, there would always be an element of doubt; it was the way Hitler worked.

Canaris found the experience frustrating. He sometimes felt that part of the pattern formed a trap for himself. Anything he was handling which involved Walter Schellenberg must be handled with extreme care. He sat back; he had always felt there was treachery in the air but now it was only the amount he was not sure about.

Schroder crouched at the upstairs window watching. From across the room Jacqui said in bad German, 'They will see you.' The two had found that they could converse better in Jacqui's halting German than Schroder's poor French.

Schroder, once alone with the girl, had been quick to get the measure of her distraught state of mind, had understood her fears completely. She seemed to him frail even though her slim body was firm. There was an elfin quality in the fragile smoothness of her face that portrayed so easily what she had suffered.

As soon as Fuller had gone Schroder had set out to reassure her, making fun of his own atrocious French accent and telling her how good her German was. He tried her with English and told her he would teach her.

At first she had been disturbed by his Saxon appearance, coupled with the uniform, but he had poked fun at that too and even raised a laugh from her. She had been near to breaking point and he marvelled that she had survived this far. It was going to be a delicate battle to build up her courage again.

Right now she was cutting across his concentration as he watched a group of soldiers make their way towards the beach. He tried to shut out her voice and held up a restraining hand. What particularly held his attention was the mine detector one of the men carried. He waited until they were out of sight beyond the rise then carefully scanned the direction from which they had come. There was nobody else. He crawled to the door. 'I'll be back. Don't worry,' he murmured softly in an agonising mixture of French and German.

Jacqui looked frightened again but he gave her a thumbs up and hurried down the stairs. He was careful as he left the house and did not follow the direction of the group but went straight to the rise that sheltered the house from sight of the beach. He crawled up it carefully and lay flat to peer over the edge.

Schroder could see the beach and the men who were now strung along the rear of it; as far as he could judge they were above the high-water mark. An officer was barking orders and appeared to be in a bad temper as he instructed the man with the detector to line up on a particular rock below and to the right of Schroder, who groped quickly in his pockets to produce a pencil and a still damp notepad.

There were five men including the officer and they all appeared to be disgruntled. The man with the detector started to pace forward slowly while another counted his steps. The detector was slowly swept from side to side. They were either plotting the minefield a section at a time or were establishing a definite safe path down to the waterline. From the mood of the officer it seemed to Schroder that this was something that should have been done at the time of laying.

One soldier called out direction and the number of paces, another wrote them down and a third man studied a sheet clipped to a board. Schroder concentrated and counted and made notes.

He was suddenly aware of someone behind him and turned quickly. It was Jacqui crawling up the rise to join him. Momentarily annoyed he realised that she was placing them in no more danger than he himself. 'Watch our backs,' he rapped out in German, not sure that she understood. He was worried now. How much had he missed? It was important to learn of a safe approach to the waterline which might mean a path to freedom.

There was a period when there appeared to be confusion among the soldiers. The detector bearer seemed reluctant to move at all at one point. From what was shouted between them and from the irascible comments of the officer Schroder guessed that there had been a query on the original plotting; the officer had noticed what he considered to be a discrepancy and had insisted on a check.

When this was finally finished the officer, perhaps out of pique or to mete out punishment for neglect, changed the detector bearer and then did spot checks in other areas of the beach. On one of Schroder's courses he had been taught how to search for tell-tale signs of mines but whether it was standard German practice to keep a plotted record of a minefield he had no idea. It could be an enforced exercise in mine detecting. If it was he hoped that it had been accurately performed. Nobody had been blown up anyway.

He slid down the rise and saw that Jacqui had positioned herself just below him so that she could watch both ends of the gulley. Once below the skyline he helped her up.

'Are you warm enough in that thing?' The dress seemed so flimsy.

She got the gist of what he said and told him that Claudie had supplied other clothes which were in a cupboard upstairs. She held on to his hand as if she was afraid of losing him. As they returned to the house she haltingly explained that this was the first time since arriving that she had dared to go out in daylight and would not have done so had he not been there.

When they were back upstairs words poured from her. He let her talk on realising her need to offload. At one stage he was certain that she wanted the physical contact of him, someone, almost anyone, to hold and comfort and protect her.

He was afraid to touch her; it could quickly send her the other way if he made one wrong move and Fuller had told him that her fiancé had drowned. He wasn't sure what she wanted so he listened and watched as she talked on endlessly, tension and fear flowing out of her.

When night fell she lent him a blanket for a pillow; blankets had been smuggled to her one at a time by the Fullers. He stayed well away from her not wanting to frighten her and even offered to go into one of the other rooms. But that prospect scared her too. She had a protector whose very presence kept the Germans at bay and to whom she could pour out her fears.

She came to him in the middle of the night and sobbed as if it would never end. Her fingers bit into him painfully but he said nothing and did nothing except to hold her as she buried herself into him, and to murmur comforting words he doubted that she heard. After her young body had ceased to wrack and the tears had finally stopped she slept like a baby in his arms.

He was propped in an awkward position but he did not want to disturb the girl; it was probably the first sound sleep she had managed since arriving. One of his arms was cramped as she lay against it and he wondered how he might change position without waking her. Her body warmth had penetrated his jacket. He was uncomfortable and realised that he still had his jackboots on.

As he lay there in the darkness cradling the girl and trying to figure out how best to ease his own discomfort he heard movement downstairs. Then he heard voices, low-pitched but unmistakable. He kept perfectly still. There were men below.

At first he was not sure what to do. It might be wisest to stay where he was. But then he realised that it would be better to find out what was happening. There might be danger; something was going on and he'd better discover what.

Something of his tension communicated to the girl. She stirred and he moved and as she awakened he felt the panic run through her. He quickly put a hand over her mouth and held her lightly. 'Keep still,' he whispered. 'Someone's downstairs.' She shuddered and struggled and he held her to give her time to grasp what was happening.

After a while she calmed down, and he whispered, 'I must see what's happening.'

'No.' She clung to him again. 'Don't leave me.'

'I won't do anything stupid. I must find out what's going on.'

He was not sure if she understood him. He eased her away from him, whispering, reassuring. He kissed her lightly on the cheek and squeezed her hand. There was no doubting her terror and he was aware of his own rising fear as he reassured her once more before slipping off his boots.

He crawled across the room on all fours, trying to recall whether there were any creaking boards. Reaching the door he raised his hand to open it. It groaned as he pulled it back and the sounds below became more distinct. He crept across the landing, stopped above the stairs, then eased his legs forward so that he was sitting with his feet two stairs down.

The sounds now were more recognisable but at first he could not identify them, or was disbelieving what he heard. He went halfway down the stairs in a sitting position, not putting too much weight on any stair and he stopped again.

Schroder froze. At first he was stunned and then, as he took in what was happening, lost his surprise at the sounds of increasing ardour taking place below him. On an island of men cut off from normal life he supposed that the inevitable was happening. He wondered how long they had been there. Was it a regular tryst that Jacqui had been unaware of or had they simply found another place to discharge their lust?

As passion passed its zenith and the voices made more recognisable sounds, Schroder thought it best to get back up the stairs. It was unlikely that the two men below would come up. And then one of them spoke and the other laughed awkwardly. There was movement and the rustle of clothes and Schroder knew that the young ears below might now pick up any sound he made. He thought of them as young because the timbre of their voices was youthful as was their present reaction to their clandestine meeting.

It became clear that they were now in a hurry to get back to their billets. Listening to their soft exchanges Schroder learned that they came from the same house and that it would be prudent if they arrived back there separately, as they had probably done here. One of them left in a hurry and Schroder saw the pale reflection as the front door opened. He decided it was safer to stay where he was until the other man had gone.

He sat waiting, listening to the hurried movement. Something metallic struck the floor. There was shuffling followed by some swearing as groping hands failed to find whatever they were seeking. A click was followed by a flash of light.

Schroder drew back. The tiny flame of the German lighter was like a fire in the darkness. Shadows spread from the light bowl and Schroder could see clearly a drawn face in the flickering glow. And then he noticed the belt near the foot of the stairs.

It was too late to retreat. The soldier bent down for his belt and straightened with it in his hand. The light went out and the darkness was total. Schroder held his breath unable to see a thing. And then the light flashed on again and the soldier was staring up at Schroder, the glow illuminating a mixture of alarm and disbelief on the young man's face.

Neither made a move and it flashed through Schroder's mind what the soldier was confronting: sitting on the stairs was a German officer with his boots off. Had he . . .? The soldier, realising that he could not pretend not to have seen the officer, clicked his heels and threw a salute. Schroder was thinking quickly. It could not be left like this. There might be talk. The soldier might become over-curious, if not immediately, then later. He was about to climb to his feet, to bluff it out and put the fear of God into the man as an interim measure when he saw the expression change to one of amazement.

Without looking round Schroder was certain that Jacqui had crawled on to the landing to see what was happening. She had been silent but the soldier had glimpsed her. A woman? Schroder picked up the innuendo of doubt and suspicion and could see that the soldier was about to run. The youngster was bewildered and had seen something he could not grasp, but his instinct warned him that something was drastically wrong.

Schroder dived from where he sat and landed on the German with tremendous force. They crashed to the floor as Jacqui cried out. The lighter went out as it dropped. There was a terrible crack as the soldier's head hit the floor and his body cushioned Schroder's fall.

Schroder clung to the German's throat. While he squeezed in the darkness, listening to Jacqui's panicking cries from above, he had the sensation that he was trying to take the life from someone already dead. Afterwards, as he crouched panting over the body, he was not sure whether the fall had broken the soldier's neck or whether he had strangled him.

It was a little while before he took his hands away. His fingers were clawed up with tension and it took time to straighten them. 'It's all right,' he called up the stairs. 'He's dead'. There was no need to test the pulse, to do any checks at all. Jacqui began to cry and he felt for her, but he himself was knotted up and he was finding it difficult to come to terms with what he'd done. It was over and that was that.

He searched around for the lighter but could not find it. Wherever his fingers groped they always finished up on the body. 'Christ!' He experienced relief and self-disgust but there could be no recrimination. War was war. He located the back of the stairs and pulled the body into the recess. It was the best he could do for the moment but he would have to get rid of it.

He called up the stairs again before he climbed them to Jacqui. At the top they clung together, the need mutual. It was some time before they talked and when they did it was in the dreadful mixture of languages that they had learned to adopt; the essence was clear.

'Are you sure he's dead?'

'Absolutely.' Their grip on each other had loosened but he felt her shudder.

'We can't leave him down there. They will search for him.'

'I know.'

With a crisis to consider Jacqui was calmer, her mind acting positively. 'What was he doing?'

'He was with another soldier.' He gave her time to work it out.

'Oh!' And then she said hesitantly, 'But the other soldier will report where he last saw his friend.'

'It's highly unlikely, Jacqui. I guess he'll keep his mouth shut.'

'He might come back to look.'

'He might. We must get rid of the body.'

'How?'

'I'll dump him in the sea,' he said casually, not wanting her to dwell on it.

'*No.*' She stiffened immediately. '*No.*'

'It's okay. I've got the notes of the clear lanes.'

'You'll kill yourself. If I lose you I'll give myself up to the Germans. I could not stand being alone again. Not now. We can bury him.'

'Dig a grave with our fingers? And where could we do it without being seen?'

'At night. We'll find something to dig with.'

'This night is nearly over and we can't wait for the next one. Don't worry. I'll be okay.'

He could feel her fears return. He thought they were mainly for herself but he tried to understand; he had not suffered what she had suffered. The fact that he had killed the German seemed not to worry her at all.

There was no more sleep for them that night. They stayed close together because they did not want to lose physical contact and to be separated by the darkness. It was easier to talk in whispers like this. At times they dozed as they waited for the dawn.

At the first tinge of grey Schroder got to his feet. Jacqui rose with him. They could barely see each other. He went down the stairs and she hurried after him. 'I must get it done,' he said.

It was not until he stripped to his trunks at the foot of the stairs that she really accepted that he intended to go through with it. He took the notes of the minefield from his pocket and tucked them into the top of his trunks. She could not believe what he was doing and it was fortunate that he could not see her despair.

He pulled the body from the recess and out of the front door. It was still dark but the larger shapes were beginning to take on hazy outlines. He bent down and raised the soldier in a fireman's lift and Jacqui scampered after him to the rear of the beach where he put the body down.

'You can't see in this. You'll be blown to bits. And then they'll come and find me.'

'While I'm getting rid of him,' he said, 'as soon as you can see properly you look for that lighter. It's a giveaway, and, anyway, it might be useful.'

She put her arms round his neck. 'Don't go. Don't leave me.'

'I must. And don't do that.'

She pressed herself into him and found his lips and clung and moved her hands over his body in a desperate bid to stop him.

He forced her head back and said viciously, 'Just where did your fiancé drown?'

She broke away and slapped his face and the sound carried across the sands like a whiplash.

'That's better,' he whispered.

'What's wrong with you?'

'Your timing is lousy. Wait till I get back if you're that eager.'

The beach gradually emerged like a break in cloud. It was barely discernible and beyond it mist clung to the sea. But he could pick out the rocks now and he bent to lift the body again. He leaned against the rock and produced his notes; it was awkward with the dead weight on his shoulder. The soldier's hat fell off and, Jacqui making no attempt to retrieve it, he bent again and rammed it on his own head. He was shivering from the cold.

'You can't see in this light.'

'I can count. And I can see enough.' Even when he held the paper in front of his face he could barely read it. He would have to wait a little longer. He lowered the soldier. The wraiths of mist were rolling back yet there was no breeze.

'How will you know the length of each pace?' Jacqui, still close to him, illustrated as she stepped in front of him.

At last she had got through to him. He had taken particular care in noting the length of pace but distance and perspective had been against him. It was his main worry.

It was light enough now to see her as she stood in front of him but still sufficiently dark for the rising ground at the end of the bay to be hidden. It was time to move; he dare not leave it longer.

Once more he bent to pick up the soldier and Jacqui flung herself at him, crying and scratching in an effort to stop him. She raised her voice and was becoming hysterical, unaware or unheeding of the noise she was making. He clipped her on the jaw and she fell at his feet across the body of the soldier. He dragged her clear. There was no time to take her back to the house and he could only hope that he would return before it was really light. If he got back at all.

He could now read his notes as he adjusted the weight of the corpse on his shoulder. He lined up hoping that he was precisely facing the right way. This was not what he had expected to use

127

the notes for, nor so soon. Without another glance at Jacqui he strode out towards the pale, wide stretch of sand and the shrouded sea.

Had he allowed himself to consider the consequences he would have gone no further. Now totally committed his concentration was absolute and this helped stave off his fears. He closed his mind to everything except following explicitly the detail he had jotted down.

He trod carefully yet he dare not take too long. He stopped at the end of the first leg and pivoted exactly at right angles, his only guide to accuracy the faint impression of his own footsteps behind him. Ten paces to the left. In spite of the early morning chill, he started to sweat.

Turn right. He checked his footprints and made a slight adjustment. Twenty paces. Left fifteen paces. After seven he stopped. He was not sure why but his nerve ends were strumming. Making sure the feet of the corpse did not touch the ground, Schroder squatted on his heels and finger brushed the sand in front of him. He touched metal and found the mine he had been about to step on.

He looked towards the sea. It was still misty but he could hear it lapping at the shoreline. There was one more dog leg to go and he could not see the high-tide mark in the murk. He scanned the notes again.

Rising slowly he gazed back at his footprints and noticed that about five paces back they veered slightly. He stepped back carefully into his own tracks and then corrected his direction before setting out again. In spite of his concentration the hair on the nape of his neck bristled.

He did the last leg almost in a daze, counting the final twenty paces and afraid to put one foot in front of the other. He was still treading delicately when he noticed the high-tide mark. His relief was so immense that his legs almost lost strength but he kept going and then hurried as fast as he could to reach the sea. When his feet splashed in the water he tried to run but his legs would not respond and the weight of the corpse was now bearing him down.

He hit the grey, placid sea clumsily. Swimming on his back he gripped the soldier under the chin and grabbed the hat which fell from his own head. The going was difficult and slow. The corpse had lost air and was starting to sink but Schroder needed deeper water; he did not want the soldier finishing up on the beach. What worried him most was the rising mist; it hovered over the sea making a grey sandwich of cloud, air and water.

Believing he had gone far enough and that he had no time to go further out, he trod water, held the corpse round the neck, pushed hard under its rib-cage to force the remaining air out, then let it go. The soldier slipped away, odd air bubbles plotting his course. Schroder had to swill the cap around before it would sink and even then it drifted down all too slowly. Wearily, he swam back to shore.

He ran along the high-tide mark until he found his footprints and then followed them back. Nearer to the rear of the beach where they might be seen he took the time to footbrush the sand over them as he continued. When he reached the rock Jacqui was sitting up, rubbing her chin.

'I'm sorry,' he said. 'You were making too much noise. I had to stop you.' He held a hand out to help her up but she ignored it. 'Come on,' he said urgently. 'We're pushing our luck.'

Jacqui made no sign that she understood and climbed slowly to her feet to stare at him sullenly.

'What's the matter?' he asked. 'Are you afraid that I might take you up on your offer? Don't worry. I'm getting back to the house to look for that lighter. You'd better get out of sight damned quick.' He pulled the sodden paper from his waistband and it came away in pieces. 'Well, that's that.'

Jacqui turned her back on him and headed towards the house. Schroder was not sure whether it was her pride that had been hurt or her chin but what he did not like was her sullen indifference, that could be dangerous for them both.

On the morning that Schroder killed the soldier Fuller found alternative accommodation for the fugitives. The house was just inland of the mid-south section of the island, near a bridle path roughly between the coast and the middle artillery site being excavated. There was a good deal of work going on in the vicinity but the house itself was isolated. Part of the roof was down and no one had troubled to repair it. It was small and in generally bad shape and had probably been part of a small-holding.

Because of its bad condition nobody went near it. Fuller had known of it for some time but it was the discovery of its cellar that really swayed him. An old garden shed had been built against the southern wall. It was a depository for discarded equipment; a broken shovel, rusted garden fork, withered hosepipe, an old mower and pieces of worn carpet scattered haphazardly. Hooks set into the roof beams had probably been used for hanging onions. There were three old tea chests full of junk and it was under one of these in a filthy corner that Fuller had found the trapdoor.

The trap, at one time, must have been just outside the house in the open cobbled yard. Its original purpose was probably to store farm stocks in the cellar without going through the house. The shed may have been built when the trapdoor became less weatherproof. There was one broken window and the roof let in water where the slates had come loose.

The cellar, reached by a wooden ladder, was cluttered, dirty but dry. And there were bales of straw for beds. He would have to wait until night time before he could lead Jacqui and Schroder to their new home. But first he had to tackle Gorkov about the tunnel he had mentioned; it had been playing on his mind to an extent that made him believe it to be crucial for him to find it.

'Tell me everything you know about the tunnel.'

Gorkov turned his gaze from Fuller to Kremple. 'Never mind about him,' added Fuller. 'What do you know?'

'We worked on a section at a time. As each batch finished a section they were taken off the work and were exterminated.'

'Which tunnel are you talking about? The main one to the hospital or the secondary one to the big chamber?'

'I don't know either of those tunnels. We worked from above ground. The tunnel went straight down.'

Fuller turned to Kremple. 'Do you know anything of this?'

'Nothing. We knew a hospital was being built. None of us were involved in it or saw it.' Kremple gestured at Gorkov. 'I don't know what he's talking about. There are tunnels being built all over the place.'

Gorkov glared. 'When I realised what was happening to my comrades I knew what to do when the batch I was in was taken off work. When a colleague collapsed and died I dropped near him and feigned death. I might have got a bullet in the head to make sure but I was lucky. I slipped away before they came back to remove our bodies. I don't know where the tunnel went or how far down. We concreted the sides as we went. I think we may have reached the bottom but we were taken off before I could be sure.'

'Could you show me where it began above ground?'

'No. We were taken part way by a small bus with blacked-out windows. Then we were blindfolded and formed up in a single file each holding a hand of the man in front. We were led the rest of the way on foot to the tunnel. It could have been anywhere.'

'In woods, open ground, near town?' Fuller reflected that he had seen the small blacked-out bus on occasion and tried to recall its direction.

'Woods, I think.' Gorkov spread his skeletal hands in exasperation. 'Do you imagine we cared where it was? Do you think we were making notes?'

'I'm sorry. If anything comes to mind let me know.' But Fuller was convinced that Gorkov had nothing else to tell him; he would have to find out for himself. As the secret had been kept by killing all those who had worked on it locating it would be far from easy. But he still believed it was connected with the hospital complex.

When Fuller told Claudie she suffered the despair of knowing that there was nothing she could do to stop him.

10

Lord Arden had a final meeting with his son and the key people involved in his scheme to bring peace back to Britain. It had taken months of planning and secret meetings to have arrived at this point of no return. The timing was right: the hold up of the German advance on the Russian front should aid his proposals.

He flew from London to Lisbon with the comfort of knowing that Portugal was Britain's oldest ally, a bond which was to show itself throughout the war in Portugal itself and in her colonies. Extra fuel tanks had been fitted to allow for the circuitous route of a commercial aircraft; the Portuguese could not allow a military plane to land without loss of neutrality.

He sat hunched and cold and felt exposed at being airborne in unfriendly skies off the French coastline. Even with the knowledge that instructions had been issued that this was one plane to be left alone it was an uncomfortable experience. But he could face his fears, subjugate them with undoubted courage.

Watching his huddled, lean body, one could imagine him feeling the chill; but there was nothing in his face to betray the cold terror he felt as he listened to the drone of the engines.

Arden greeted the loss of altitude on the approaches to Lisbon with relief. He was met at the airport by a senior member of the International Red Cross who was not convinced that he was not being used but powers greater than his had decreed his action. And Arden's papers proclaimed him to be Swedish. He caught a Spanish plane to Madrid on the morning of the third day and the following day a German plane to Paris with a touch down at Bordeaux. At Paris he was met by a high-ranking German officer who checked his false credentials knowing no more about the real purpose of his visit than his papers revealed.

Arden was taken to a luxury apartment block off the rue du Caumartin. Brandy, cigars, and strangely, a bottle of French perfume were on a table under a gilt mirror. An expertly arranged basket of fruit occupied the centre of a Louis XIV card table. These were no luxuries to Arden but their presence in wartime showed that the Germans, those who mattered anyway, did not lack for anything. He glanced at the perfume and hoped they would not be foolish enough to try to foist a woman on him. He had lost interest in women once his son was born.

He bathed, changed, and rested on the canopied bed, unable to doze in spite of his wearying series of flights. His mind was sharply active, going over the details again and again. He reflected upon the reaction his visit would produce from Churchill, Roosevelt, Stalin and Hitler. Without doubt it would affect all four dramatically and in quite different ways.

Captain Jürgen Heyden sipped the brandy in the small, sparse office. There was a cheap desk, a chair behind it and two in front, in one of which the SS captain sprawled, legs out, jackboots shining. The house in Victoria Street, St Anne, was one of a terrace and, like the others, housed the occupation forces. This particular building, with no outside notice to identify it, was Gestapo headquarters.

Behind the desk was a weasel of a man, sharp of speech and feature with darting brown eyes. Erich Kratz was paid on the scale of a lieutenant colonel. He had been in Alderney only six months and had quickly learned that the island could not really sustain someone of his position in his particular field. There was really no one who could effectively harm the Reich in any way, except perhaps the English doctor. The labour force was politically ineffective; it did not matter whether they lived or died and there were none fit enough for subversion. Which left only the forces of the Reich, including the TODT organisation. Quite simply, there was not enough for him to do and he could foresee the day when he would be withdrawn.

Potentially Kratz was the most powerful man on the island but unless he could show something for his position his superiors in Cherbourg would eventually catch up with him. At least Heyden, sitting opposite, could occupy himself with the TODT group, dispense with those who held up progress; but the Gestapo was political and none knew better than Kratz that there was no political situation here. Jersey, Guernsey, even tiny Sark, the other Channel Islands were different. They still had sizeable civilian populations. Alderney was unique among them. He often wondered why the island had been cut off from the rest. When the working parties from Guernsey had been allowed over he had at least been able to justify his existence, but now they had stopped and there was little to occupy him. Because of the ultimate query hanging over his position, he was exceedingly interested in what Heyden was saying. He asked in his dartlike way, 'Has Hoffman anything specific against the doctor?'

'Not that I know of, but Hoffman has a good nose for trouble.'

'Do you know why we can't touch the doctor?'

'I don't think even Hoffman does but he thinks it is a situation that will change.'

'Let's hope he's right. Fuller gets away with far too much.'

'Hoffman says the same: he does not like the doctor.' Heyden produced cigarettes and a lighter.

'Do any of us? He doesn't hide what he thinks of us. It's intolerable. Yet there's nothing we can do. No one knows why he's protected but everyone knows it's on the highest authority. We dare not violate that protection. I think Hoffman knows more than he says.'

'Which is why I came to you, Herr Kratz.'

Kratz held his head at an angle. His gaze was so disturbing that Heyden straightened, pulled in his feet. 'What's on your mind?'

'It's not the major's affair. Fuller is political. Couldn't we be prepared for when his protection is withdrawn?'

'Are you trying to teach me my job?'

'No, sir. I know Major Hoffman would like to drop the dear doctor into the foundations of one of the sites. There is also no doubt that the major carries privileged information; more than anyone else on the island. I felt that in relation to the doctor you should know at least as much as the major.'

Kratz said icily, 'Is it the major you're after or the doctor? Be careful, captain. Anyway, I am already prepared for the doctor.' Kratz was pensive, his pointed chin cupped by very thin fingers. 'We can help it along, of course. Incriminate him. We might possibly dislodge him from his privileged position.'

Heyden sat up eagerly but his expression froze as Kratz added, 'I trust your lust for the good doctor's wife has not influenced in any way what you have told me? Nor your ambition for Major Hoffman's job?'

Heyden recognised that this was not the time to lie. 'I'll admit the woman interests me. But I certainly wouldn't risk anything for her.'

'But you'd like her just the same?'

'Yes.'

Kratz nodded. 'That's not impossible. Now, I want a good man. One you can utterly rely upon. I think what we must do is bait the doctor. Trip him. This is strictly between you and me, captain. I don't want Hoffman to know and no word must ever reach Captain Brocker. I don't trust his association with the doctor. I want them both to hang themselves on the same piece of wire.'

Fuller guided Jacqui and Schroder on the difficult journey to the new hideout which was much nearer his own house. It was not until they reached the cellar that Schroder had a chance to tell him what had happened during the night and that he no longer had the route through the minefield.

It was the first time a German soldier had been killed and Fuller wondered what the reaction would be. When he had deposited the French girl and the American, leaving with them an old oil lamp, he went to his own house to fetch Kremple and Gorkov.

The atmosphere was tense when he got back and introduced the four different nationalities but once they began to talk a feeling of security grew in the huge, brick-pillared warren of the cellar.

Earlier, Fuller had opened the trapdoor to let in fresh air and then nailed one of the chests to the lid of the trap, shaving along one bottom edge of the chest so that it did not foul the floor on the hinge side of the trap when it was raised.

The cellar needed cleaning and tidying and a separate niche was found for Jacqui to sleep in. Jacqui seemed to have gone within herself. Fuller noted that she was not on edge as she had been before Schroder's arrival, but that she seemed to have cocooned herself and had barely uttered a word.

Fuller gave no explanation of Schroder's presence except to say that he had just arrived. 'We need food desperately. There's plenty of darkness left. Max knows the way and you'd better go with him, Rod.'

'Okay.'

Fuller nodded, watching the reaction of the German and the American together. Ironically, Kremple who now wore rough civilian clothes was uncomfortable with Schroder, who was still dressed as a German officer.

After they'd gone Fuller turned to Jacqui and Gorkov. The girl had retreated to the furthest corner of the cellar where the light from the solitary lamp barely reached her. Before Fuller could speak Gorkov said, 'I understand. I frighten her. I'll keep out of her way. But she had better get used to me.'

Schroder kept close behind Kremple. The American had no knowledge of the island except for the map he had memorised. He was suspicious of the German whom he felt Fuller had taken at face value, and he did not like being so reliant upon him.

Kremple displayed his knowledge of the island and of the many danger spots. He moved well, skirting sentries and sites as they made their way across the island to the small township of St Anne. It was a long, variable route and Schroder was quick to appreciate the sergeant's skill.

Kremple slowed right down as they neared the town; night patrols were standard procedure. As they crouched on the outskirts Schroder realised that he was completely in the hands of the sergeant, but they had no language problem.

They heard a patrol some distance away; jackboots on cobbles, but precise location was difficult to pinpoint. The trick was to anticipate direction. They advanced further into the dark, empty streets and reached Victoria Street, the main street of the township. Schroder glanced at his watch: 1.30 a.m. He had slept little during the last three nights but there was no time for tiredness now. The streets and pavements seemed terribly narrow to him, the dark, uneven shape of buildings crowding in to give an even more cramped impression.

Kremple was moving on, doorway to doorway, and Schroder kept close behind him. The place seemed dead, a rising wind whistled down the street eerily.

Kremple put out a hand and froze. He was wedged between a

telegraph pole and a bush behind a low wall fronting a shop which lay well back. The patrol was audible again; Schroder tried to shrink beside Kremple. Across the street on a corner, was a sizeable shop by St Anne's standards, with its windows boarded up. He remained very still as he caught sight of the sentry outside the front door.

The patrol approached, a dark blob growing more distinct as it emerged from the dark backcloth. They marched slowly, led by a sergeant with an MP-38 slung over his shoulder. The men carried rifles. Their free arms swung loosely in rhythm. As they passed the sentry the sergeant called a greeting but did not stop.

Kremple stayed still. He was listening. If the patrol turned left at the lower end of Victoria Street they would be going towards the church at the foot of the incline; if they turned right and then left then they would head for Braye harbour. He squatted and listened and tried to pick up their change of direction. The route they took could affect the time they could be expected to return. They turned left, which was a pity.

Kremple led the way back to a facing intersection. He looked back. The sentry was not in sight. He signalled Schroder to cross the street and they ran, crouched and silent. Suddenly they were a team and understanding began to show.

Kremple went down the narrow intersection, turned right and right again. They now approached the shop from the rear. If they continued to the end they would find themselves back in Victoria Street with the sentry just to their left.

They did not go so far. They passed padlocked double gates at the end of which was a wall. Kremple, the shorter and stockier of the two men, indicated that he wanted to climb the wall. Schroder cupped his hands for the German to step into. When Kremple was astride the wall he leant over to help Schroder up, but the long-armed American had less difficulty in climbing.

Below them was a yard in which there were two army trucks. Backing on the rear of the shop was a low annexe with a gap of two or three feet from the wall. Kremple stepped on to the sloping roof of the annexe and waited for Schroder to follow. They reached an old-fashioned sash window and Kremple produced a clasp knife supplied by Fuller. He slipped the window catch and lifted the lower frame.

For some seconds they lay flat on the roof peering into the room. There were crates almost in front of them. They found a gap and climbed through, closing the window behind them. After making sure the panes were boarded Schroder produced the lighter he had recovered.

The room was full of crates stacked in rows. 'Clothes and blankets,' explained Kremple. They could do with both but food was the priority. Easing their way through the narrow gangways between the crates they reached the landing and crept along to the top of the stairs. It was pitch black and the place smelled musty.

Schroder was using the lighter only when necessary; the flame was already losing strength. They groped their way down the stairs and Kremple seemed to know his way about once below. Although the shop windows were blacked out it seemed slightly less dark.

The shop was a big through room. Crates were stacked at the rear but along all the walls were wide shelves holding a mass of cans. There was a long L-shaped counter at the front with empty cartons under it. Next to the counter was the front door with the sentry the other side of it only feet away from them. They took two of the sturdier cartons and returned to the shelves.

It was necessary to use the lighter to examine the cans but once they knew the contents they operated by touch. They loaded as much as they could carry comfortably then went back upstairs.

Kremple climbed through the window first and Schroder heaved the cartons to him and then got out and closed the window. There was no tension between them at all now.

While Schroder held the cartons Kremple went down the roof backwards and then Schroder pushed one carton at a time down to him. Schroder slid down and stepped over the gap to the wall which he straddled while Kremple passed the cartons across.

Satisfied that the cartons were properly balanced Schroder remembered that the sentry was just round the corner, just as the soldier himself appeared. With his gun over his shoulder the sentry walked slowly to the double gates, passing below Schroder. Afraid to move Schroder knew that he must warn

Kremple who was about to step across the gap; he held up an arm and Kremple stopped, poised awkwardly.

The sentry examined the padlock for something to do, expecting to find nothing wrong. The two cartons lay balanced above him but it seemed to be the jackboot dangling down the wall that caught his eye. It was impossible to say why. Nothing had moved, it was dark, yet he glanced up.

He slipped his machine pistol from his shoulder as he tried to identify the figure straddling the wall. He was confused. His gaze swept from the jackboot to the uniform of an oberleutnant. *An Officer stealing rations?* They were the only ones who were well fed.

'Congratulations,' said Schroder swinging his other leg over. 'I will recommend you to your commanding officer.' Schroder dropped down in front of the sentry and brushed his breeches.

The sentry was speechless. Was he being tested?

'There has been pilfering from the stores,' added Schroder. 'We decided to check the vigilance of the guard ourselves.'

We? Ourselves? The officer was not SS. It was true that there had been pilfering. Where there were stores there was always pilfering. At no time did the sentry consider Schroder to be anything other than a German officer. But there was something wrong. He was trying to see Schroder's regimental tags but the light was too bad. He reached for the lamp fixed to the back of his belt and as he did so he glanced up again as if to reassure himself that that was where Schroder had come from.

He saw the overhanging cartons like two dark shadows and his machine pistol pointed at Schroder's middle. Holding the gun with one hand he reached for his whistle with the other.

'Attention,' rapped Schroder.

Discipline was hard to break. The sentry half-lowered the gun but he did produce the whistle.

'Put that whistle away at once.' The raised voice was really for Kremple who was now standing on the wall above and behind the sentry. The sentry put the whistle to his lips as Kremple dropped behind him. Kremple acted as he'd been taught; he placed one arm round the sentry's neck and pulled back on the helmet with the other and the chinstrap cut off the air in the sentry's windpipe just as he was about to blow.

Schroder grabbed the gun and had to break the man's

forefinger in the trigger guard before he could tear it away. Kremple still applied pressure and the sentry tried to break his grip. It was all or nothing now. While Kremple kept up the pressure on the windpipe Schroder gripped the man's arms. It was a little while before the sentry buckled. They laid him down quietly and made sure he was dead.

They stared at each other across the body. Kremple was breathing heavily; he wiped his mouth with the back of his hand and stared down at the body. Schroder knew the feeling but it was worse for Kremple who had just killed an ex-comrade.

'We must get the cartons down.'

Kremple nodded slowly. He was still squatting over the body. 'We must get rid of him, too.' His voice was unsteady.

Schroder was sorry for him and Kremple had just uttered almost the same words that he had used on Jacqui. Dead soldiers could not be left around.

'Cartons first.' Schroder wanted to snap Kremple from his remorse. He cupped his hands again and Kremple climbed the wall. Schroder reached up and took the cartons from him. When Kremple jumped down Schroder said, 'He doesn't look too heavy. I can sling him over my shoulder if you'll take the gun.'

'What shall we do with him?'

Schroder knew that Kremple was still dazed but they had to get their minds back on the job. 'I was hoping you could tell me.'

'I'm sorry. We'll have to take him back with us. And then over the cliff. Can you manage him that far?'

'With the odd rest.'

They helped each other load up. They could not discard any cans without disclosing what had happened. Kremple took the gun and the helmet and Schroder gave the body a fireman's lift. It was the second time in less than twenty-four hours that he had carried a corpse in this way. He held the carton in both arms.

They had not got far before they heard the patrol returning. It was impossible for them to hurry while weighted down and in the back streets they were cut off from the better hiding places. Finally they had to stop. The doorways were so narrow here that they took one each. Schroder propped the corpse on the carton pushed back against a door. He prayed that no one would wake up in the house. The corpse hovered over him like some grotesque sightless watchman.

The patrol sounded as if it was marching straight up to them. Kremple, who was two doors away from Schroder, had pulled back the bolt of the machine pistol. If they were caught it was better to get it over quickly. He had not visualised that deserting could be like this and yet, as he squatted, he had regrets only for the man he had killed.

The patrol passed the top of the intersection and continued on, its tread growing fainter. But it had gone in the direction Schroder and Kremple must go. By unspoken consent the two men stayed in their flimsy cover eventually to venture out almost simultaneously. Whatever the risk of continuing it could be no more than staying. The sound of loading up again seemed to them to echo round the streets.

The advantage they had, and that Fuller had used during his nocturnal excursions, was that at night the troops retreated to St Anne for sleep or entertainment. The labour force was returned to Sylt camp near the airport. The sentries on the gun sites, except those on the coast facing Britain, bordered on the indolent; they saw the duty as a military chore and not as a necessity. Provided the sites were known, and that one was careful and silent, it was possible to move about the island at night without being seen.

Sense of direction was essential and so was a good memory for the danger areas. Kremple had both these qualities. Their present problem was the addition of the corpse. From time to time Schroder had to rest. He refused Kremple's whispered offer of help; it was important that the German should concentrate on direction and he still had a heavy carton of cans to carry.

They continued on, thankful that they did not hear the patrol again but aware that they were slowing down and prone to the odd stumble. They had one more long rest before the final leg to the cellar hideout. They sat in silence, their breath rising on the cold air. It was almost possible to believe the whole island was dead; there was the wind and darkness and nothing else but themselves.

The guard dogs at Sylt started to bark and the two men realised that they did not have far to go, but first it was essential to detour a huge site. Schroder learned as he went.

When they finally reached the old house they left the cartons outside the lean-to and carried the corpse to the nearby cliff top. It was exposed and dark and dangerous. They felt their way carefully to the edge guided by the sound of sea breaking on rocks. Not far from here was the point where Schroder had landed.

When they were as near to the cliff edge as they dare get, they lowered the corpse and then undressed him. If the body missed the sea and landed on the rocks it was less likely to cause comment naked than it would in German uniform. Even at this height the wind brought with it the smell of putrefaction from the decomposing bodies below.

Schroder took the legs and Kremple the arms and they swung the body to and fro before letting it go. The white flesh made a streak in the darkness as it arched out over the edge. Although they listened, the breaking surf covered the sound of landing and they did not know whether the body finished up in the sea or on the rocks. They gathered up the uniform and the gun and trudged back to the house.

They had killed one man each on consecutive nights. Schroder was well aware of this but he kept to himself his own deed; he did not know how Kremple might take it.

Major Carl Hoffman almost over-reached himself in front of the colonel. He had become so used to his power that he saw the island commandant as nothing more than a general administrator. When Private Sonnen and Private Mueller were missed, Hoffman's reaction was one of deep suspicion, although strictly it was not his problem.

Lieutenant Colonel Helke, the commandant, was less positive. He was a soldier and while officially he condoned the brutal torture and suffering that went on in the island privately he disagreed with it. He had long considered making an official report to Berlin but what dissuaded him was the very occasional visit of more senior officers from the Fatherland, who had seen everything but made no complaint. The English doctor had protested to him but when he had passed this on to the visiting German army doctors they had received his news with silence and disdain. As he had no inclination for demotion or worse he tolerated what he found intolerable.

When Private Sonnen and Private Mueller disappeared from the face of the island, the last thing Helke wanted was upheaval. Both disappearances were a mystery. There were no enemies on the island except the labour force. There was Fuller, but what could he have done? Sonnen was thought strange by his colleagues. For all anyone knew he might have walked off the edge of a cliff. He had gone to bed and in the morning his bed was empty. Nobody knew why or would suggest a reason. Whatever had happened to him had been self-induced. He could not have been taken from a room with other soldiers in it.

Sonnen had been a second-line soldier with an indifferent record, and, it was rumoured, odd habits. Forget him. There could be no reason for suspicion; the strain must have been too much for him.

It was true that Mueller's disappearance was much more baffling; he had simply vanished without trace while on sentry duty. An extremely serious crime. But no one except Hoffman considered it was foul play. How could it be? A patrol sergeant had twice spoken to Mueller during his rounds and the patrol had not heard or seen anything suspicious. Both incidents were on different nights in different parts of the island. There could be no connection between them.

Helke conceded that there must be an enquiry. But he refused point blank to turn the island upside down to look for two private soldiers, which was what Hoffman demanded. There was another reason for keeping a cool head at this time as Helke was fully aware. Top VIPs were due on the island from Berlin. A Swede named Ardense from the International Red Cross was also arriving soon, though for what reason was a mystery. This was top secret information which only Helke and Hoffman shared. So why did Hoffman want to disrupt everything at such a time? What was he afraid of?

Helke was well aware that if he backed down from Hoffman he might just as well relinquish command. Without doubt Hoffman had special powers but he was a tactical specialist and was not SS, and he was only a major. Helke clung to these crumbs of comfort. 'What exactly do you suspect, Major?' It was the second time Helke had asked the question but Hoffman had yet to answer, and still he could not satisfactorily do so.

Hoffman stood in front of the colonel's desk and took off his spectacles to wipe them. It was a retaliatory move of insolence which Helke duly noted. 'I find it strange that two men should disappear just before we are expecting some very important people.' Hoffman realised that what he said had come out differently from how he had intended. The truth was he instinctively felt that something was wrong.

Helke looked up with disdain. 'I fail to see the connection between two private soldiers disappearing and the arrival of VIPs. Had *you* gone missing, or *I*, or even Hauptsturmführer Heyden, then I might agree. I'll instigate the usual enquiry. I will not have the island searched for two men of that calibre.'

'Yes, Obersturmbannführer.' Hoffman saluted, stiff armed and left the office burning with resentment. He had handled it badly, he realised that, but the colonel was a blind fool. Something was going on under their noses, and, as always when he had no answers, his mind turned towards Fuller, the butt of his frustration and hate. There were times when he had to keep tight control over his own feelings and to remind himself of his orders. But his day would come; of that he was absolutely certain.

He walked into Royal Connaught Square, in St Anne. The trees at the end were already turning golden brown and leaves were spiralling down gently in the light breeze. Half-tracks were parked in line in the small square like grotesque taxis. As Hoffman left the square he noticed Captain Heyden leave the Gestapo office. The liaison of Heyden and Kratz was something else that rankled him. The SS and the Gestapo both resented the power that Hoffman held on the island and both would like to break it. But in this respect Hoffman knew that he had something in common with Fuller; his source of protection was far too powerful for Heyden and Kratz to destroy. But they would try. And for this, too, he somehow blamed Fuller, whom he was convinced was at the root of all his problems.

Hoffman strode out purposefully. It would be a bad day for slave labour. He would see that a few more than usual would die slowly and in agony.

Walter Schellenberg and Klaus Wendel flew to Paris with fighter escort on the early morning of the 23rd September. They were given special rooms at the George V hotel. Lord Arden was still in Paris but no contact was made.

There were several reasons why they did not hold their meeting there. Paris had too many unfriendly ears and eyes, and news could travel fast. There was also the matter of checking Arden's bona fides. What was really the crux, however, was Hitler's insistence on the meeting taking place on British soil, and the security on Alderney was infinitely better than Paris – a sealed unit with no indigenous populace.

While Arden waited in his luxury apartment, Schellenberg and Wendel were flown on to Cherbourg and from there to Alderney. They did not become friendly at any stage. A resentment had built up in Wendel; he believed that the head of RSHA VI was there to spy on him, and Schellenberg's presence would cramp his style.

Sitting side by side in an aircraft only exacerbated the growing tension between them and the silences became longer on each leg of the journey, until on the final flight they did not converse at all. Hitler, who had foreseen this, would have been delighted. It kept both men on their toes.

They were met at Alderney airport, especially cleared to make way for the Junkers, by Lieutenant Colonel Helke and Major Carl Hoffman. In the background, Captain Heyden had a small guard of honour of his SS men, and lurking on the perimeter was Erich Kratz, who kept his distance throughout. Both men had been advised of the visit only that morning.

Rooms had been prepared for VIPs in the best private house in the centre of St Anne. A buzz spread right through the garrison. On such a small island it was impossible to keep the visit a secret beyond this point. Wendel was not well known but it soon leaked out that he was Ribbentrop's deputy. Walter Schellenberg was quite a different matter; he carried the kind of authority that was understood and feared. That fact suddenly brought the Fatherland, even the Führer himself, much nearer.

Wherever the two emissaries went, and they were shown the workings right round the island, they were accompanied by an SS guard all armed with submachine guns, and motorcycle outriders front and rear covered the staff car provided for them. Both men forgot their unspoken resentments of each other; for the moment they were royalty, fêted as royalty should be.

The hospital was left until last. As word flared round the island faster than the small convoy could travel, Fuller turned out to watch its approach. Claudie stood near him, Blanco in her arms. They were joined by Captain Brocker. The open tourer went past quite slowly. Speed was difficult on the island lanes. The passengers were clearly visible. Fuller said, 'Do you know them?'

'Certainly. One is Klaus Wendel. He used to be with foreign affairs. The other is Walter Schellenberg, a close friend of both the Führer and Himmler.'

'You sound as if you don't much care for him?'

'I can't make any sense of it. Schellenberg won't be here just for the trip. Nor will Ribbentrop's deputy. They're a strange combination. It seems they are interested in inspecting the hospital.' The three of them strode along the street in the wake of the convoy, Claudie dropping Blanco to run beside them.

Something was brewing. And Fuller could see that Brocker did not like it either.

When Schellenberg and Wendel were escorted down by Major Hoffman they were shown areas Fuller had not seen. Most rooms had been equipped; most had carpets and beds. All furnishings were of a high standard. Walter Schellenberg placed on a long table in the briefing room the wrapped, personal items Hitler had entrusted to him to bring over.

The two men sat in leather armchairs and surveyed the room. Ventilation was good and Major Hoffman had assured them that the room was virtually soundproof. In any event there would always be guards at the end of the corridor. Their complete privacy was guaranteed. He did not show them all the rooms, nor a well hidden feature for which he had received his instructions direct from Berlin, and which only he knew about. He believed that all the men who had worked on it were now dead.

Schellenberg and Wendel expressed satisfaction. Part of their mission was to report back what they saw directly to Hitler. Both were careful not to voice any conclusions they might draw from their inspection. Nor did Hoffman offer any enlightenment. They were shown a hanging wall cabinet containing spirits and wine. Crystal glasses fitted into racks.

Wendel covered his reaction to some of the horrific sights he had seen on his way round the island. The usual tidying up job had been done for VIPs but there were some things overlooked; a leg protruding from set concrete had caught his eye. Bodies at the foot of cliffs, the sea lapping over broken frames. It made him wonder what was happening here but he had no intention of discussing it with Schellenberg whom he believed would have nothing to add. Hoffman poured out drinks and they toasted the Führer.

Lord Arden, who had no idea that Schellenberg and Wendel had already passed through Paris, wanted to protest about the length of his stay there but found no one he could complain to. There were many high ranking officers, even a Field Marshal, in the apartments, but nobody with authority to send him on his way. A colonel had been allocated to his welfare but his instructions were merely to see that Arden was cosseted.

Arden felt isolated; he was living an unreal life in enemy territory. Every street view was the same; German soldiers, vehicles, flags, tanks. But for the familiarity of the buildings it was almost impossible to believe he was in Paris, except, perhaps, for the women. There was something about the women here that would always be Parisienne; the way they walked, dressed, behaved. If there was a certain grim melancholy about the men, then the French women somehow lifted the dignity with a sometimes arrogant defiance.

Yet the vast military presence almost undermined him and he supposed that this was their intention. The greater his uncertainty the more he would concede. If that was the theory it was hopelessly wrong; Arden and his conspirators were well aware that there was only one deal the British would accept, only one way of removing Churchill. There could be no possible compromise. It would depend on how important it was to the Germans who were now stumbling badly in Russia.

When he considered his position it was easier to accept that he was meant to feel alone, helpless, even impotent. It would make him malleable. Arden saw himself in the Florentine mirror. He hated looking at himself, aware that, unlike his son, he lacked both looks and personality. He glanced away but before he did he caught sight of his brittle smile, catching himself in mid-thought. Without self-deceit or conceit Arden knew he was steel all through. There was no situation that could soften or scare him. If Hitler wanted to think that delaying would work then the mistake was his. Arden would endure the wait.

Fuller now ran his surgery from the hospital and although each time he went in he was tempted to go down the tributary tunnel it was impossible to do with the SS guard.

Captain Brocker called at the hospital on the morning of the day after the arrival of Hitler's two emissaries.

'They want to meet you this evening, George. Here. Before dinner.'

'Who?'

'Schellenberg and Wendel.'

'Tell them to get stuffed.'

Brocker laughed. 'It's not your style to get someone else to do your dirty work.'

'Will you be here?'

'I don't know.'

'If you are, keep your eyes open, will you?'

'If I am I won't be here as your friend.'

'You'll be dressed like a German officer, you'll act correctly, but your neck is already on the block. You'll be here as my friend.'

Brocker tipped a salute. 'You'll take that view once too often. That's twice I've warned you.'

They called soon after Fuller had done the round of his bedridden island patients. He was busy topping up the drugs in his medical bag when the entourage arrived. While the motorcycle escort remained at the entrance, the Mercedes Benz tourer came down the tunnel to the ambulance turnabout. The tunnel had been built wide enough to take an average-sized ambulance which could reverse at the junction of the two tunnels.

Fuller heard the engine echo and the tread of jackboots, their rhythm broken by one uneven tread. He quickly donned a surgical coat.

Major Hoffman was there as escort, the peak of his high crown hat and his boots brightly polished. With him was the stocky, comparatively shabby Klaus Wendel, and the more soldierly, dark-haired, strong-faced figure of Standartenführer Walter Schellenberg. Behind them were six SS guards and beyond them as an isolated tail, Captain Brocker, shorter, mature, less polished but still smart. Brocker could never be slovenly but that was a personal, not a military, trait.

Fuller was pointedly sitting at his desk when the party entered the office. Incredibly, Major Hoffman proffered the 'Heil Hitler' salute, to which Fuller failed to respond. Nor did he rise. For a moment he continued looking at a mounted X-ray photograph. When he raised his eyes it was with quiet reserve. 'Gentlemen?' The tone of enquiry was questioning and was not lost on Hoffman.

Schellenberg smiled coldly; his eyes uncompromising, the old duelling scars evident on his chin. He waited for the formal introduction from Hoffman and then said to him, 'Wait outside, Major, and close the door. Take your men with you.'

Captain Brocker asked quietly, 'Do you want me to stay?'

Schellenberg was not quite sure of Brocker's brief; it had not come from him. 'I'm sure Herr Wendel and I can cope, Captain. Equally. I'm sure the doctor would prefer his office less crowded.'

When Brocker gave a military salute and turned, Fuller made no comment. The last thing he wanted was to get Brocker into trouble.

Schellenberg and Wendel stood in front of Fuller's desk. Fuller, still seated, did not make it easy for them. Schellenberg pulled out a chair and Wendel followed suit. They sat opposite Fuller at each end of the desk. Schellenberg said with professional politeness, 'It's a pleasure to meet you, Doctor. We've heard much about you in Germany.'

'In Germany? Surely not.'

Schellenberg eyed Fuller with interest; his image was solid. 'You underestimate yourself. You're a very clever man. Our own doctors say so, and they don't give praise lightly. You are doing the job of both physician and surgeon. Also you operate from one of our few British possessions, so we are interested in what goes on here. Certainly your reputation has reached us.'

Fuller inclined his head in acknowledgment. 'I do what I can.'

Klaus Wendel was making an effort to smile, be the diplomat he once was. The presence of Schellenberg did not soothe his mood. He wanted to kick the Standartenführer from the room. He tried to take up from where Schellenberg left off. 'A lot of information about you is held in Germany.'

'I can't see why.'

'If you under-rate yourself you should not under-rate us. As the Standartenführer has told you, your skill has not gone unnoticed. Nor your friendship with Winston Churchill.'

Fuller went rigid. What were they getting at? 'I've met him a couple of times, that's all.'

'Your modesty really is unbelievable. Did not Mr Churchill invite you to many of his private parties?'

From whom had they obtained their information, Fuller wondered. 'You're exaggerating the issue. I was sometimes invited because my father knows Mr Churchill quite well. That does not make us friends.'

'I would have thought so. Small, intimate parties. Oh, yes. You can't be ashamed of such friendship? We ourselves may hate Churchill but we have great respect for him. Tell us about these parties.'

Fuller was puzzled. What did they want from him? 'The parties? Full of cigar smoke, brandy and port wine. Decadent, really.'

'What did you talk to Churchill about?'

'Bricklaying mostly. He was very keen.'

'Bricklaying? I thought that was propaganda.'

'Oh, no. He is a great bricklayer.'

Wendel's expression had stiffened. He produced cigarette and holder and lit up without offering his cigarettes round. Fuller groped in a drawer and produced a tin ashtray; he hated ash on the desk.

'Bricklaying is not important. Who was at these parties?'

'How can I remember? I haven't seen England since '38.'

'A man doesn't forget his friends, Doctor Fuller.'

'Mr Fuller. In England surgeons are called Mister.'

'Whatever you are called you have not answered my question.'

Fuller gazed at Schellenberg who was quietly watching him and said, 'I'm not being deliberately obtuse. You should really be talking to my father. I went because the booze was good. Churchill's friends weren't my friends. We moved in different circles.'

'Perhaps. Yet it would be natural to remember. Did you know, for instance, Lord Arden?'

The warning crept over Fuller like a chill. He suddenly felt they were near the crux and Schroder's message shot into his mind. He remembered Arden well. He had not much cared for him but they had certainly discussed a variety of subjects. He did not answer because he could not see where it was leading or what damage it might do.

'I can assure you that your answer will not harm Lord Arden in any way. It's a simple question.'

'I don't understand why you need to know.'

'Perhaps that is answer enough. You make no denial of meeting him.'

Fuller was thinking quickly. 'Why do you want to know?'

Wendel concealed his feelings. There were quicker ways to get an answer. 'Within two days it will become self-evident. You will tell me then, I can assure you.'

Fuller concluded that whatever he said could do no harm. Reticence would annoy Wendel; the man was showing flecks of temper. What could it matter? 'I met him a few times.'

'Ah. Thank you, at last. You would remember him if you met him?'

'Of course.'

'And he you?'

'I would expect him to. If he didn't, I couldn't have made much of an impression.' Was Arden the man Schroder had meant? He felt more confused now than at the beginning.

'Thank you. That is all we need for the moment. It's been a pleasure to meet you.' Wendel did not make the mistake of offering his hand as he rose. Schellenberg responded more slowly, his dark eyes thoughtfully gazing at Fuller who was left worried and uncertain. Why had Schroder insisted on the name being Ardense?

II

Blanco suddenly pricked up his ears and growled. Fuller and Claudie had long learned to stop speaking whenever that happened. The dog jumped down from Claudie's lap and ran to the rear door yapping and snuffling.

Fuller rose slowly, motioning Claudie to stay where she was. He went to the shelf by the fireplace to reach for the flashlight issued to him for night calls. The lens had been papered over to leave the usual slit. He opened the door and Blanco ran to the yard door at the end of the kitchen. He picked Blanco up, took the struggling terrier back to Claudie and returned to the kitchen, opening the yard door a fraction. He stepped out carefully, and slowly shone the narrow beam round. The cow was lying under cover. The chickens fluttered and he wondered if it was they who had roused Blanco. He shone the torch on the shed door but the restricted beam was so bad that he could not be sure if it was open. He stepped softly across the yard, wishing he had some sort of weapon.

The shed door was ajar. He knew that he had closed it, as he did every night. He weighed the torch in his hand; it would have to do. He pushed the door with his foot, keeping to one side. He poked the torch round and a German soldier stood crouched at the back with a machine pistol pointing straight at him.

Fuller kept his voice steady. 'I'm the English doctor. What is it you want?' The narrow beam was playing on the soldier's chest so that Fuller could see the general reaction and the lips trying to form words. The machine pistol was still levelled at him.

'Herr Doctor, I know who you are.' The voice was mature but shaking a little, nervous. There was silence and Fuller was about to speak again when the soldier said, 'Don't send me back. Please.'

Fuller was uneasy. The voice wavered but it was a man's voice, a basic sureness about it. So many of the troops were youths. 'How can I send you back? You have the gun.'

'I'm sorry.' The gun was allowed to drop on the shoulder sling. 'At first I didn't know who it was. I thought they were looking for me.'

'They? Looking? I don't understand.'

The soldier shuffled forward a few paces, knocked against a piece of metal. He held a hand up to shade his eyes as Fuller moved the torch. 'Doctor, I am desperate. I have deserted. I didn't know where to go.'

'Why here?'

'Where else? If I return they'll shoot me.'

'Not if they don't know you've gone. And if they do they'll search and find you. You'd better go back.'

In the darkness of the shed it was a strange encounter. Fuller was still uneasy. He could not see the man properly.

'That's impossible. They wanted me to strangle one of the wretches at Sylt.'

'You're SS?'

'No. It was the SS who ordered me to do it. Then they jeered at me when I refused.'

'What happened?'

'One of them did it himself with a piece of wire. The man had broken a leg. It sickened me.'

'You'd better come in.' Fuller pushed the door back and allowed the soldier to pass in front of him. Fuller closed the shed door. The chickens were still fluttering. The cow did not stir. He followed the soldier through the kitchen into the living room where Claudie was trying to calm Blanco.

Fuller explained, 'This young man has deserted.' He was still behind the soldier looking over his shoulder trying to send Claudie a warning. But Claudie needed no warning. 'With his gun?'

'I'm sorry.' The soldier unslung his MP-38 and placed it on the table. 'I had it when I decided to go.'

'Sit down. We have to straighten this out.' Fuller felt there was something wrong; he had got to know Kremple over a period of time before helping him; this man was an unknown quantity.

The German sank to a chair and their doubts communicated to him. He looked uncertain. 'There was nowhere else to go,' he repeated.

Fuller sat down, so did Claudie; Blanco was growling softly. 'What's your name?'

'Gerhard Holmeir. I'm with the heavy flak unit near the airfield. That's how I got caught up with the SS at Sylt. They are demons, those men.'

'Well, you can't stay here. I'm sorry.'

Holmeir was alarmed. 'Where can I go?'

'Back where you came from. It's your army, you try to sort it out.'

'You don't believe me?' Holmeir swivelled in his chair from one to the other. 'Why would I come?'

'I didn't say I didn't believe you. I said you can't stay here.'

'They will look for you here,' Claudie added.

'Why? You are respected. Everyone knows you.' Holmeir struggled, 'No one here looks upon you as an enemy.'

'Tell me again why you left.'

Holmeir told them.

'What was the name of the SS man?'

'I don't know. There were two of them laughing. I don't know their names. I don't want to know.'

Fuller said flatly, 'You're not likely to be asked to strangle a labourer again. It's the SS's kind of sick joke. Go back. Tell your commanding officer. He will understand.'

'No. He's almost as bad as them. All the officers go round with their eyes closed, pretending nothing is happening. I can't stomach it. I'm a soldier, nothing more.'

Fuller eyed the gun. 'Is that loaded?'

'The magazine is full. There's nothing in the breech.'

'I can put you up just for tonight. Tomorrow we'll have to decide what to do with you.' Fuller ignored Claudie's alarm. 'Leave all ammunition and the gun down here. My wife will show you your room.' He paused before adding, 'I'll have to see about blankets. There is a spare bed.' Claudie knew that they had spare blankets and would understand that he had something in mind. 'And we'll have to lock you in your room. It might give you a chance to drop from the window if they come searching for you.'

Holmeir rose. 'I'm sorry to bring you trouble, Doctor.' He looked pleadingly at them. 'I'm not the only one who feels this way but the others haven't been asked to garrotte someone.'

Fuller signalled to Claudie who led the way upstairs still holding the grumbling Blanco. Fuller waited for her to return and she whispered angrily, 'I don't trust him.'

'Nor do I. Did you lock the door?'

'Of course.'

When he picked up the MP-38 and the spare magazine she knew where he was going. 'Be careful, cheri.' She always said the same and always feared that one night he would be caught and would not return.

Fuller had not grown careless. As the garrison grew so did the danger. When he neared the house he could smell the freshness of the sea. He stepped towards the house from an oblique position. A voice said behind him, 'One night it will be too dark to recognise you.' Schroder stepped from behind a gorse cluster.

'I need Max urgently. Send him up and take these down with you.'

Schroder took the gun and ammunition without comment. He climbed down through the hatch while Fuller held the tea chest back. The low mumble of voices floated through the gap before Kremple climbed up the ladder. Fuller told him what had happened and Kremple immediately found it suspect.

'What do you want me to do? Look him over?'

'There's a chance you might know him.'

They reached Fuller's house late, having been forced to detour by an unexpected patrol. Outside the door Kremple asked, 'Are you suspicious of Holmeir or do you just want me to see if I know him.?'

'He doesn't strike me as a private soldier. Keep out of sight.'

They went in. Claudie was still trying to keep Blanco quiet. She had the blankets ready. Fuller went up the stairs heavily to cover the sound of Kremple's footsteps right behind him. The key to the spare bedroom was in the lock. He turned the old fashioned tumbler and squeezed an arm through the door to switch on the light. He went in, leaving the door ajar. Holmeir was sitting on the edge of the bed. He rose slowly. Fuller threw the blankets at him. 'It's the best we can do. But you may not need them. Be ready to move.'

Holmeir caught the bundle. 'Thank you, Doctor.'

Fuller had come halfway into the room between Holmeir and the door. 'I'll see what we can do for you.' He switched off the light, locked the door behind him. Kremple crept down the stairs ahead of him. He went into the living room. Kremple, already seated, was stroking Blanco's head but his eyes were on Fuller as he entered.

'Well?' Fuller demanded.

'He's an SS sergeant.'

No one spoke for some time. Finally, Fuller said, 'I'll get rid of him tomorrow.'

'One night here is enough for them; that you took him in at all.'

'Then I'll get him out now.'

'Without his machine pistol?'

Fuller swore silently. He was angry that he had allowed himself to fall into the trap.

'What are we going to do?' Kremple wanted to know.

Claudie slipped an arm through Fuller's. What scared her was that they all knew there was only one obvious way to deal with Holmeir.

Lord Arden was roused at 4.30 in the morning and told to be ready to travel in half an hour. He was taken down to Cherbourg by car and was partly relieved, because of his dislike of flying, and partly angry, because the long drive was all part of the psychological battle ahead. He was right to assume that he could have been flown to Cherbourg; but by so doing he would have missed the constant reminder of German power, of their occupation of France, evident all along the route. He was impressed, as he was meant to be, but at no time was he enticed. Whatever Arden was, whatever his personal ambition, he considered himself to be an Englishman to his backbone, every bit as much as Churchill, and as an Englishman he simply believed that British interests would best be served without the economic strangulation of war. And that this could be achieved with honour.

He was eyed with curiosity as he boarded the German E-boat for the short run to Alderney. The weather had worsened but he marginally preferred the element of sea to that of air. The German crew treated him as a VIP and he was shown into the main cabin. The boat lifted her bows and they travelled at speed over the choppy, slate grey sea. Right to the last his hosts were out to impress him.

When they berthed at Alderney Arden found a guard of honour waiting for him. Lieutenant Colonel Helke had been instructed to show him every courtesy, to see that he was looked after. It was difficult for him to believe that he was on captured British soil. He was taken by car into St Anne's and housed separately from Schellenberg and Wendel but no less comfortably. Herr Ardense of the International Red Cross had arrived.

Fuller had a carving knife tucked into his waistband. He felt exposed in front of the SS sergeant and was uneasy about having to lead the way. Although Max Kremple was behind Holmeir he was following at some distance, for if Holmeir heard him he would act quickly, and the carrot had to appear real to Holmeir.

Near the cellar headquarters, knowing there were no Germans close by, Fuller made sufficient noise to alert Schroder. When the tall American loomed up Fuller whispered. 'I've brought someone else to join you.' He squeezed Schroder's arm as a quick warning.

Schroder saw the dark shape of Holmeir behind Fuller and said brusquely in German, 'We'd better get you out of sight.' He led the way into the shed and Fuller now fell behind Holmeir. Schroder tilted the crate and said to Holmeir, 'I'll go first, to get a lamp going.' He went down while Fuller held on to the crate and watched Holmeir at the head of the ladder. He sensed Holmeir's unease and wondered how he would feel when he saw that Schroder was in a German army officer's uniform. Holmeir made no move. He stood staring down into the cavity until the suggestion of light filtered up and Holmeir's face was filled with pale shadows. Schroder called softly, 'Come down. Watch your step.'

Holmeir stepped on to the ladder. Kremple entered the shed as Holmeir disappeared. He patted Fuller's back as he went past. Fuller lowered the trap before Kremple could step on to the ladder.

'You're quite sure?' Fuller's voice was very low.

'Absolutely.'

'There'll be complications.'

'Whatever we do there'll be complications.'

'Don't underestimate him.'

Kremple was standing by the crate waiting for Fuller to pull it back. 'Anyone who underestimates the SS is dead.'

In the cellar the old oil lamp was burning with a foul smell. The wick was black and couldn't be trimmed any more. The paraffin had been pilfered by Fuller. Kremple went down the ladder backwards as they all did. Below him Holmeir could not take his eyes from Schroder; there was no news of a missing German officer. Behind Schroder Jacqui leaned against one of the arches in the background. Holmeir did not know whether to spring to attention now that he could see Schroder properly. He was wondering what he had been led into. He had expected Fuller to come down to explain. And the girl; where the hell had she come from? Having just arrived Holmeir wanted to get out fast. This was a hornet's nest and he had now learned what he had come for; the doctor was harbouring enemies.

Kremple was well built but he had not Fuller's height or breadth. His clothes, supplied by Fuller, were too big, so, as he slowly climbed down the ladder, Holmeir thought there was something a little incongruous about him. He reached the bottom, steadied himself and turned. The light was not good; it flickered and changed the shadows as though small animals were darting in and out of the far corners. But it was good enough for Holmeir to see Kremple.

Holmeir, thinking at first that Fuller had come down at last could not believe his eyes. He saw a familiar face, and his stomach churned. But it wasn't until Kremple greeted him that he really recoiled.

'Hello, Sergeant. Where's your SS uniform?'

Holmeir stepped back but Schroder had moved and prodded him forward. He turned and saw that Schroder was holding a machine pistol and his fear was complete. 'What is this? What's the matter? The doctor said I would be among friends.'

'And the doctor is right, Holmeir. You *are* among friends. But not yours.'

'For God's sake what are you saying? Get the doctor. He knows about me.'

'He does indeed.'

158

Full recognition dawned and with it Holmeir lost all hope. He pointed at Kremple. 'You're dead. You were buried at sea.'

'I've come back to life. We're going to kill you, Holmeir, when you've told us who sent you. Whether we do it slowly or quickly is up to you. No one will hear your screams down here.'

As if to prove the point Jacqui, suddenly realising that she was to witness murder, started to scream. Schroder wheeled, moved back to Jacqui, shook her, and then, as she continued to scream, slapped her hard. She collapsed at the foot of the arch, half-dazed, half-sobbing. Holmeir dived forward to grab the gun which Schroder was now holding one-handed and pulled hard. Schroder, feeling the gun being wrenched from him, turned and butted Holmeir under the chin with the heel of his free hand. The SS sergeant fell back, then jumped away as Schroder kicked out at his groin. Holmeir flew back against Kremple who was stealing swiftly up behind him.

The SS man, fighting for his life, rolled off Kremple, who fell to the floor. Schroder stood where he was, the machine pistol still held one-handed following Holmeir like a pointing finger. Behind Schroder, Jacqui rose shakily pushing herself up against the rough brick arch. Her only thought was that the American had struck her again. Filled with rage this time she threw herself at his back and started pummelling him with her small fists. After the initial shock he just stood there letting her punch away to get it out of her system but not taking his eyes off Holmeir.

Kremple, annoyed at being knocked flat, made the mistake of going after Holmeir when Schroder had him covered. The two men rolled and Holmeir had weight on his side. As he grappled with Kremple, Holmeir used his full range of crippling tricks and Kremple squirmed with pain. Meanwhile Jacqui had exhausted herself against the placid Schroder. Resentment had built up in her to an obsessional degree; he had insulted her womanhood and had hit her. It was all she could think of. What was happening on the floor did not touch her. The strain of her weeks of virtual incarceration was taking its toll in a way nobody could have anticipated. She looked around for something to hit Schroder with.

Holmeir knew that beating Kremple would not be enough; he could not hope to overcome the tall man with the gun. As he sought frantically for a means of escape he applied his thumbs and knees on Kremple who found himself in agony, having the life choked out of him. The pressure eased on Kremple's windpipe and he gasped, his throat burning. Then they were rolling again and, hazily, Kremple realised that it was Holmeir, clinging fiercely to him, who was making them roll.

Schroder watched closely in the poor vacillating light; he realised Kremple was losing but was waiting for them to break apart so that he could tackle Holmeir without complication. When he saw there was no sign of them breaking and that Kremple was in a bad way he became suspicious. He noted the direction of the roll and that Holmeir was using the semi-conscious Kremple as a shield. He stepped forward just as Jacqui hit him round the back of the head with a well-rusted spade.

Schroder dropped to his knees, his grip still on the gun, blood eddying through the hair at the back of his head. A terrible wail escaped from Jacqui who dropped the spade at the moment that Holmeir kicked at the lamp which was perched on part of a dismantled brick oven. The glass broke and flames gushed up as the paraffin escaped. A pile of hay they used for sleeping flared up immediately and with frantic speed spread to some old storage sacks.

Kremple, dazed and rasping, wasn't sure what was happening. Schroder, still in a position of supplication, was trying to shake off the effects of the blow. Holmeir ran for the ladder, deciding not to push his luck in an attempt to get the gun. He was halfway up when Jacqui, realising too late what she had done, picked up the spade and hurled it at him. It clattered ineffectively against the ladder and dropped on to the quarry stone floor. The flames, rapidly devouring the dry hay, had now reached the badly plastered ceiling above which was the wooden floor of the house. There was a crash of the trapdoor as Holmeir let the crate drop behind him.

12

Fuller left the shed. In a few hours' time he was due in his surgery and there were operations to perform. He felt mentally exhausted.

He rested a little outside the shed, not looking forward to the journey back yet knowing he could not delay it. But he was worried about Holmeir and about those who had sent him. It was important to know who and why. He felt he should be down in the cellar with the others, sharing the responsibility of extracting information in a way that would be unacceptable to many whose lives did not depend upon it. This worried him too. He could see no reason for sacrificing Claudie, himself and the others, to obey the rules of decency in order to protect one treacherous bastard.

He steeled himself and set off with the wind at his back. Had it not been for that, Jacqui's screams might have gone unnoticed. The house was actually out of sight when he stopped, crouched in the grass to listen again. The sound was so fleeting that he thought it might be in his head. Then he heard another scream and realised that it was too high-pitched to be Holmeir's. He waited, listening, clearing his mind of fatigue.

Then he heard something quite different. Someone hurrying, making a good deal of noise. Running. As the footsteps came nearer he realised that they were from the direction of the house. Someone so careless could only be Holmeir and he would run to the nearest military post. Fuller knew where that was, too. He rose and started to run obliquely from his original route. The wind was in his favour and carried Holmeir's movements to him. Occasionally he stopped to listen for a bare second and then he would race on. He dare not think what had happened for Holmeir to escape.

Fuller closed the gap and saw the shadow stumbling up the incline towards him. Immediately he dropped down out of sight. Holmeir was putting as much distance as he could between the house and himself; he would shout once he was near enough to be heard and Fuller knew that moment was not far off. Something had gone drastically wrong and Holmeir had to be stopped. Fuller dived at the panting Holmeir as he went past.

The fight was uglier than when Holmeir tackled Kremple. Fuller was powerful but Holmeir was highly trained. The German tried to yell but Fuller stopped him. Fuller knew that if Holmeir broke away he would not be able to catch him again. It was not until he realised that Holmeir was getting the better of him that he remembered the carving knife in his waistband. He wasn't sure if it was still there.

He had to get a hand free to grope for it. This enabled Holmeir to roll on top, straddle Fuller and start to choke him to death; fear and hatred hardened his strength. Fuller stopped struggling. He had seconds left before he would black out. He found the knife handle and squirmed to pull it out. Holmeir's body angled above him and Fuller plunged the blade under the ribs. Holmeir opened his mouth to scream in agony but died before he could. He dropped on top of Fuller and the knife plunged further in from his weight.

For some time Fuller could not move. The hands had loosened from his neck but Holmeir's body had driven out what little breath he had left. Eventually he half-rolled and Holmeir dropped away. Fuller rose to one knee, checked that Holmeir was dead, pushed him on to his back and withdrew the knife.

He retched beside Holmeir's body. After a while he thrust the knife into the soil and finished cleaning it on Holmeir's shirt. He rose very shakily.

He could not leave Holmeir there; he dragged him along with a leg held under each arm, pulling him like he would a wheelbarrow. He wondered what had happened to the others.

Gorkov had been watching the scene from the shadows. Once Kremple had identified the SS swine, Gorkov was ready to see him suffer. There was little feeling of revenge in him, little feeling of anything. He just wanted to see if Holmeir could take it as well or as badly as some of the slaves had done.

A few days of what was to him luxury feeding had not changed his outlook; he had considered his situation hopeless from the outset. He had started feeling better though, and had even begun to enjoy the company of his new friends. But his physical limitations were brought home to him with a jolt when matters started to go wrong.

At first, Holmeir had been lucky in knocking over Kremple. After that, though, Gorkov had seen the cunning of the man but with Schroder standing there remained unworried.

Gorkov knew that Holmeir hadn't seen him. The Russian had learned to use shadows and recesses as an animal does. Jacqui had acted much too quickly for him, however, and when Schroder fell instinct made him keep back when he realised he couldn't reach the ladder before Holmeir. Self-preservation sensibly rooted him until the flames exploded beyond the initial modest fire. Either he got out or fought the flames. Schroder and Kremple were still groggy so Gorkov moved as fast as he could, calling to Jacqui for help.

He reached the old sacks and between them they beat at the flames. In a matter of seconds Gorkov discovered how physically depleted he was. But he waded in as if proofed against flame, urging Jacqui on.

Jacqui needed no urging, knowing only too well that she was responsible for what had happened. She was fighting as hard as she could, sweat pouring from her. By the time Schroder and Kremple joined in the flames were licking the ceiling. The four of them beat frantically at the ignited straw.

When Fuller reached the shed he could smell the smoke filtering through the floorboards. As flames flickered through the cracks in the floor he pulled Holmeir's body across to block off the air. He knew that if he opened the trap oxygen would pour in to feed the fire. He could hear the others beating, swearing, calling to each other. They were alive.

There was a water butt in the yard which they could use. He ran out, found he could not move it by himself, then ran back. He stamped his feet and called through the boards. It was some time before they heard him. He yelled about the water and within seconds Schroder had pushed himself through the trap, closing it immediately. Between them they got the butt into the house, into the kitchen beneath which was the seat of the fire, Schroder said. They tipped the butt over and the water gushed out, cascading into the cellar, soaking the smouldering boards. They dashed back to the trapdoor and climbed down.

Up until then the fire had barely been contained but now, with the water, it was brought under control. It was some time before the last flame was out and there was still plenty of smouldering. The cellar was a warren of smoke, the haze drifting and spiralling from the straw. They set about raking and beating.

They ended up breathless and soot-covered and when they were satisfied the danger had fully passed they went upstairs for some air, leaving the trap open. They went as near to the cliff edge as they dared in the dark. The sound of the sea lapping on the shore was restful after the strain of the night. The wind whipped at their over-heated bodies and made them feel cleaner. They sat close to each other, silent and disconsolate.

Kremple put a hand on Gorkov's bony shoulder. He squeezed gently in tribute; Gorkov could have run out, instead he had driven himself almost beyond his limits. Schroder took off his jacket and placed it over the thin shivering body.

Her voice tremulous with emotion, Jacqui said, 'I'm sorry. I don't know what else to say.'

Schroder put an arm round her shoulders. 'You knocked half my brains out.'

She began to sob quietly into his shoulder. Fuller rose wearily. 'I must leave Holmeir to you.'

Kremple was still fingering his throat. 'We'll take care of him.'

'I'll get you another lamp.' Fuller swayed a little.

'Are you all right?' Schroder asked the question that all of them were thinking.

Fuller looked down at the small huddled group. 'I'll survive.'

He moved off with a faint wave of the hand and they watched until they could neither see nor hear him. After a while, as the pre-dawn chill really bit into them, they went back to the house. Gorkov and Jacqui started the long tedious and dirty job of clearing up while Schroder and Kremple stripped Holmeir and returned to the cliff edge with the naked body. They swung Holmeir like a sack and sent him to join the man they had already killed on the rocks below.

Kremple looked up at the sky. It was still dark but he could now make out the dim shape of the deserted house.

'The doctor is in grave trouble.'

'Holmeir?' Schroder glanced back towards the cliffs.

'We didn't find out who planted him.'

'Does it matter? Gestapo, SS?'

'It does matter. Holmeir has disappeared and someone deliberately sent him to the doctor.'

Schroder said, 'I didn't mean to sound callous. I'd have been shot by now, but for him, but there's nothing we can do. In this he's on his own.'

Lord Arden awoke to a crisp morning. He had been allocated a batman, his clothes had been pressed, his underwear and shirt washed and ironed, a change laid out on the seat of a chair and he was served a full breakfast in his room. But his impression of being deliberately isolated remained. He did not complain, however.

When he was dressed he was told a car would call for him. He was asked to wait in his room meanwhile. He could understand that his hosts would not want him to see what was happening on the island. Had he seen the progress and size of the fortifications he might have been both puzzled and alarmed at their magnitude. He noticed, too, that his room view was confined to other buildings in St Anne. He had been nicely tucked in by bricks and mortar. All this he expected. If positions were reversed he would have done the same.

Yet it was no easier for him to wait in the confines of the room. He had been deprived of conversation for several days; it was beginning to penetrate his considerable psychological armour. He had nothing to read. He realised he should have brought something with him. He had asked his batman for books, magazines, newspapers, English or German, it did not matter, but promises had not produced the goods. As in Paris, he had nothing to do but to wait and think and examine his plan for weaknesses. But it was his position they were trying to weaken, and he knew it.

The car arrived mid-morning and the SS captain Heyden greeted him formally and joined him in the car which another SS man drove. In front and behind them was an SS escort, every man with a submachine gun.

It was drizzling. The journey took longer than Arden expected and he assumed that the route had been carefully planned so that he had minimum view of what was happening on the island. The one insight he was offered was clearly designed to impress. The side of Fuller's old house was closed as they approached and the hydraulic gear operated just when he thought they were driving straight into it. The side rose and they drove into the lighted tunnel, deep under the earth until they reached the turn-round. The car stopped and the door was opened for Arden. Captain Heyden handed him over to Major Hoffman who escorted him on foot down the much narrower, right-hand tunnel as the sentry sprang to attention.

He was shown into what Fuller had called the briefing room. And Hoffman stayed with him.

It was another half hour before Klaus Wendel and Walter Schellenberg arrived. They entered without ceremony and closed the door after Hoffman had left. Wendel made the introductions but Arden had already recognised them both. For years he had made a study of the Nazi hierarchy and of those close to Hitler. The presence of Schellenberg surprised him considerably but then no one knew how Hitler's mind worked. They shook hands and sat down.

Fuller was in his surgery when Major Hoffman called. The major came straight into the inner room where Fuller was examining a sailor. Fuller glanced up, annoyed, but Hoffman was coldly polite.

'I'm sorry to burst in, Doctor, but you are wanted in the other section.'

'Other section?' Fuller's fingers were gently exploring the sailor's stomach.

'Herr Wendel would like to see you.'

Fuller was thinking fast. Why the other section when they'd been keeping him out? 'I still have some patients waiting.'

'They do not appear to be in imminent danger of dying, Doctor. This is very urgent.'

'All right.' He told the sailor to dress. He kept on his surgical coat as a reminder of interruption and followed Hoffman out. They walked side by side along the corridor. The major, pointedly looking to his front, had no intention of being drawn. Fuller did not try; he walked in silence with some apprehension. They turned left at the junction, continuing to the end door. Hoffman knocked crisply and on the command 'enter' opened the door and stood aside for Fuller to go in. Fuller had his hands in his coat pockets as he stepped forward. Wendel and Schellenberg both rose, but it was Arden who gave him the shock. Arden, who was never a focus of attention and always the last man to attract it. Fuller's mind raced.

'Good God. Lord Arden. What on earth are you doing here?'

Arden came round the table smiling, his hand out. 'Mr Fuller. George. How good to see you looking so well.'

'Am I? It's not easy on this island fortress.' Fuller was feeling the effects of the long night. He was thinking that Arden must be the man he had been asked to watch and that many lives and a submarine had been put at risk so that he could receive this instruction.

'I heard you were here. On the island.'

'Really? Am I so important?' They had vigorously shaken hands and were standing at one end of the room as if Wendel and Schellenberg weren't there. But Fuller was constantly aware of them and wondered how far his questioning could go.

'The island is important. And what happens to any prisoners,' replied Arden.

'But how did you learn I was here?'

Arden shook his head with a smile, glanced over Fuller's shoulder. 'You wouldn't expect me to answer that.'

Fuller noticed the strong innuendo of British concern in Arden's replies. 'You're not a prisoner here, I hope? I don't recommend it.'

'It's no deep secret, George. I'm here in an attempt to arrange an exchange of sick prisoners. Many of our lads in German PoW camps will never be fit enough to fight again. They present no risk to the Axis who should be glad to be relieved of the responsibility and the cost of keeping them alive.'

'A quid pro quo?' Arden was already volunteering his reason for being here?

'Exactly. It takes time to arrange these deals.'

Fuller hid his qualms. 'I thought the International Red Cross handled that sort of thing?'

Arden shot a glanced warning. 'They do. I'm representing them. I'm here as a Swede named Ardense. The reasons are too complicated to explain but it does cut red tape and save an awful lot of time. It's important that you forget who I really am. Only the four of us here know. Not a word to anyone, George; for everyone's sake.'

These three men to discuss an exchange of prisoners? Arden using a false name with the knowledge of the Germans? Suddenly Fuller felt the focus on himself. 'Of course not. You know you can trust me.' So Schroder *had* got the name right.

'I would not have asked to see you had I thought otherwise. I knew you were here. I knew that your father would want to know how you are. He's fine, by the way. I couldn't possibly have gone home without seeing you.'

'It's good to see someone from the old country. Do we meet again?'

Arden glanced over Fuller's shoulder and Schellenberg came halfway along the side of the table to say, 'I can see no reason why not. This is a meeting of mutual interest on humanitarian grounds. I'm sure it can be arranged, Doctor.'

Fuller nodded. The meeting was over, as brief as it had been. He offered his hand to Arden again. 'You can tell my father I'm doing what he does so well, mending bodies. But if he can influence the Prime Minister to lift Claudie and myself from this island prison, I would, of course, be delighted.'

'I'll tell him, George. I'll tell him you haven't changed one bit. I'm only sorry this meeting is so short and in such difficult circumstances.'

Fuller shrugged, sensing that they were all waiting for him to go. He looked round the room, at the frame on the rear wall and his gaze dropped to the foot of it. There was a little pile of brick dust on the carpet below.

When he had left the other three sat down again. Arden said stiffly, 'I hope you are now satisfied.'

Wendel was impassive. He sat with elbows on table, his hands clasped, the wide shoulders hunched. A document case lay in front of him. 'Reasonably so, Lord Arden. We must not forget that using the doctor to confirm your bona fides was your own idea.'

'For God's sake, do you imagine I planted him here?'

Wendel shrugged. 'The good doctor had a point. How did you know he was here?'

'You had better ask your Führer.'

The two men gazed placidly at each other. Wendel broke off and aware that the more relaxed Schellenberg had not notice his irritation. 'For the moment we will accept or's reaction. You are who you say you are. You have friends in high places.'

'I have friends with more power than most who occupy high places.'

'As you say. It would be better if you didn't see the doctor again.'

'Provided you are completely satisfied, I agree.'

Wendel undid the lock of the document case. 'We won't dispose of him until you have left the island. It might be embarrassing for you.'

Arden knew that Wendel had tried to shock him, to test his strength. 'I agree. It's essential to me to conceal any involvement.'

Wendel nodded approval. 'You are a careful man, Lord Arden. It becomes clear why we know so little about you.' He took out a carefully stapled sheaf of papers from a sturdy folder. He held them up, and then returned them to the folder and pushed it along the desk to Arden. 'I suggest you take these back to your room and digest their contents.'

Arden picked up the folder. 'These are from your Führer?'

'He, I and Standartenführer Schellenberg are the only people who have seen them. Which is why we have had to run so careful a check on you.'

'When do we meet again?'

'At the same time tomorrow.'

Arden opened the cover, flipped through the pages. 'I can be ready by this evening. There's no room for bargaining.'

'Digest them, Lord Arden. With respect. You will be locked in your suite until tomorrow. Meals will be brought to you. If there is anything you need, please ask.'

'Am I a prisoner as Mr Fuller suggested?'

'No, not at all. The security is for the documents. I'm afraid you must suffer a little to protect them.' Wendel closed his case; the first session was over.

'He says he's here about an exchange of prisoners.'

Claudie watched him, aware of his deep concern as she tried to hide her own. 'Is this possible?'

'I doubt it. He's here as Ardense. A Swede. And that's how you'd better refer to him if it crops up.'

'Rod Schroder risked his life to bring you that name. So he's an English lord. It stinks.'

'I must find out why he's really here or Rod's stuck his neck out for nothing.'

'Be careful, George. *Please*.'

He took her by the shoulders. 'It would be natural for him to want to see me, to take a message back to Father. What isn't natural is that he's here at all. I think I was wanted to identify him.' He felt her stiffen under his hands.

'Is this why they have tolerated so much from you over the past few months?' She dreaded what would happen now.

'It looks like it.' He was thinking back to the occasions when they could have reprimanded him, or got at him by withholding rations or liquor. How long was it since they had placed Claudie and him on officers' rations? 'They do need me medically.' But that was not true any more. He was convinced that other doctors and surgeons would be brought in very shortly.

For a while Fuller cradled Claudie, then he said, 'Someone in England isn't sure what Arden is up to. *But they knew he was coming.*'

'If the Germans knew Schroder was here they'd kill us all now.'

It would be useless to try to reassure her. 'Get your coat. We're going to search for that bloody tunnel.'

Claudie grabbed a jacket and called Blanco.

Fuller took the short route to the hospital. There was nothing unusual in this but on reaching it he led Claudie round the back of the old house, circling widely. Beneath them were the tunnels and he tried to gauge how they ran but it was almost impossible.

They continued on to a wild area of bushes, trees and clumps of gorse. It was an area that might possibly have been cultivated and he wondered why it had not been. He watched Blanco running in and out of the clumps in his endless quest for rabbits. Claudie hung back a little to watch their rear; occasionally she had seen Hoffman head this way.

It was not until after lunch that Captain Heyden could get to Gestapo headquarters. Kratz was impatient and annoyed and came straight to the point.

'What's happened to this reliable man of yours?'

With the VIPs on the island and the involvement of his men on escort duty, Heyden had little time to think about it. 'Holmeir? Hasn't he reported to you?'

'I wouldn't be asking if he had.'

Heyden tried to bring his mind back to his collusion with Kratz. 'I've been so busy. All he had to do was to implicate the doctor and return to you some time this morning with a report. I took him off all other duties.'

'I haven't seen him, Hauptsturmführer.'

But Heyden was thinking that only that morning Fuller had been taken to the tunnel where even he was not allowed to go.

'Perhaps he couldn't get away from the doctor.'

'Are you saying the doctor has locked him up?'

Heyden recalled that the doctor had looked tired; but he had been interviewed by the VIPs. He must tread carefully and so must Kratz. 'Would you like me to organise a search?'

'That's what is needed but it could raise questions while the Führer's representatives are here. Yet we need to know. Your own men will note Holmeir's absence. Can you arrange a *discreet* search?'

'It will not be easy if we're to disguise its purpose. I can cover Holmeir's absence for a time. Will you see the doctor?'

Kratz had considered it again and again. 'It will be difficult without showing some knowledge of what Holmeir was supposed to do?'

'Would it matter?'

Kratz did not answer at once. He was tired of being a one-man unit. He had two assistants but they were minions, useless to his line of thinking. He would rather deal with Heyden but the captain was now displaying his limitations. Yet he needed someone to talk to. 'At the moment it matters. The man is being treated like royalty and none of us know why.'

'The Führer would know.'

Kratz glared. He did not want to be reminded that he might have slipped up. 'What could have happened to Holmeir? Surely he must have gone to the doctor's? He was either taken in by the doctor or turned away.' Kratz's face was lined and sunken but his dark eyes were bright with thought. 'Perhaps our doctor has more to hide than we realise. Perhaps Holmeir saw more than he was prepared for.'

Heyden was worried now. Kratz must be under strain or trying to justify an idea that had gone wrong; he should have avoided trying to help him. What could the doctor seriously get up to on this island? The doctor's views were well known. Britain would win the war. He had enjoyed protection for so long that everyone had got used to his occasional pronouncements. A few even admired his courage.

Kratz was still thinking, fingering the deep lines of his face. 'I wonder if the doctor is not quite as open as he's led us to believe? His skill may not lie solely on the operating table.' Kratz glanced up quickly and caught Heyden's look of doubt. 'By sending in Holmeir we may have stirred up a hornets' nest.' He pushed his chair back, gazed evenly at Heyden. 'Holmeir might even be dead. If he hasn't reported by tomorrow we must assume that he is.'

Heyden was shaken. Kratz's cold logic was at last getting through to him. 'What shall we do?'

Kratz cupped his fingers, satisfied now with his own line of reasoning. 'Normally the answer would be easy. While we wait for a return to normality we had better keep an eye on the good doctor. When they are out search his house. Watch his movements.'

13

Captain Brocker cycled mainly for exercise but partly because motorised transport was limited. He had thought Fuller might be at home as it was just after lunch, and so was surprised to catch sight of him and Claudie disappearing into the woods behind the hospital. He recognised the little white streak darting in and out of the trees as Blanco. He dismounted and propped his cycle against a tree. The entrance to the hospital was open, a sentry just inside. He set off after Fuller.

Brocker was about to call to the doctor when he noticed that Fuller was searching for something, kicking into odd clumps of growth. Claudie seemed to be acting as lookout but she had not yet glanced his way; a fickle breeze tugged at her hair.

Brocker dropped back and trod more carefully. Blanco would have long since picked up his scent but for the terrier's preoccupation with rabbits. Brocker moved behind a tree to watch. Fuller's actions worried him. The doctor was hiding too much from him.

Claudie suddenly caught sight of the cycle and called to Fuller who stopped kicking at clumps and bawled, 'Are you spying on us, Joachim?'

Brocker came forward sheepishly. When he was near enough he called: 'You look like a golfer who has lost his last ball.'

'Searching for a special kind of wild flower. Only grow in these woods.'

'Yes, of course. I was fascinated by the delicacy of your search, George. Boots are clearly best for botanical study.'

Claudie smiled tensely; she had not been nervous of Brocker before. Could she afford to trust him now?

'What are you actually looking for, George?'

Fuller bluffed it out. 'I'm not going to tell the enemy.'

'Ah! Today we are enemies. Then, as my prisoner, I demand that you tell me.'

'Rank, name and number, Joachim.'

Brocker tapped with a boot. 'Somewhere underneath here is

the hospital. You think there is danger of the roof collapsing?'

'What do you want with us, Joachim?'

'I wondered what our illustrious visitors wanted of you. And the Swede?'

Fuller glanced at Claudie who quickly understood his alarm. She called Blanco and put him on the lead. 'You two carry on while I take Blanco back.'

Fuller and Brocker, aware of some of the old suspicion creeping back between them, climbed to higher ground where they could look out to the north-west towards Casquettes lighthouse, some six miles off the coast; the two towers, joined by a low building, sprouted from the elongated rock base like trained fungus. From this distance they could just see the hazy detail. About half a mile out to sea four German soldiers were fishing from a large rubber dinghy which they seemed to be having trouble in controlling.

The two men stood looking out to sea. Fuller was satisfied that he had nothing to lose, that the die was already cast.

'He's not a Swede. He's English. More English than Winston Churchill, who had an American mother. He's Lord Arden.'

The news came to Brocker as a shock and he did not like the implications. 'He has a Swedish passport in the name of Ardense. Who else knows that he's English?'

'Schellenberg, Wendel, me, and now you. It's highly dangerous knowledge.'

'If it's so dangerous to know, why tell me?'

'Because I believe that you and I are irretrievably linked. What happens to one will happen to the other. I fear we've played our parts.'

They were quiet for some time before Fuller unexpectedly changed the subject. 'Is that from Fort Clonque?' He pointed to the rubber dinghy which seemed to be in difficulty.

'How your mind switches. You know they keep a couple there as part of the life-saving equipment.'

The old fort lay below them at the bulbous end of a short peninsular whose finger pointed to the lighthouse.

'Where exactly is the life-saving stuff kept?'

Brocker was mystified by the continued change; his mind was still on Fuller's revelation. 'Just inside the gates. A store room.' He looked up curiously. 'Obviously as near as possible to where they might be needed. Are you thinking of stealing a dinghy to reach England? You wouldn't get far in one of those in these currents.'

'That's obvious. They're having trouble out there now. As a doctor I should be told where any aid to life saving is kept. I haven't seen them being used before.'

'They shouldn't be. But boredom here is a problem and a blind eye is occasionally turned. I have the feeling that you deliberately changed the subject. English or Swedish, you still haven't told me what happened between you.'

'Arden? I know him slightly and he knows my father. Ostensibly I was taken to see him to exchange greetings so that he could tell my father that I'm alive and well. He says he's here to arrange an exchange of prisoners.'

Brocker's silence was condemnation of the notion. Fuller said drily, 'So you can't stomach it either. Will you help me find out why he's here?'

'Is *that* why you told me? Anyway, how can I? You apparently think the secret lies in the woods somewhere behind the hospital.'

Fuller was not drawn. 'Don't make me lie to you, Joachim. Do you know where Arden is billeted?'

'He's in a house in St Anne.'

'Is it possible for me to see him?'

'No. Nobody sees him other than his batman.'

'He's a prisoner then?'

'A very well treated one.'

'Couldn't you help me see him?'

'That's impossible. I understand there's a guard outside his door.'

'Will you take me to the house?'

Brocker considered this. 'I'll take you past it.'

'That's very good of you.'

'I'll go no further than that.' Brocker hesitated. 'What Lord Arden is here for is no concern of mine. Why should it worry you?'

They began to walk towards St Anne. 'I don't know,' said Fuller. 'I think I was used to identify him. Which means they have to be sure of him.'

Brocker made no comment; he was sorry that Fuller had told

him about Arden; he could see it as both compliment and danger.

It was a little time before they reached St Anne. They went along the cobbled streets, turned from the High Street, passing a sentry who sprang to attention. As he returned the salute Brocker said, 'That's the house.' A little further on he added, 'Three floors. He has an en suite room at the back of the top floor. It is usually kept for visiting officers or a senior officer of the garrison. The two lower floors are officers' billets.'

'Formidable,' remarked Fuller. 'How can I get in?'

'You can't. Try force and you'll be shot by a sentry. Orders for his protection are very explicit.'

'Doesn't it make you wonder why?' They had now turned a corner and Fuller headed for the back of the building.

'Yes. But I'm a minion. And I have come to terms with it.'

The house was the centre of a terrace of three, all differing in height. The rear gardens backed on to those in the High Street. Scattered behind was a haphazard collection of buildings spreading back towards more open country.

'There's no way in for you, George.'

'Which is the room?'

'I think that's the window, there. Come, I must retrieve my cycle.'

On the way back Brocker was thoughtful. He said carefully, 'You asked me if I was spying on you. Let me tell you that if I was you would have been shot by now.'

Fuller gazed down at Brocker, aware that he was looking into the face of a friend. 'Have I hurt or upset you in some way?'

'You've deliberately misled me. Lively as Blanco is he cannot scuffle about upstairs while he's sitting on my lap. Nor can Claudie make noises in the bedroom while she's standing in the doorway behind my chair.'

'Why didn't you say something at the time?'

'I wanted to think about it. I like you well enough to have given you the benefit of doubt.'

'Am I making it too difficult for you?'

'That depends on what you are up to. You had someone up there. Who was it? An escapee from Sylt?'

Fuller did not want to involve Brocker but realised that he already had. 'I'm deeply sorry. Will you accept my word that at present there is nobody in the house except Claudie and me?'

'I accept that as truth. It's what you are not telling me that I find worrying. And now you intend to get up to something else.'

'I only want to speak to Arden.'

'You're playing a dangerous game, George. You have real enemies here. Hoffman, Heyden, Kratz.'

'I know. But I don't think it will make any difference to what happens to me.'

'You could be wrong; your usefulness may not yet be over.'

'Perhaps. The answer lies with Arden.'

'George, you can't fight a war on your own on an island like this.' Brocker stopped. He adjusted his cap as he looked Fuller straight in the eye. 'I've told you before that there will come a time when I will have to take sides. Just remember that *I am a German officer*. Don't force my hand. For your own sake.'

Fuller gazed round. They had transformed the cellar from a near wreck to a clean home. They had salvaged some of the straw and had stolen some hay. They were better than back to normal for among the rubble in the cellar they had found old tins of paint and brushes and some of the brickwork was now blue and pink. The clash of colours was appalling but it brightened the place.

Fuller said, 'We have three machine pistols with limited ammunition. Can we get some more?'

Kremple pointed to the MP-38s hidden under sacks in the corner. 'To get weapons like that would be difficult. Main units have their own armouries, the Wehrmacht, Marine, Luftwaffe. Pistols and grenades are locked away; rifles, machine pistols, chained and locked.'

'We don't want to use force. It would take very little now to advertise your presence here. Once they suspect, they'll find you.'

Schroder said, 'Has something gone wrong?'

Fuller ignored the question; his nostrils twitched at the combined smell of paint and paraffin. 'We've got to think of escape.'

'We think of nothing else.'

'I know. I've dreamed of it for over two years.' Fuller turned to Kremple again. 'When you Germans first came here you had a most peculiar assortment of arms. Now they are different. What happened to the others?'

Kremple pondered. 'The first arrivals were second-line troops and were armed with almost anything. The ROA had Russian rifles. SSSR 7.62 mm. There were bolt-action Mausers, KAR 98ks, 7.92 mm. Marvellous rifles. Some are still used here. There was a variety of pistols. Polish 'Vis', W 235 or Radoms, what we call P 35s. Old Mauser C96s. Do you remember those? Broom-handles is the name we gave them. They were obsolete before 1939. Others I remember, Lugers, PO8s. They were a quartermaster's nightmare. A mixture of our own old and captured arms. Even the Zielfernrohre were ancient.'

'Telescopic sights? So what happened to them?'

'They were called back. I think they are now down by the harbour. An annexe to the cement works was used as an armoury.'

'I know the place, a small building on its own which housed a generator. The generator broke down and a replacement was installed. As it was too much trouble to rip one out and put in another they built a new housing. To the left of the main complex?'

'That's it. It's always guarded.'

'I'll take a look.' Fuller turned to Schroder. 'Did they teach you climbing in your outfit?'

'Sure.'

'I need your help. I want to break into a house in St Anne. Still got the rope?' Fuller had supplied most of it; there had been lengths available on various farms in the early days. They had used it to explore the cliff face.

Schroder went to the darkest end of the cellar and came back with two coils of rope. 'You going to tell me what it's about?'

'Ardense has arrived.'

Fuller and Schroder each slung a coil of rope over their shoulders and climbed the ladder, leaving behind them an uneasy air of speculation amongst the other three.

Fuller led the way past the sites and slowed on approaching St Anne. It was not yet late enough for everyone to be asleep and, to confirm this, raucous singing came from somewhere in the centre of town. It started to rain. Fuller said, 'We walk in. They know me and nobody will examine your uniform in this bloody weather.'

The risk was not too great. Although there were sounds of life the streets they used were empty and Fuller kept away from those that might not be. He led the way round the back of the gardens. There were no lights to guide them and the rain became persistent.

They climbed a fence and approached along the garden of the end house. A strident sound of music came from inside. The garden had been cultivated and they carefully picked their way between crops. The soil was soft and the rain was making it worse. They reached a small dilapidated greenhouse from which a slabbed path led to the back of the house. The rain was heavier now and they lost sight of the murky shape of the buildings. Everything was black.

Schroder asked, 'Where do you want to get in?'

'Third window along on the central building.' They had to creep closer for Schroder to see it.

'I can get up the end building to the roof and work my way along. I'll take both ropes.' The rain was dripping from the polished peak of Schroder's cap.

'How long?' Fuller unhitched his coil and handed it over.

'Twenty minutes?'

'Don't slip.'

Schroder patted Fuller's arm. He went down the path and was lost almost immediately in the murk.

Fuller rose. Night in St Anne could be uncanny. Apart from sentries there was virtually no sign of life. Sometimes, but rarely, a car or half-track would rumble past. But it was not yet midnight and he could still hear the distant sound of German army songs. And, from the direction of the quay, the faint growl of armoured vehicles sometimes reached him. He wondered if there was an exercise on. He groped his way to the boundary fence, keeping between the vegetable lanes, and climbed over. The wire squeaked as he pressed down on it and he cursed himself for being so noisy.

The American was cursing too. He had tested the drainpipe for strength. His cap was a nuisance but, as there would be times when he might need it, he rammed it hard on his head. He pulled himself up the wall, hands on the pipe, his feet some-times slipping.

He reached the guttering and held on. Hooking a leg over he heaved himself up. There was an awful moment when the guttering took his full weight and he felt it give but he reached the slates, squatted, afraid to move; the pouring rain made matters worse. Using his hands as suction pads he steadied himself then sat facing outwards. Gradually he pushed his way up backwards to the angle of the roof.

He straddled the roof top as if it was a heavily flanked horse. From here he, too, could hear the distant clank of armoured vehicles. Below, the sentry had stopped pacing outside the officers' quarters, presumably to take shelter. Schroder worked his way along the roof until he reached a chimney stack. Getting round it was difficult and he was aware of taking too long.

At the end of the house he faced the problem of a different roof height. He pulled himself up to the new level and hitched himself along again. The rain was now driving into his face. He advanced in a series of small movements until he reached the middle chimney stack.

There was little he could do until the rain eased and he worried about Fuller waiting below. Eventually, as he had hoped it would, the heavy shower faded to the earlier drizzle, but he had lost time. He held one rope like a huge skipping rope and cast it over his head to clear the tall chimney stack first time.

He sat there until satisfied that nothing had been heard by the sentry below, then he knotted the two ends and looped the second rope over the first which he paid out slowly so that it would fall below gutter level. The pulley rope now dangled in a long hoop down the side of the house; he tied the free end to the stack.

Fuller could neither see nor hear the rope coming down. From time to time he checked, going as near as he dared. It was unfortunate that the back door was central to where the rope would fall.

When the rope did come snaking down he tugged lightly to warn Schroder then stepped over the loop, finding he was almost touching the door. Pulling on the loose end brought the loop up. He held tight and sat on the rope, lifting himself just clear of the ground. He began to sway as the rope slid under him and he had to adjust his position.

Upward movement was slow and he had to have short rests while he wound the loose end round his body to steady his position. It was difficult to keep his feet clear of the windows and he had to inch past them carefully. The method was primitive but it worked.

He reached what he believed to be Arden's bedroom window and, steadying himself against the sill, wound the rope round. He stretched to get a fingertip support under the sash window overlap and got as close to the frame as he could. It was impossible to see whether or not a light was on in the room. He tapped gently on the glass. He thought he heard a movement and whispered, 'It's George Fuller. Open up.' He tapped and whispered again raising his voice.

Suddenly he was aware of music in the room, at first loud but quickly turned down. A radio or gramophone. Fuller almost lost his grip as a voice from the other side of the glass demanded, '*Wer ist das?*' Christ. A German. No. A German officer would have called the guard out immediately. 'George Fuller,' he responded as loud as he dare. The window was unlatched, the bottom part raised. There was no light. A smudge of face appeared, unidentifiable, but the incredulous whisper was Arden's. '*Fuller?*'

Fuller realised what he must look like if he could be seen at all. 'Give me a hand. I'm coming in.'

There was little else Arden could do except to sound an alarm. He grabbed Fuller's jacket as the doctor awkwardly lifted a leg over the sill. Fuller was concerned about the music escaping and drawing attention to the window.

'God, man, you're soaking wet. What on earth are you doing climbing ladders in this weather?'

'A rope,' said Fuller. 'I was on a rope.' As his feet touched the floor and Arden helped him straighten, he turned to close the window and made sure the heavy drapes were pulled. 'Can we have a light on?'

Arden crossed the room, switched on the light. He blinked and stared at Fuller in amazement. 'Good God, just look at you. You're staining the carpet.' He was in pyjamas and dressing gown. 'You'll get us both shot.'

'Only if we raise our voices. Leave the radio on. But you'd better come away from the door.'

Arden came forward and they faced each other by the window wall. 'I can't ask you to sit down. You'll mark the chair and I'll have to explain it away. As it is the carpet will cause comment. This is a crazy thing to do. We'd have met again before I leave.'

'Would we?'

'What on earth do you mean by that?' Arden went into the bathroom to fetch a towel. He sponged up the pools at Fuller's feet; the water was still running off the soggy trousers and shoes.

'It means that I've served my purpose.'

Arden rose, the wet towel between his hands. His gaze was piercing, affability suspended. 'You mean by identifying me?'

'Wasn't that the object?' Fuller's gaze was wandering the room.

'Of course. I told you we knew you were here. You surely haven't placed us both in jeopardy to ask a silly bloody question like that?'

'No. I don't suppose you have a drink?'

'Schnapps?'

Fuller's face lighted up. 'Fine.'

Arden remembered; Fuller was like his father. 'It must be difficult for you. There's a shortage at home too, you know.' He opened a cabinet and poured liberally. 'Neat, I seem to recall.' He passed Fuller the tumbler.

Fuller swallowed with relish. He kept hold of the glass, as if putting it down would be to invite it to disappear. 'How's the war *really* going?' he asked.

'Things are very bad.'

'We're losing?'

'We're certainly not winning. It's probably worse for the Americans; we've had three years to get used to it.'

'You speak as if there's no hope. Aren't the people behind Winnie?'

'I find it difficult to believe you made your perilous journey just for a news bulletin.' Arden lowered his voice as Fuller signalled a warning. 'Of course the people are behind him but they're fed up. Winston is under constant pressure. It's inevitable. The tide of war has been against us.'

'That's very depressing news.'

'They're very depressing times. Will you get to the point?'

Fuller respected the fact that Arden was a lifelong friend of Churchill's but it did not make him like the man. He appreciated his shrewdness, could admire his sharp brain, the mental ability to grasp a situation while most others saw only its periphery; he could do that and plan a solution at the same time. Fuller had listened to his appraisals in the past but they had mainly been financial, rarely political and then only in a general, non-party, sense. What he did not like was the coldness, the apparent lack of emotion of any kind. This meeting for instance; Arden had displayed surprise and concern for the carpet and furniture but not once had he remarked how difficult Fuller's entry must have been; not once worried about his discomfort.

'So you're here on a prisoner exchange?'

Arden showed signs that he would prefer to sit down but they had to be close to communicate at so low a pitch. On the radio someone was talking in German. Arden's face did not change expression, his bony hands were thrust into his dressing-gown pockets. 'You surely didn't believe that?'

'Why say it?'

'It's what people must believe.'

'What people?'

'Come, George. Stick to medicine.'

'I've been a prisoner on this bloody island for two and a half years and I've carried the flag. No one here is in any doubt where I stand. I want to know what's going on.'

'It's none of your business.'

'Anything to do with the war and this island *is* my business.'

'I'm sorry. I understand your feelings and your frustration but this is a matter of State. Top secret. I really can't tell you.'

'Don't be so damned pompous. You mean you can't trust me? You think I'll run round the island telling everyone?'

'I know that you won't. Nobody resident on this island knows what this is about. Not even the commandant.'

'You say my father knows I'm here; does anyone else?'

'Because of your father's friendship with the PM I informed him too.'

'*You*? You're in intelligence?'

Arden did not reply. He stood as if the strain was almost too much, shoulders rounded, stance limp. Only his eyes in the sunken face were alive.

Fuller felt like striking him. After the journey, endangering Schroder and himself, the difficulty and discomfort, to be met by a stone wall was almost too much. He had nothing to lose. He said,

'You're a cold-blooded bastard. I can perhaps understand your need for secrecy, whatever the reason. But I can't stand your attitude. You haven't asked me a single question on what it's been like here. Don't you want to know that they're butchering the labour force and what else they're doing here? I don't believe you're interested.'

Arden sighed wearily. 'You've always been outspoken, but you should not pass judgment on something you can't be expected to know about. I know more of what's going on here than you realise.'

'Marvellous. You must have the Germans in your pocket.'

'I think you'd better go back.'

Fuller finished his drink, handed back the glass, turned to the window. 'That's what I thought. I've served my purpose. Wasn't much of a part, was it?'

'You're being ridiculous.'

'Naturally. I'll find out why you're here, one way or the other.'

'If you have any regard for Winston at all you'll try no such thing.'

'Oh, he knows you're here?'

'He instigated it. You've always shown high regard for him. Don't spoil it now. You would be doing him a great disservice.'

Fuller seemed at last aware of his wet clothes. He shuddered then gazed at Arden thoughtfully. 'You'd better turn the radio down while I get out. And switch off the light.' He had learned nothing and his mood was bitter.

Arden helped him on to the rope, holding the end while Fuller coped with the difficult balance. When Fuller had gone Arden closed and locked the window, pulled the curtains, felt his way across the room to switch the light back on. He went to the bed, lifted the pillows and extracted the papers Klaus Wendel had given him. He would remind Schellenberg of what must be done to Fuller.

Schroder sensed Fuller's disquiet. The rain had stopped but they were drenched and shivering by the time they reached the lean-to.

Schroder said, 'Don't you like what he's here for or didn't you find out?'

'I didn't find out. His name is Lord Arden, he travelled as a Swede ostensibly to arrange a PoW exchange. He admits that's rubbish but that's as far as it goes.'

They could barely see each other inside the shed. There was no sound from the cellar. Schroder would bang out a signal on the floor before entering and then wait for an acknowledgment, knowing that at least one gun would be trained on the trap.

'Well, you learned what he's *not* doing.'

'That's not what they sent you to find out. It's time you told me who actually *did* send you?'

'David Bruce. He heads the OSS in Britain. But I guess he did it for your crowd.'

'I can see why. Arden knows a lot of people in high places. If it had gone through our own machine he might well have heard of it.'

'You'd better get back,' said Schroder. 'You can't go on like this night after night.'

'No. Another thing that worries me is the possibility of Arden waking up to the fact that I could not have reached his room without help.'

'What can he do?'

'That's the big question isn't it? We're back to why is he here at all? Look, I might need your help again. There's a hidden tunnel somewhere that leads into the hospital complex. I've got to find it. I'll be in touch.' But on the way back the thought that recurred incessantly was Arden's claim that Churchill had sent him. That did not match up with Schroder being sent to ask Fuller to find out what was going on. Somewhere there was a double-cross. He hoped he would have time to find out before they killed him.

14

Fuller went to bed after stripping and drying down. Claudie had stayed awake. He briefly told her what had happened but hid his mounting fears.

When he rose at dawn she knew how worried he was. He looked tired and irritable. When he said he was taking Blanco for a walk she was certain he was going to search for the tunnel again. When she suggested she should go with him he seemed relieved but she knew it meant that he thought they might be watched.

They went into the copse behind the hospital again. The skies had cleared and it was fresh though still wet underfoot. Claudie took pains to check if they were being observed.

It was the terrier who made the find. Fuller heard him scuffing and then the little paws worked faster and the growls increased.

Fuller couldn't see the dog and Claudie called to Blanco. In this part of the copse the ground shelved. The trees, thinly spaced, still had plenty of leaves on them in spite of shedding. The sound of scratching paws came from somewhere below. They reached the incline then Fuller suddenly slipped down a shelf of dead ground that had not been apparent under the leafy blanket. He swore as he landed on his back. Blanco, distracted for a moment by his master's distress, dashed over to give a few perfunctory licks at Fuller's face, then scuttled back to his digging. Claudie clambered down to help Fuller who was now raised on an elbow to watch Blanco.

The bank was only three feet deep, narrowing until it petered out further along. Gnarled tree roots protruded like grotesque arms. Part was grassed, part covered in gorse and ragged-leaved bushes. It was behind one of the bushes that Blanco was frantically burrowing, as though he was trying to bore into the bank itself. Claudie called to the dog again but Blanco ignored her.

Fuller rose slowly, shaken but unhurt. Claudie helped to brush him down, then they picked their way to where Blanco was scratching. Roots twisted from the earth behind the bank but Blanco was sniffing and tearing at the grass. When Fuller saw the small pieces of concrete rubble behind the bush his interest sharpened. He asked Claudie to put Blanco on the lead and to keep guard.

He made sure they were alone before dropping to his knees. There was nothing but the small quantity of rubble yet Blanco had found a scent of some kind. Perhaps a fading human scent.

Running his hands through the grass, along the bank, over the roots Fuller explored and found no answer. Behind him Blanco was struggling on his lead, and trying to yelp, and Claudie, hand over his muzzle, was becoming increasingly concerned. But she knew that she could not stop Fuller now. Fuller probed with his clasp knife where Blanco had dug out a patch of turf. The blade went so far then stopped against something solid. He gave a quick little dig. Metal? He cut out a small piece of turf and ripped it off. He explored with his fingers, tapping. It *was* metal. He was satisfied that he had found the tunnel Gorkov had told him about; the one for which Major Hoffman had found it necessary to exterminate all those who had worked on it.

Fuller rose slowly. He turned to see Claudie's expression. 'I'm sure it's Gorkov's tunnel. I must go down.'

She was too scared to speak. The risks were growing all the time yet she did not know how to stop him. 'I'll keep watch for you,' she eventually said.

'It's metal under the turf. Bang on the lid if anyone comes.' He could see how she felt. 'I'm sorry, Claudie. Try to understand.'

She nodded miserably and averted her head.

He turned away and felt wretched about what he was doing to her. But there was nothing else he could do; personal feelings, love, had to be shut out. He sliced a larger patch from the turf. A tree root had been cut, partially hollowed, then treated and positioned over the short handle of the metal door. He pulled upwards and the door lifted; it was quite heavy but the hinges were well oiled.

A perpendicular metal ladder ran down the side of the

circular tunnel. He could not see the bottom and the tunnel was narrow for a man of his size. He swung down on to rungs, having to turn in Claudie's direction to do so, but he avoided looking at her. He went down slowly.

The sides of the tunnel were concreted and at the bottom was a small, square chamber. A suggestion of light showed at its base and Fuller was convinced that facing him was the map frame on the wall of the briefing room where he had met Schellenberg, Wendel and Arden.

It was unlikely that anyone would be in the room at this time but he listened carefully before pushing the frame back on strong hinges. The door from the annexe tunnel faced him and fixed to the wall above it was a night light which emitted the palest of blue glows. He jumped on to the carpet to avoid bringing concrete dust down with him and wiped his feet to disperse traces in the pile.

He had twice been in this room before but now he could see that there was a door at each end of the room in addition to the main door. He put his ear to the main door before stepping past the long table and the row of chairs, to one of the secondary doors. He listened again before opening it.

It was dark inside and he groped for a light switch. He caught his breath as he stared round. He was not a technical man but he realised that he was looking at a highly sophisticated radio operations room. A mounted desk ran round three walls of the room with eight equally spaced swivel chairs in front of it. Above the desk, virtually covering all the wall space, were banks of equipment; a mass of apparatus.

He stayed there longer than was wise. Numbly he switched off the light and closed the door.

He went down the other end of the room in a daze. Carelessly, he opened the door without first listening, but luckily the room was unoccupied. He found a switch and stood in the doorway. This was the most luxurious of the rooms he had so far seen. There were only two beds. On a writing desk against one wall a framed photograph of a woman with a dog stared at him. He stepped forward and picked up the photograph and noticed that his hands were trembling. For a long time he could only stare at the smiling face which gazed back at him. He had seen that face before in the army newsheets. It was Eva Braun. He put the frame down carefully, making sure that it was returned to the same position.

His confused thoughts were penetrated by the sound of footsteps. In panic, he switched off the light, closed the door, hastily rounded the table, knocking against one of the chairs, then drew himself up quickly into the small chamber, pulling the map frame back with him. He knew he had dislodged some dust; there was nothing he could do.

Someone entered the briefing room and the scraping of a chair was quite audible. It was still early morning and Fuller supposed that someone was doing a routine check. He wondered if it was Major Hoffman.

Fuller resisted the urge to escape. The air was foul in the chamber, breathing difficult. He tried to get comfortable but each tiny movement was like thunder in the confined space. The main door opened and closed again and then there was silence the other side of the map frame. He waited a little longer and climbed the ladder. Halfway up he felt something and he groped round the rough walls and located stapled radio antennae.

He was totally confused by the time he reached the top, but his alarm was deep. He poked his head out and drew in air. Blanco started to bark on seeing him and Claudie came forward.

Fuller climbed out, closed the lid and wadded back the turf. He did not know what to say to Claudie. Before rising he fondled Blanco in order to gain time.

'You've been ages. I've been scared to death standing here.' And then Claudie caught full sight of him as he straightened. 'My God! You look as if you've seen a ghost.'

He stood there shakily. He was still confused but a great depression had seized him. He wiped his eyes not knowing what to say.

'You've been crying.' All the love, the anxiety burst from Claudie in the few words.

'It's the dust down there.' He put an arm round her and they started to walk back to the house. A new problem faced him and he sensed it was the crux of all that was happening on the island. But he could not sort his thoughts out; it was as if the whole matter was beyond him. 'Stick to medicine, George.' Perhaps Arden was right; he was out of his depth. He suddenly felt like an old man instead of someone in his early thirties.

'You look so pale, cheri. Are you all right?'

He nodded slowly. 'There was not much air down there. I could hardly breathe.'

She looked up at him. His voice was so strange; he seemed to be in a state of shock. 'Was it worth it?'

Fuller glanced down. 'I don't know. There's a radio room and a bedroom.' He was not sure why he did not mention the photograph.

The significance of the radio room passed her by. 'So what happened to scramble your brains? What's happened to your English sang-froid?'

He smiled awkwardly. 'The same that has happened to your French *savoir-faire*.' And then, as his partial stupor lifted, he suddenly knew what had to be done. It was difficult to see a connection between Arden's presence on the island and what he had just seen. Yet he felt there was one. He stopped walking, looked around the woods. They still seemed to be alone.

'I want you to see Schroder,' he said.

'Now? In daylight?'

'Keep Blanco with you. Be careful. If you think you're being watched then go back to the house. If it's okay, take Schroder to the tunnel. Tell him there's a chamber at the bottom concealed by a map frame. The briefing room is the other side. That's where Schellenberg, Wendel and Arden met and I'm positive that's where they'll meet again. I want him to listen.'

'It will be terribly dangerous for him in daylight.' She did not add that the danger would extend to her if she was caught with Schroder.

'He has his German uniform. Being with you should keep the others away.'

Now she knew just how serious he considered it to be. He knew the danger he was placing her in yet he still wanted her to do it.

'Claudie, if I could do it myself I would. But I dare not miss surgery and then there are my calls. I wouldn't ask you if I could get away with it.'

'I know.'

She reached up and lightly kissed him and then turned to

head south through the copse, Blanco trotting contentedly beside her.

Fuller's disquiet increased on the way back to the house. He had just placed Claudie in peril and that also meant Schroder, Kremple, Gorkov and Jacqui. If one was caught, they would all be caught. And yet he felt the danger was already there and was closing in on them whatever they did.

As soon as he reached the house he started to pack a grip for himself and Claudie; essentials in the case of emergency. It was a ridiculous thing to do for there was nowhere to go but he followed his impulse, as he always did. During the course of the packing he realised that the house had been searched. Items had been moved or not returned correctly to drawers.

At first he was not quite sure, but his suspicions grew as he realised that Claudie could never be so untidy. And then he discovered that Schroder's broken radio was missing. There could be nothing more incriminating than that; it was damning.

He considered who might have done it. Hoffman would have brought a company of men up and would have made Fuller and Claudie stand by to watch them ransack the place. Captain Heyden, even with the power of the SS behind him, would not blatantly cross Hoffman's path. It smacked of the small Gestapo unit; Fuller had only met Erich Kratz twice and had barely spoken to him.

Fuller sat on the side of the bed. The net was closing. He could see part of the reason for this but the big mass of questions were still unanswered. Even now, with the discovery of the bunker, he was groping in the dark.

He left the house. Some distance away two SS men clumsily turned away as he appeared. So he was now being watched. He entered the hospital, checked some X-ray plates, and then went into the main ward with the duty medical orderly to visit the patients. There was one minor operation to be performed later that morning, but if he found it necessary postponement would cause no problem. He performed his duties as he did every day. The orderly may have noticed that Fuller was more reticent that morning, perhaps a little less friendly, but his efficiency was not impaired.

Fuller worried about Claudie and Schroder. His concern increased when the car and escort came down the main tunnel.

He left his office. The sentry at the entrance of the subsidiary tunnel had sprung to attention as Arden climbed out of the tourer, and then behind him came a second car with Schellenberg and Wendel. The footsteps of the three men faded as they neared the briefing room. Then the motorcycle escort withdrew to the main entrance and the exhaust fumes crept towards Fuller. With considerable anxiety, he wondered if Schroder was in position. Just after mid-day the cars and escort came back to collect the three VIPs. Fuller never left the hospital before 12.30 and it took him all his determination to endure the twenty minutes that were left. When he did return to the house Claudie was not there.

The wait was the worst he could remember. He had a light lunch but he had no appetite. Claudie returned just before he was due to go out on his rounds. The moment he saw her he knew something was wrong. 'Thank God you're back,' he said. 'Thank God.'

Claudie sank wearily to a chair. 'There was no trouble. I don't think we were seen at all. Going round the naval battery took the time. He wants to see you at once.'

'Schroder?'

'Of course, Schroder, my darling.'

'Well aren't you going to tell me what happened?'

'I don't know what happened. I collected him, he went down the tunnel and was down there a long time. That was the difficult part, trying to keep Blanco happy while acting as sentry. When Schroder came up he looked worse than you did. He was white and in a state. But he refused to tell me anything. He said he will tell only you. Then I had to escort him back.'

'Did he wad the turf back over the lid?'

'Of course. George, I'm scared.'

'So am I. This house is being watched.'

'Are you sure?'

'They searched the house this morning and took the radio.'

'Oh, my God!'

'I've packed a bag. Check to see if there's anything else you'll need.'

'But we've *nowhere* to go!'

'Just do it, Claudie. At worst we can join the others, but not until we have to.'

'You sound as if you *know* that they will come for us.'

'We must be ready in case they do.'

'What's going to happen to us?'

'All we can do is to try to prepare for the worst.'

'Will they follow you on your rounds?'

Fuller stood up helping Claudie to rise with him. 'I'm about to find out.'

She leaned against him, weary and frightened. 'Get yourself some food,' he said, 'whether you want it or not. I've packed some tinned rations. And keep the bolts on until I'm back.' He went to the door. 'I *will* be back, Claudie.'

His more serious cases were now in the hospital, but there was a scattering of patients in billets in St Anne and at sites around the island. It was some time before he was certain that he was being followed. An SS soldier was cycling behind him.

On higher ground in the more open country Fuller stopped. So did the SS man. Fuller turned his cycle round to head the way he had been coming. The SS man decided it would be better to let Fuller pass first but Fuller did not pass. He pulled up beside the SS man and said, 'Tell Captain Heyden that if I find you following me just once more I will report it to Major Hoffman and Colonel Helke. Good day.'

Fuller turned his cycle round again and pedalled off. He did not look back until after he had topped a rise and free-wheeled down the other side. He braked at the bottom of the slope and waited. The SS man did not follow. Fuller thought that he may have gained only a little time. He cycled off as fast as he could, occasionally checking his rear.

Fuller was ultra cautious near the cellar. It was now late afternoon. He took the bike into the shed, rapped out the signal on the floorboards then lifted the trap. An agitated Schroder came to the foot of the ladder. As Fuller stepped into the cellar the American tried to take him to a corner away from the others, but the doctor stopped him. 'We're all in it together now. You may just as well tell us all.'

Schroder was not keen to tell everybody. Then he realised the utter futility of their position. 'Okay. They must know something's up. You took your time. I've gone crazy just waiting.'

'I was being followed. I had to get rid of him.'

Schroder briefly told them what he had done that morning.

Even in daylight it was dark in the cellar but a little light filtered through the floorboards above and they could at least vaguely see each other.

Schroder's voice shook as he said, 'This Arden guy is trying to make a peace deal with the Germans. It comes down to this: Britain and Germany disengage and sign a peace treaty. All European troops in Britain will have the choice of going back to their own countries, which would mean virtual suicide, or staying in Britain as civilians, or emigrating to America if we'll have them. All American troops will be sent back; they'll have no European base from which to continue the war there. That's it.'

Fuller could not believe his ears. At no time had he imagined anything as monstrous as this. The magnitude of the betrayal was almost impossible to grasp and Schroder was affected as deeply as he.

Fuller asked shakily, 'Did the Germans buy the idea?'

'There was a lot of arguing! I thought I'd gone mad and much of the detail passed straight through my head. The Germans are finding it tougher in Russia than they thought. It should've been all over out there but the Ruskies are standing up. There is also the fact that in the longer term, although America is being roughed up now, we have the money, the men, and the technical know-how to endure and eventually to win. These were Arden's points. The biggest blow to Germany in the long term is America's entry into the war. With Britain out, America is out. That leaves Germany with a lot of extra men and equipment they can use on the Eastern Front.'

'Did Arden say why he's seeking peace?'

'He wants Britain back on its feet before it's too late. Otherwise you'll be paying for the cost of the war, one way or another, for decades. He even offered an arms deal for the Germans to fight the Russians, and, of course, no more arms' convoys would sail for Russia.'

Fuller was almost afraid to voice the next question. 'Did he say who he represents?'

Even now Schroder was having difficulty in grasping the implications of what he had heard. 'It seems that not everyone in your Parliament is behind Churchill. He has political enemies. At the moment his position is far from strong. With

194

the right deal he could be overthrown. This guy Arden has his knife right in Churchill's back. And he has chosen his men carefully; there is no doubt that he has support. Whether he succeeds depends on what deal he can pull off here.'

'He told me Churchill knows that he's here.'

'If he does he can't know the real reason. I guess that's why I was sent to contact you.'

'We've no way of letting them know.' Fuller leaned back against one of the pillars. Numbed and shocked, Arden's treachery was difficult to accept. And yet he could see the cold logic of Arden behind it. Arden had always been logical; he would not see it as betrayal but as salvation. Too many thoughts crowded his mind, too many implications were implanted into the main theme. There was too much at stake in too many directions. All he could fully grasp was that what Arden was trying to do was against what he personally, and his father in England, had ever stood for. That thought brought the whole issue much nearer home. Wearily he said, 'They'll have to kill me and anyone who might be friendly with me. They can't risk any chance of this getting out.'

'They don't know that we know. They don't even know the rest of us are here.' But Schroder saw only too clearly Fuller's own position.

'I've had contact with Arden. He knows I don't believe him. It's enough. Apart from Schellenberg, Wendel and Brocker everyone else on the island thinks he's a Swede in the IRC. Arden knows me well enough to know that I'll do everything I can to find out why he's really here. It's best I don't come here again.'

'No.' It was Kremple. 'You come.'

'We stay together.' Gorkov insisted.

'Just what the hell would we do without you?' Schroder wanted to know.

'Please don't leave us. We need you.' The most timid and the most convincing plea of all was from Jacqui.

Fuller was touched by their loyalty and friendship. He reflected that really, in the end, it would make no difference. But it was the monstrosity of what Arden was trying to do to a nation that had been fighting for its life that largely occupied his thoughts. 'There's something else,' he said. 'Something even you don't know, Rod. Beyond the chamber is a radio operations room and a bedroom with Eva Braun's photograph in it. What can they have to do with a peace deal?'

The silence was protracted. Fuller had taken them by surprise and the information took a while to sink in. Fuller and Schroder would probably have arrived at the same conclusion as Gorkov but it was the Russian who so clearly saw the web of deceit. Life had become one big round of pain and treachery for him. 'This is a big radio room?'

'Very big. I speak as a layman, though.'

'And the other room has two beds and a picture of Eva Braun?'

'Yes.'

Gorkov began to laugh light-headedly. It was a terrible sound escaping from a larynx shrivelled from disuse. 'Oh, Doctor. Even you are fooled. Don't you see? It will be Hitler's bunker.'

'I realised that.'

'But not why. Don't you see?' Gorkov was enjoying himself in a situation where he had nothing to lose. 'You are not devious enough. And you, American, what do you think?'

Schroder was confused; he had the feeling that he was missing the obvious and when he turned to Fuller, at present an unmoving shape lost against one of the pillars, he received no help.

Gorkov could not resist a chuckle in his moment of ascendancy. Jacqui had no idea what was going on and Kremple's thoughts were still concentrated on their immediate danger. Fuller and Schroder were too shocked by Arden's treachery to see the much deeper treachery of Hitler. Gorkov said emphatically, 'Your Lord Arden will get his peace deal. They will bicker with him, not make it appear too easy. But Germany and Britain will break off hostilities. There will be a treaty. While Germany continues against Russia, Britain will send home the foreign troops on her soil. And she will slowly disband her armies.'

Gorkov peered into the gloom, trying to see their reaction. But if he could not see it, he could feel it like an air of dread and death creeping into every dark corner. 'And when Germany has finished with Russia, aided by the extra armour and divisions released from the West, she will then invade a much-weakened

Britain. The bunker will be the nerve centre of the invasion. Hitler will operate from one of his few British colonies. And it will amuse him that the negotiations for peace took place in his invasion centre. You now know why the fortifications here are ridiculously out of proportion to the size of the island.'

Fuller was stunned. His stomach, his whole nervous system, contracted to a single, ever-tightening knot. Schroder had lowered his head to his drawn-up knees and was shaking it slowly as if in disbelief. But nobody in the cellar disbelieved. Gorkov had made his point and now he was quiet, even sorry that he had so drastically disturbed his friends. His only surprise was that they had not seen matters as clearly as he had; but perhaps they had been too close to it, too involved in risking their lives to learn the facts to which he had so adequately provided a reason.

'I've got to stop him,' said Fuller quietly. He did not recognise his own voice.

'Arden? You'll not get near him again. He won't open the window next time. He'll have the guard out.'

'Not that way. But somehow.' Fuller rose, surprised at the weakness of his legs. He held on to the pillar behind him. 'I've got to stop him,' he said again as if speaking to himself.

This time nobody commented. Schroder did not like the way in which Fuller had spoken. Fuller walked to the ladder like an old man. Gorkov called after him. 'Doctor, there is nothing you or anyone can do. There is too much against you. Use your sense as you have always done.'

But Fuller seemed not to hear. He slowly climbed the ladder while the others silently grouped at the foot of it. He said nothing as he went through the trap. When Schroder started to follow him Gorkov put out a restraining hand. Whatever Fuller had in mind to do there was nobody capable of stopping him attempting.

Fuller's mood was so bleak it was impossible for him to hide it from Claudie. And what was the point? She above all people deserved to know the truth. He told her and watched her increasing distress and then he said, 'If you see anyone approaching the house, leave by the back way and go to the cellar and wait for me.'

'Where are *you* going?'

'To the hospital. They'll be expecting me there. And then to see Brocker.'

'Is that wise? He must now think of himself.'

'I know. I'll try not to be away too long.'

They embraced. She did not know what he had in mind and she was afraid to ask; but Claudie knew Fuller better than anyone. Sometimes it was a disadvantage for she worried endlessly for him, but she had known very early in their relationship what Gorkov had so recently perceived in the cellar; Fuller would do what he believed he must even if it killed him. Claudie did not want him dead but she did not want him to change from what he had always been. There would never be an easy way for men like Fuller, nor for those who loved them.

He went back to hospital on foot. He toured the ward, had a word with the orderlies and then went into the dispensary. He was behaving reasonably normally in spite of a pounding headache. He took some aspirin and then checked through the drugs' cabinet and all the time two words hammered through his head. *Hitler's bunker. Hitler's bunker.* He took a piece of tissue paper and poured a minute quantity of powder on to it. He folded the paper carefully.

Fuller was certain that Gorkov was right. The Russian had seen at once what was really going to happen. Could Arden be so obsessed that he could not see the possibility? Now more than ever it was necessary for Fuller to act out his part, raise no suspicions. One good point seemed to be that nobody was watching him anymore; he had successfully played on the rivalry between the SS, the Gestapo and Major Hoffman, and it was the latter who carried the backing from Berlin. It might not last but at the moment it helped.

Brocker was in the officers' mess when Fuller called. Although the official liaison of Brocker with Fuller was well known, Brocker knew that he must not appear to pander to the doctor; Brocker was older than most of his contemporaries and his duty had always been seen as an easy number by his colleagues. They knew him to be friendly with Fuller. For this reason when Brocker received the message that Fuller was outside he instructed the orderly to ask Fuller to wait. He knew that Fuller would not call at the mess unless it was vital but he forced himself to linger longer than he wanted to. The young surgeon was impatiently pacing the cobbles when Brocker emerged.

They strolled out of St Anne by silent consent and Fuller did his best to hide his agitation. The weather had cleared and the early evening was crisply breezy.

'You're showing your feelings too freely, George.' Brocker spoke without turning his head.

'I've never done anything different. Anyway I can't talk to you like this.'

They moved off the road, across some wet grass to a large beech tree, its golden leaves shedding.

'Well?' demanded Brocker. 'You're in a terrible state.'

'I'm placing my life in your hands with what I have to say.'

Brocker saw that Fuller was totally serious. 'Then you'd better not say it. It would not be fair to either of us.'

'Joachim, you're the only person I can turn to. I desperately need your help.'

'George, if it cuts across my duties forget it. Don't compromise me, you'd put me in danger.'

'You're already in danger. Anyone who is remotely friendly with me is in danger. Even my patients. I couldn't make it worse for you. I'm already under sentence of death because I know Lord Arden. And he'll guess that I don't believe what he claims he's here for. He's negotiating a peace deal with Schellenberg and Wendel.'

'Good. I'd like to see us at peace with Britain. Did you expect my reaction to be the same as yours?'

'He's selling the country out, betraying his lifelong friend, Winston Churchill.'

'I'm sorry you told me this, George. I'm not an Englishman, you can't expect me to support you.'

'Joachim, please, listen . . .' Fuller looked about them but all movement that he could see was normal.

Before he could continue Brocker said, 'You don't want peace between us?'

'Not this kind of peace. It's a sell-out. But that's only part of it. The . . .'

'George, stop it. I'd personally welcome peace so don't tell me any more. Anyway what do you think you can do about it?'

Fuller was satisfied that he had got Brocker thinking; he had planted the hook. He had to take a chance. He told Brocker about the bunker and the radio room and put forward Gorkov's conclusions as his own. 'It's Hitler's bunker,' he finished. 'Eva Braun's photograph. The bastard intends to invade when our guard is down. The perpendicular tunnel is an escape hatch cum emergency air shaft, cum bolt hole, cum radio mast.'

Brocker shot Fuller a look of warning. 'Keep your voice down. You could be shot for referring to the Führer like that.' But Brocker was disturbed; not with the same angry fervour of Fuller because his position was quite different. Hitler was well capable of such an act of treachery; Germany had already lost credence on too many occasions. Honour was important to Brocker and he saw none here from either the British or German standpoint. He had paled slightly and placed his hand against the tree. 'I'll respect your confidence. It's the best that I can do. I should report you but if questioned I'll say that you've told me nothing.'

'I need your help.'

'You won't get it. You've implicated me for reasons of friendship but it will probably turn out to be a very unfriendly act.' And then reflectively, 'Our magnificent Führer has a very devious mind. But you could be wrong. The bunker could be a precaution against failure to find peace terms or a clever intimidation to make certain that there is no failure.'

'All I want is an opportunity to have a few words with Lord Arden. Then I'll know one way or the other.' Fuller was aware that Brocker did not know that he had climbed to Arden's room.

'I can't get you in to see him. And would he see you, anyway, in view of what you believe?'

'That's why I need your help. I know I've strained our friendship to the limit. And I'm about to stretch it further. You're right, he won't see me even if you can get me in. I want you to drop something in his coffee.'

Brocker laughed spontaneously, 'George, you're mad. I can't take that seriously.'

'It won't hurt him. All he'll get will be a stomach ache, enough to call in a doctor.'

'I see. Ingenious. But he's guarded.'

'I can handle that.'

'Are you really serious?'

'Never more so. I could not ask such a thing of you if there was some other way.'

'Supposing he dies? Is that the idea?'

Fuller shook his head. 'I wouldn't do that to you, Joachim. For God's sake, you know that. It will give him pains, no more. There's no danger.'

'You're asking far too much of me.'

'I know. I trust you and I'm desperate.'

They stood silently, uncomfortably aware of an unspoken regard for each other, an affinity they both felt. In an odd way the alienation of war had made their bond stronger. One friend was asking another to do something against his sworn duties. If it were the other way round Fuller knew he would help, just as he hoped that Brocker would. If it was against Brocker's own conscience, a conviction that what Germany was doing was right, he would not have asked; but he knew that Brocker hated Hitler and what he had done to Germany and Europe and to himself and his family.

Brocker said calmly, 'I suppose, for you, this is a normal request from a prisoner to his jailer.'

'I've never seen you as my jailer.'

Banter was a safety valve. Fear wouldn't stop Brocker. He had resigned from real purpose a long time ago. 'What, precisely, are you asking me to do?'

'I have some powder in my pocket. Drop it in his coffee and stir it. The coffee's so atrocious he won't taste the difference. It's very simple.'

'*If* he drinks it. And *if* I can get near it first.'

'I recall he used to drink gallons of the stuff, black. Your own quarters are next door; surely you can find an excuse to visit another officer? Borrow a book or something? His batman takes his food.'

'How do you know that?'

'You told me,' said Fuller smoothly.

Brocker thought it out. 'Will the powder show?'

'Not if you stir the coffee. The quantity's minute.'

Brocker looked up at Fuller and shrugged. 'What is it about you that makes me even consider your crazy ideas?'

'I'd do the same for you. And you know it. A condemned man's last wish, Joachim.' Fuller pulled out the folded tissue.

'Perhaps that's the reason.' Brocker tried to reject the truth of it and quickly put the packet away. 'And it will give him nothing more than stomach ache?'

'You have my word.'

'I won't place myself in difficulty. I will try. That's my sole promise.'

'Thank you, Joachim. I'll never forget you.'

They left the tree and were slowly walking back. 'That sounds like a farewell. You really do believe you're condemned.'

Fuller stopped walking. 'I'd better get back to Claudie.' He groped for words then said, 'I won't shake hands because there are soldiers down the street, but if by some miracle we survive this war I would like to make contact again. Over a bottle or two.'

'That would be nice. If we believe in miracles. But we don't, do we, George?'

'Perhaps not the kind that we need. You've been a good friend to both Claudie and me, Joachim.' Fuller was about to move off when he observed: 'I've told you you're in danger; you've taken it very calmly.'

'When an old soldier like me is used to cosset a prisoner like you there has to be a solid reason. People like me are expendable, George. I knew something was going on but I didn't know what. Anyway, what can I do? Swim away? We're both in the same trap.'

Fuller inclined his head and then walked sadly away; Brocker was right; he accepted that there was no chance of survival.

15

The paraffin lamp was low and the flickering light cast the palest of bowls beyond their shadowed faces, highlighting their eyes and their cheekbones. The wick had been cleaned but the smell lingered in the cellar with that of the paint. No one had spoken for some seconds.

On leaving Brocker, Fuller's mind had remained on the German captain. It was not his own fault that Brocker was now a marked man; Fuller himself had been predestined for his role as Brocker had been. There seemed no way that he could help the captain.

What distressed Fuller more was the way Brocker accepted his fate; without query, without visible concern. It worried and upset him that he had left Brocker the way he had, asking a virtually impossible favour without adequate thanks.

Fuller had told none of those in the cellar what he had asked of Brocker; it was better that they did not know. Confined as they were he did not want to give them more to worry about. Just for a moment he brooded on what would happen to Claudie once he himself had been executed.

Gorkov saw through Fuller's mood and his unusual quietness. The long-suffering Russian had learned to interpret almost any form of danger. He could sense it, see it, feel it, hear it in so many different ways. Innuendos, omissions, inflections, all conveyed their own messages to him. A smile could mean death or torture. It depended on the curl of the lips, the expression or lack of it in the eye. Even the movement of a man's fingers was a signal. He saw through Fuller's reticence and he observed quite softly, 'You are expecting death, Doctor.'

His quaint phraseology had a strange impact. It broke a silence which was immediately restored and drew everyone's gaze to him. Gorkov spoke rarely but when he did the others had learned to heed him. As if by signal the attention switched suddenly to Fuller.

Gorkov said, 'He is preparing himself for it.'

Fuller and Gorkov stared at each other across the feeble island of light. Gorkov did not flinch. With Fuller he had no need to be devious. Fuller said, 'I don't think they'll try to kill me until Arden, Schellenberg and Wendel have left. I'm sorry you read my mind.'

'Why so? Don't you understand we're behind you? We all face death. Not one of us doesn't realise that we can't go on for ever like this. We can only survive if we get off the island and reach England. And that's impossible.'

'What's your point?'

'You join us here now. We fight it out here when we have to.'

'You take it very philosophically.'

'No more than you, Doctor. At Sylt I was doomed. I would be dead by now and I would not have died comfortably. This way I take a good few Nazis with me.'

Fuller looked round at them face by face. He could barely see them, the shadows were so deep, the light so bad. Schroder said, 'I agree with Vassily. If you're not sure when they'll come for you, it's better that you come here now.'

Kremple and Jacqui gave him backing.

Fuller was touched again by the group. 'With Claudie there will be six of us. With three machine pistols.' He was about to add that he had been down to the armoury when Kremple said, 'We are planning a raid tonight. After midnight. I did a recce on my own last night. There is only one guard. It can be done.'

'I'll come with you,' said Fuller. He listened to their scheme which Jacqui had expounded.

It had already been agreed that it was too risky to use Schroder with his out-of-date insignia; the bluff would not work.

From the rise above the harbour they could see the spread of the old armoury and, occasionally, when he shifted position, the sentry; Fuller was close to the main door and so far had stayed there. The moon was out at last. All five of them were lying flat and they all knew that Jacqui wanted to make up for her earlier lapse.

They had come as far as they could without being seen and now everything depended on the girl. She took off her blouse, shivering a little. The moonlight cast grey half moons under her small breasts. She slipped down the bank on to the concrete.

They watched her go, a pale vulnerable figure. They took up positions along the bank, Kremple with one MP-38 and Schroder to the right with another, and Fuller with the third. The possibility of Jacqui being shot on sight depended entirely on the sentry and the strength of his eyesight.

Jacqui felt the cold. She wanted to put her arms over her breasts to try to stop the shivering which was not solely due to her half-nakedness. As she walked on, her fears mounted and she would have given anything for the comfort of Schroder just then, a need she had left undeclared to him. Her legs trembled when she was halfway across and when she tried to walk faster she found that she couldn't.

The sentry shuffled and she stopped, but surprisingly he had not yet seen her. She stepped a little nearer and pleaded in French, 'Can anyone help me?'

The sentry sprang to life, his machine pistol jerking up, harness creaking. 'Halt! *Wer da*?'

'Please help me.' German this time with a delightful French accent, the voice weak with despair.

A *woman*? He was going crazy. Apart from the doctor's wife he hadn't seen a woman since he had last had leave in Cherbourg. Month after month went by without one to look at. The island was a prison unless you were lucky enough to have visiting duties on the main islands and that privilege was usually for officers. Anyway they were cold bitches. What was approaching him now was a dream. God, she was *naked*. What a body. Young. Beautiful in the moonlight. She was in trouble, limping. Where the hell had she come from?

As Jacqui drew nearer Ernst Wegel shouldered his gun. It did not occur to him to sound the alarm; he had a whistle for that because the guard room was a little distance away and also served another part of the harbour. The girl was unarmed. You'd have to be blind not to see that. And she got better all the time. Discipline held him back. Then she lurched. When he thought she was about to fall he stepped out to catch her. God she was soft. But firm too.

'Help me.' Jacqui had an arm round his neck and she let him support her. He was being over-zealous and she could feel the fever mounting in him but she bore his exploring hands. He was trying to be gentle with her in a rough inexperienced way and she had literally placed herself in his fumbling hands. A natural trembling of apprehension helped her. He was holding her, trying to warm her. She moved and his hand was on her breast. 'Please take me inside. I'm so cold.'

'Where have you come from?' He hardly recognised his own voice. He had never held a girl so exciting.

'The boat . . .' She tailed off and went limp against him so that his grip had to tighten to prevent her from falling. She stirred. 'I must get inside.'

He wanted to unsling his machine pistol and put his jacket round her but he had been too severely trained to do that. The obvious thing for him to do was to sound the alarm and for her to be taken to the guard room and questioned. He convinced himself without too much difficulty that she was not quite fit enough yet. After a little rest she would probably manage. He agreed that she needed to get out of the cold but the armoury was locked and the key was in the guard room. Meanwhile she was driving him mad. He had her all to himself and there was no one around. There was still an hour and a half of duty to do before a sentry change.

He eased her towards the door and she was still clinging to him for support and warmth. As he turned her round his face touched hers, very close to the lips and he was tempted. She didn't seem to mind but his damned helmet was in the way. She shivered violently and he held her tightly. Oh, my God. He wouldn't force himself on her. Somehow he couldn't do that. But he didn't believe he would have to. She moaned, her face turned and brushed his again.

Ernst Wegel moaned too. He pulled off his helmet and lowered it by the strap so that it wouldn't clatter. He placed his gun against the wall and propped Jacqui against the door. She could feel the haft and the padlock against her back. Instinctively she knew that this was the time she must not overdo it. He was struggling with his conscience and she was winning, closing her mind to his ever-heavier breathing, his excited movements. 'I'm so cold.'

'I can't open the door. I haven't got the key, Fräulein.'

'Please call someone who has.' It was the right thing to say and it came with another slight sagging of the body.

Her German was poor and halting, but he understood. He didn't want to call anyone else. Not yet. Oh my word if she moved like that again he would not be able to answer for himself.

'Can you not open the lock without a key?'

He'd been considering it. There were piled-up blankets in there. Dare he do it and could he get away with it? And then the simplest of solutions struck him. He dare not break the lock but would his clasp knife undo the screws of the haft? Were they rusted in too much? 'Fräulein, sit here. Just for a moment.' He pushed her into a sitting position at the side of the door, looked down at her, tore off his jacket and placed it round her shoulders. She glanced up in gratitude.

The knife was bulky, with two blades and the curved tool that was supposed to be for getting stones out of horses' hooves. He dug the tool in behind the lock haft to find that the wood had gone soft. Using the larger blade he nervously undid the four screws, working feverishly and reflecting that there were only obsolete arms inside, anyway. He managed to prise the rusted screws. He pulled back the haft and opened the door.

Jacqui was pushing herself up against the wall, the jacket held rather carelessly in front of her. He propelled her to the door, easing her through in front of him. He reached to grab his machine pistol as he went in and at that point Schroder hit him with clenched fist at the base of the skull. Jacqui turned to help catch him. Fuller and Kremple came crowding in behind Schroder.

The windows were in a permanent state of blackout, heavily shuttered, with steel bars across them. Fuller produced matches and the stub of a candle once the door was closed. They bound and gagged Wegel with a short rope and his own handkerchief. And then they worked fast.

They ignored the rows of rifles with padlocked chains running through their trigger guards but they forced open two padlocked chests and found Bergman 18s 'blow back' sub-machine guns. Kremple inspected them quickly. 'Very old but reliable.' The snail magazines were in a separate compartment and would hold a thirty-two round reserve. They took four guns.

Ammunition boxes were forced open and again they had to rely on Kremple to sort out the correct calibre. They used one metal box for their own ammunition and redistributed the contents of the other boxes. The 9mm rounds could also be used for the MP-38s.

Speed was essential. They found a few blocks of ammonal, gun cotton with fuse wire and detonators and crammed these into the ammunition box. Schroder and Kremple tested its weight. With frequent stops Kremple was satisfied that he could manage his end with Fuller acting as relief. Schroder closed the boxes and lifted the untouched ones on top of them. Fuller, who was watching the time, insisted that they moved out. Before leaving, Schroder jammed the padlocks tight with twigs he had brought with him.

They carried the arms outside, then Wegel. There were two courses open, kill him or leave him. The latter might have a doubtful advantage. They untied him, put his jacket back on, his helmet, laid his gun beside him and propped him against the door. Kremple quickly screwed back the haft. He slipped the knife back into Wegel's pocket.

Jacqui, clothed again, carried two guns. Fuller carried three, one of which was for Gorkov, who was keeping watch on the high ground. Schroder and Kremple carried their own MP-38s but they had to cope with the heavy ammunition box. Kremple fixed the snail magazines to the guns before they moved off. Each gun weighed over nine pounds and the old-fashioned magazines made them awkward to carry. They started the hazardous journey back.

Ernst Wegel regained consciousness with little recollection. One moment he was taking the girl into the armoury the next his brain had burst. When his head began to clear, panic rose quickly. Standing up groggily, he propped himself against the wall while he rubbed the back of his neck. Christ! The time. Ten minutes before his relief was due. He peered at his luminous watch again.

The girl! Had he gone mad? He turned to the armoury. The door was locked, the screws were back. Had he had some crazy dream? He could almost believe that he had but he could still feel her, sense her, see her beauty in his mind's eye. So what had happened? Where had she gone? Who had struck him? Wegel belatedly bent to retrieve his machine pistol and immediately went giddy.

Time was running out. His relief would be here. What was he to do? Wegel inspected the door again. When he looked closely he could see nothing wrong with the lock. He suddenly ferreted for his knife. It was in the wrong pocket and he knew he hadn't put it there. It *had* happened. The girl had been there all right. My God, she had. He felt the frustration of holding her. But who had been with her and what had they wanted? Arms? The island was a fortress.

Wegel thought it through with little time to go. If he reported it he would be in deep, deep trouble. He had neglected his duty, opened the armoury he was supposed to protect, whose lock he had actually forced in order to rape some half-naked French girl who had appeared from nowhere. That was how it would sound.

On the other hand if he did not report it who would know? How could they know? If the lock was later examined, if arms were found to be missing, who could say that it had happened while he was on duty? The armoury was never examined; it was all old stock from the original garrison, most of it from the last war. Wegel weighed duty against personal safety. Had he believed there to be a real danger to the island he just might have spoken up and taken the consequences. As it was he decided to hold his tongue. And to carry through his conquest of the girl in his young mind.

Claudie had long learned to respond to Fuller's moods but she had not known one like this since the early occupation of Alderney. Then, to a large extent he had lost himself in drink, but now there was so little of it his depression deepened.

They talked it out. The successful arms' raid hadn't lifted him. He was pleased about it but in the end he saw it merely as a means of going out in a blaze of glory. There was nothing she could do to pull him from the very depths of despair. She had to repeat herself two or three times before he heard her at all. She dreaded what was passing through his mind, how reckless he might become. She was certain that he was about to do something crazy.

Joachim Brocker arrived at the hospital by car mid-morning with the message that Lord Arden was ill. Brocker showed concern as he drove Fuller into St Anne. 'It's much worse than I thought it would be. The man is clearly in pain; he's writhing.

'It'll be all right. Did you have much trouble?'

'It was surprisingly easy to slip powder into his coffee. The batman wasn't looking for trouble. The breakfast was prepared with others in a normal way in the kitchen.'

I told you they would have to send for me.'

'Not without trying Kossl, the warrant officer medical orderly first. The last thing Wendel wanted was to bring you into it but in the end he had to.'

'Kossl is a good man who, if he wasn't trapped like the rest of us on this bloody island, would be at medical school. They trained him on Jersey to be a stop-gap anaesthetist. I've used him many times.'

'It was he who insisted on fetching you.'

'They'd hardly have time to get someone over from the larger islands.'

Brocker, gloved hands on steering wheel, shot him a suspicious glance. 'Let's hope no one finds out what's happened.'

'They're not likely to from me, Joachim. Thank you for what you did. I'm surprised they sent you. I thought, at this stage, they would separate us.'

When they arrived outside the officers' quarters in St Anne, Wendel had clearly given explicit orders. He had personally collected Arden's file on the peace terms and Schellenberg had instructed Captain Heyden to place SS guards both outside and inside Arden's room. Fuller was not to be left alone with him.

Fuller was hustled into Arden's room. A guard stood by the window and Kossl, the senior medical orderly, was there by the bed. Arden was pale, holding his stomach and grimacing with pain. He was clothed except for his jacket, which Kossl had taken off to examine him. Fuller gazed across the bed. 'Have you given him anything for the pain?'

'No, Doctor. I thought it better for you to examine him first.'

'Good man. Let's lift his shirt.' Fuller made a thorough

external examination, ignoring Arden's groans, quietly insisting to be told the seat of the pain. He felt no sympathy for Arden. The pain would pass. After the examination he pulled the shirt down. Fuller said, 'I want you down at the hospital for an X-ray. You might have an ulcer.'

Kossl was apologetic. This had to be cleared with Herr Wendel or Standartenführer Schellenberg. Fuller expected nothing less. He hated deceiving Kossl but it would be all right if Kossl remained in the dark. 'You sort out the details while I give him a shot for the pain. But please be quick.' He took Kossl aside. 'We don't want peritonitis to set in.' Kossl hurried off and Fuller opened his bag and prepared an injection. He did not want to remove the pain completely.

There was nothing Wendel could do but agree. He visited Arden again and spoke to Fuller outside the room. He had no reason to suspect Fuller but he did not like the idea of him being near Arden. The ambulance came and Arden was loaded into it. To satisfy Wendel Fuller asked Kossl to travel with Arden while he returned to the hospital in the car with Brocker.

Brocker drove in silence. With the SS guards, the personal appearance of Wendel, the ambulance, there were far more complications than he had expected. George Fuller had gone to extreme lengths to ask Lord Arden a question. He reflected with considerable misgivings that if Fuller had been truthful about the affect of the powder he might not have been about his motive. Fuller sat beside him with a set face.

At the hospital two orderlies were already on duty. Kossl sent for more. Fuller dismissed his remaining outpatients and arranged to see them later that day. Arden was undressed, a towelled dressing-gown wrapped round him. He was then wheeled on a trolley into the X-ray room while Kossl prepared some barium meal. During the whole of this time Fuller had two SS guards with him and there was always one near Arden.

Much of the work Fuller did overlapped other specialist duties. There was no permanent radiologist on the island but he had no doubt that a whole team would soon be on its way. The hospital was still very much understaffed. There were two reasons; the hospital was not yet being used to capacity, and, in Fuller's view it was a preparation for future rather than present use. The more serious cases were still sent to Guernsey or Jersey. X-rays were at present done by Fuller himself.

Arden was assisted to a chair in the X-ray room. Fuller took his pulse while Kossl looked on. Arden still looked wan but his pain had eased and he was now fully aware of what was going on.

'How do you feel?' Fuller lowered Arden's wrist.

'Damned awful. The pain's not quite so bad though.'

'I want to take a scan then a full X-ray. You'll be able to stand all right?'

'Yes. I'll be all right. You say it's an ulcer?'

'I said it might be.' Fuller smiled in a friendly way, very much the family doctor. 'I certainly didn't expect to see you again in these circumstances.' They were speaking in English. Kossl knew a little because Fuller had taught him. Fuller reasoned that Wendel would have insisted on at least one of the guards having a knowledge of English. Another orderly came in and Arden was helped to the screen. Fuller pulled up the chair and sat down. Kossl handed Arden the glass of barium and Fuller told him to drink it slowly while he studied the result, his fingers exploring Arden's abdomen behind the screen.

'All right. Now over here on the table. Stretch out.'

Fuller attended to the plates, pulled the frame down, adjusted position. 'Arms straight. Won't take a minute.' When finally satisfied he said, 'Right. Everyone out.' He still spoke in English knowing that Kossl would pass it on in German. The SS men refused to move. The second orderly had already gone. Fuller said wearily, 'Kossl, get those goons out. Explain to them that I shall be behind that screen there and that if they don't leave this room they will be exposed to radiation. Tell them it's quite normal procedure.'

Kossl told them. The SS guards still would not leave. Their orders had come direct from Schellenberg. Kossl explained again, softly, patiently; the doctor was suggesting nothing unusual.

Fuller reassured Arden. 'I'm sorry about this but I won't take an X-ray until the room is clear. I'm not going to have the German medicos complaining later. All I want to do is to get you well.'

Arden rasped out in German. 'Get out you damned fools. I

don't want to sit around here the whole day.'

Ardense was a high-ranking Swede from the International Red Cross and was friendly with Wendel and Schellenberg. If he was satisfied so would they be. They withdrew reluctantly and so did Kossl as he normally did.

'Thank God for that.' Fuller spoke softly, conversationally. 'Now we can get on.' He was making some minor adjustment. 'What do you think of the equipment?'

'Very impressive. Am I going to be all right?'

'Of course.' Fuller smiled. 'There's no need to worry.' Another small adjustment.

'Can't think why Winston didn't have your father as his personal surgeon, considering his fine reputation.' Arden's friendliness was from fear. He still felt a little pain, and the sudden attack, and the atmosphere of the X-ray room had unnerved him.

Fuller said, 'Almost ready. Hold your breath when I tell you.' He had just been about to ask the direct question when Arden had spoken of Churchill and his father; it made it easier for him; 'Tell me,' he said, 'Did Winston really send you over here?'

Arden was taken by surprise but he did not hurry the reply. 'Of course. Do you really imagine I could have got here without his help? He pulled the strings behind the scenes with the Red Cross.'

'I was just curious.' Then why had a submarine brought Schroder over?

'I know how you feel. But you must still understand that I can't confide in you.'

'I do. I've got over that.' It crossed Fuller's mind that he had taken Schroder on trust. It was now a matter of personal judgment, and the responsibility was enormous. He went behind the screen. If Arden was telling the truth then Schroder was lying. He preferred to trust the American. 'Hold still. That's it. Now let's get you to bed.'

'Bed?'

As Fuller lifted the frame he helped Arden sit up. 'Until I've checked this. The pain could get worse. I want you within easy access for treatment.' His mind was in turmoil. He called out for Kossl who came in with the guards. 'Get Herr Ardense into an isolated bed while I see to this plate. Send someone for his pyjamas.

Later, he took the plate into his office and promptly lost his temper with a guard who tried to follow him in. The guard finally stood outside the door which Fuller slammed violently. He sat at his desk head in hands. His head was drumming.

After some time he fitted the plate to the light clip and switched on. He had not expected to find an abnormality and he did not. He examined the plate closely then turned off the light. He left the plate clipped on because he was the only one on the island who could adequately read it.

Fuller was faced with a monstrous problem and he had to make a decision. He wanted to go out into the fresh air to be totally alone, to be at one with the sea and sky. He could not leave without the guards following and without raising comment. Catching himself in mid-thought he was appalled by what he was considering.

The increasing strength of Fuller's revulsion frightened him. His mind clouded, the pressure in his head increased until all thought was channelled into one narrow, terrifying direction. He had stuck by what he believed in all his life. Could he now pretend not to see and ignore the treachery going on right under his nose? He had never turned his back on anything, however distasteful. But had he nerve enough to do what was necessary?

Fuller's dilemma was one he could not share with anyone. The decision must be his alone. What happened to him did not matter, but what happened to Claudie and his friends was of vital importance to him. But he had to project himself above that consideration, and to shut them out, to shut out everything except what mattered above all.

He rose unsteadily from the desk. He felt drained and hoped to God that he did not look it.

He was shaking as he went to the door, and had to remain there a few seconds before walking along the corridor to the room in which Arden had been placed.

Standing at the foot of the bed and gazing down at Arden was the greatest effort he had ever been called upon to make. He was unaware of the two SS guards who had entered the room behind him. They did not matter to him.

He placed his hand on the bed rail, not too tightly, nothing must give him away, but he needed the support. Arden was gazing back at him trying to determine from Fuller's expression whether he carried good news or bad.

Fuller smiled, reassuring and gentle; it was effective because he noticed Arden relax a little, the gaunt face sallow against the pillows. With quiet confidence Fuller said, 'You have a perforated ulcer. Nothing for you to worry about provided we tackle it straight away. We'll operate as soon as we have you ready.' He did not know how he got the words out.

16

Arden flinched; he had not expected it to be so bad. 'A perforated ulcer? Are you sure?'

'Of course. There's no need to fret provided we get to it quickly. Delay could cause problems. Do you want to send a message back to Winston? I don't know whether they can help you to do that.'

'How long will I be in?'

'I can't really answer until after the operation. We'll start in an hour or so. You're very tough. You should be back on your feet in a few days. You'd have to take it easy, though; be careful with your diet.'

'I don't want to worry Winston. He has enough on his plate. I'll leave it until after the operation and then speak to Wendel. You'll have a better idea of my condition by then.'

'All right. I'll send someone in to prepare you.'

'George,' Arden called out as Fuller turned. 'Is there any danger in this?'

Fuller steadied himself. For a moment he felt compassion. As he replied the voice was his but he could not believe the words were.

'No. It's one of those awkward things but, as I said, you're in remarkably good health otherwise.' Somehow he smiled, 'I'm not worried so don't you be.'

Arden relaxed against the pillow. 'Then I won't. We'd better tell Schellenberg and Wendel.'

'Someone is already on his way to do that.'

Wendel arrived while they were preparing the theatre and sterilising the instruments. He left no one in any doubt how he felt and cornered Fuller in his office. 'What is this I hear?'

Facing Wendel helped Fuller. Angry, militant Nazis acted almost as a soporific to him. 'My patient has a perforated ulcer. I must operate.'

No. I'll send to Guernsey for one of our own surgeons.'

'As you wish. Of course, by the time he gets here the patient will probably be dead.'

It stopped Wendel in his tracks. He stood before the desk glaring at Fuller. 'Are you saying it's serious?'

'The ulcer is perforated. Peritonitis is the problem. That could be fatal.'

Wendel was uneasy. He could not argue with Fuller and he had to make a decision. 'I can get a surgeon over in two hours.'

'That's optimistic, and you know it. You have to find one free, he has to fly here, get to the hospital, check the plate, prepare. I intend to operate within half an hour. Any delay now is dangerous.'

Wendel felt himself cornered. The responsibility would be in his hands. Fuller was extremely capable, everyone knew that. The problem was solved by Walter Schellenberg who opened the door quietly and stood behind Wendel; he closed the door and Wendel wheeled round. Schellenberg observed quietly,

'If Herr Fuller operates and something goes wrong wouldn't it be better for us if that happened under the hands of an Englishman rather than a German? If Lord Arden died due to delay and under a German surgeon the English might miscon-strue what had happened.'

It was so near the bone that Fuller was rattled.

The perception of the Standartenführer annoyed Wendel. 'It does not matter what the English think.' But it did. To those involved in the plot to depose Churchill it could matter a great deal. A peace initiative could collapse if Arden's friends weren't satisfied about the circumstances of his death. Schellenberg said nothing more. He got no pleasure from seeing Wendel squirm on the hook of his own obstinacy; it was far too serious a situation to score points.

To break the deadlock Fuller said, 'We're wasting time.' He kept his trembling hands in his pockets.

Wendel backed down ungraciously. 'All right. Go ahead. We've talked of dying, but he'd better live.' Then, more to get at Schellenberg than Fuller he demanded, 'What do you do for an anaesthetist, Doctor? Or do you do that too?'

'Kossl is sound. I can keep an eye on him. The other orderlies are well trained in theatre drill.'

There was nothing more to be said. Wendel stormed out and

Schellenberg gave a polite bow, but his eyes were reflectively cold as he left. Fuller stood behind the desk for a few minutes, his breathing slow and heavy. He took his hands from his pockets and held them out before him. His fingers were still trembling. They would be fine once he started, they always were, but he'd give anything for a drink right now. It was too late to change his mind and he did not want to. Nothing had changed.

The lamps burned down and his hands were very steady as he had expected them to be. With his big frame and wide shoulders he was able to mask much of what he was doing but he had to go through the usual routine. He could not rush it. Everything had to be normal. He could handle the orderlies, although one of them might be capable enough of remembering later if he was in any way careless. He had made them stand back a little, making it just that much more difficult for them. But his mind was screaming at him to stop. His hands worked efficiently, as if unconnected to his brain.

Kossl was the danger. He had a wide knowledge well beyond the ordinary demands of his rank. Fortunately he was totally engaged at the end of the table. It would be difficult for him to see precisely what Fuller was doing.

Meanwhile, Fuller continued, obscuring his movements as best he could. He could not safely ensure that Arden would die quickly, but he could almost guarantee that death would be painless. Some time later he stitched up, impressing the orderlies with his dexterity. It was over. His mind had gone blank. His hands still worked because he watched them, but there was no conscious connection with them. For a short time he felt as though he was outside his own body viewing a group of strangers during the final stages of an operation, and then it was over and Arden was being wheeled away.

Fuller peeled off his gloves and everyone believed the operation had been successful. Fuller believed nothing any more. He had guarded himself against feeling. Arden was dying and Fuller was dead inside. It could not be the same again. Ever. Lord Arden died peacefully while still unconscious, one hour later.

A numbed Fuller had gone home to Claudie. He hardly spoke

to her but he had never needed her more and she knew that something terrible had happened. The SS banged on his door at precisely twelve noon. Fuller calmed Claudie, tried to allay her fears but his own deadpan acceptance of the SS men only made her worse.

They drove him back to the hospital where a strained looking Wendel and an anxious Schellenberg were already waiting in Arden's room. The orderly withdrew with the SS men. Arden lay on his back. The sheet had not been pulled up over his face but his eyes were closed. The deep-lined face was relaxed.

Wendel could hardly bring himself to speak. He was greatly agitated, his thoughts already on the report he would have to make to Hitler. Schellenberg watched quietly as he always did. Wendel jabbed at the body. 'You had better explain, Doctor.'

Fuller stared down coldly, with no regret but for the loss within himself. He had deliberately killed a man who was in his care. Worse, he had breached the solemn oath he had taken when receiving his first medical degree. 'Perhaps his system couldn't take the shock. I can't account for it.' His voice was wavering. He should be going through the motions of confirming that Arden was dead but he could not. All he could cling to was the belief that he had stopped Arden's betrayal of his country and had prevented any subsequent treachery from Hitler.

'You will have to do better than that.'

'I can't do better without a post mortem.'

'You won't touch him.'

'I thought you wanted an answer.'

'I'm still waiting for one.'

'I can't give you one without an examination.'

'Then our doctors will do it.'

That was where it ended for him. Fuller had expected it. He made a last attempt to prevent it. He went to the bed, tested the heart then thoughtfully drew up the sheet. 'If you feel that is necessary, then you must do it. But understand this, Herr Wendel. Lord Arden was a countryman of mine. Churchill was our mutual friend. I wanted to operate only because I knew speed was essential. Peritonitis had set in but only in small measure. I wiped the whole of his peritoneum. There was no residue and if there had been it could not possibly have killed him so quickly. The operation was successful. I've no doubt you've already questioned Kossl and the others.'

He turned and faced Wendel squarely.

'I had every reason to save this man. I don't know why he was here. Certainly not to discuss prisoners with you; men of your calibre do not discuss such things. It was good enough for me to know that it had to be of the highest possible importance. I did everything I could. He was not a young man.' Fuller's voice was calm and carried conviction. He was giving the performance of his life. He went on: 'I understand your position and that of the Standartenführer. If it will make it easier for you both I will make a full, detailed report which you can send to both London and Berlin. I take full responsibility and will say so in writing. But I'm guilty of no neglect. On the contrary, no surgeon could have done more.' If he went on he would give himself away.

Wendel and Schellenberg exchanged glances. There were advantages in taking the easy way out, not stirring too deeply. And Fuller would soon be killed anyway. Get his report first. Then decide whether or not to bury Arden or cut him open.

'How soon can your report be ready?'

'I can work on it now. I will do one each in German and English. Should you decide to get them typed I would suggest the original goes to London.' He saw their suspicion. 'Certain people there can confirm my handwriting.'

'How do you propose we get a report to London, Doctor?'

Fuller showed surprise before realising that Wendel was so disturbed, so scared for himself that he could not provide a solution. Schellenberg was about to speak when Fuller replied, 'The problem is yours, surely? It will depend on how quickly you want to get it there. Neutral channels will presumably take some time. I would have thought that one of your planes could drop it over London together with whatever effects Lord Arden might have here.' He waited for them to damn the idea, to suggest another but they seemed as numb as he. He went back to his office, collected the X-ray plate and some notepaper, then went home.

When Fuller had gone, Wendel and Schellenberg at last found the necessity to liaise without rancour. Neither needed telling that Hitler would fly into a rage at the news of Arden's death. They all knew that Arden couldn't have been working alone; there were some powerful men in Britain supporting him, but it would be difficult to arrange a meeting with the next in line, if not impossible; Arden had played it very close and both Wendel and Schellenberg had limited information. That fact alone illustrated the degree of importance attached to the peace deal by Hitler.

By common consent the two emissaries went into Fuller's office and dismissed the guards. Wendel sat on the edge of the desk while Schellenberg used Fuller's chair. Ever-suspicious, Wendel said, 'Why isn't he doing his report here?'

Schellenberg shrugged: 'What does it matter as long as he does it? More importantly the doctor had a point about using a plane to London. Time is the essence if we are to come through with our skins intact. We dare not use radio, and diplomatic channels would take far too long. And security would be difficult. We want no leaks, no interceptions, no interpretations by outsiders. We can send a report to the Führer by air; hand to hand. But to whom do we send a report in London?'

Wendel stared at his colleague uncomfortably. 'Churchill?'

'That would be in order if Churchill, or a responsible subordinate knows that Arden came here. Obviously if he does he would not know the true reason. And we don't know what excuses Arden used to get here; they would have had to be convincing for someone to forge Red Cross documents for him.'

Wendel said uneasily, 'Perhaps only the Führer knows that.'

Schellenberg was thinking. 'The lines of communication were set up by Canaris.' Schellenberg hesitated. Personally he did not trust Canaris but in this he would have to trust the admiral, who must surely have acted under the Führer's direct orders. Thoughtfully, he said, 'While the doctor is doing his report we had better get off a guarded top priority signal to Canaris. He must know whether we should attempt to inform Churchill.'

'If Churchill receives a report what good will it do?'

'Surely I need not answer that. The news of his friend Arden's death will filter down soon enough. Somewhere along the chain one of Arden's confidants will hear of it, be informed even, and he will know what to do next.'

'Yes,' Wendel conceded. 'It *is* imperative for Arden's friends to find out quickly that he died a natural death. If they don't, they will think the worst and we will be blamed and everything will collapse.'

'Which, my dear Klaus, would not please the Führer. He must be told what has happened and that we are doing everything possible to retrieve the situation.'

Wendel said with complete honesty, 'I'm dreading telling him.'

Their latent hostility to each other had suddenly gone; they were both on the rack and they had to salvage the situation. They went over their hastily formed plans once more and then returned at speed to St Anne to implement them.

Admiral Canaris received the signal with extreme misgivings. The signal did not state that Arden was dead; it merely posed the question that in the event of his death, who should be informed in London so that the threads might be picked up? In such an eventuality would it be safe to inform Churchill who, Arden had stated, knew he was there? The signal had been designated for his eyes only and he had decoded it himself.

Was Arden ill? Arden's son was the obvious alternative but it would be far too dangerous to try to contact him directly; in the unfortunate event of Arden's death how could the son explain his knowledge of it? And he would not be able to follow his father's footsteps without displaying such knowledge. To inform Churchill was not a bad idea for he would at once see to it that Arden's son was advised. What also worried Canaris was that there was no mention of *how* Churchill was to be informed; he would have been alarmed had he known and would have realised the degree of panic and confusion that had sprung up between Wendel and Schellenberg. As the signal had come from Schellenberg he was not too surprised at its lack of information. He coded a reply.

Fuller had fought his way through a bout of deep depression out of necessity. But nothing could take away the inner blackness he felt. For once in their association he kept something back from Claudie and that in itself changed their relationship. Claudie did not know yet that Arden was dead. When she found out she might guess what had happened and if she did he had no idea what it might do to them.

She came up behind him as he bent over the table writing carefully, and placed a hand on his shoulder. She knew that what he was keeping from her must be something dreadful. She said, 'Why are you writing in milk?' But her mind was not on what he was doing but what he was hiding from her.

'It's an old schoolboy trick. You write in milk and it's invisible. You put heat to the paper and the milk burns and shows up.'

'And who's going to read it?'

'I'm trying to get a message to England.'

'To England?'

'Don't ask any more, Claudie. Forgive me but I must get on with this medical report.'

'You usually do those at the hospital.'

'Yes, but there's no milk there, my love.'

'I'll leave you alone to do it.' She kissed his cheek and noticed how cold it was. Her heart was banging with anxiety.

Major Carl Hoffman walked slowly past the house above the hospital, and wandered into the woods. He was alone as he always was on these periodic missions. Knowing exactly where to go, he did not hurry. It was early afternoon and the rain had held off.

He was mulling over the morning's work, making a mental note that the labour force needed strengthening. He reached his destination, followed the line of the bank and squatted on his haunches, poking with his swagger stick behind the bush. This was a matter of routine, his sole responsibility.

For so confident a man his posture became suddenly bizarre. He half rose, back arched, legs bent, jackboots reflecting shafts of filtering sun. He ripped the bush aside. My God. The marks of cutting were clear all round the edges of the door. He pulled the handle and the door opened easily. The turf had been deliberately cut. He went down the ladder, pistol in hand, a cigarette lighter in the other. No one there. He went back up and closed the door to examine it again.

Carl Hoffman straightened nervously, filled with alarm. His orders had been sealed, delivered by hand directly from Hitler's Adjutant General, General Schmundt. So to whom could he refer? Schmundt might be anywhere in Germany. And what

223

could Schmundt tell him but to find and deal with the culprit. He was already satisfied who the guilty party was but the doctor still had immunity.

Hoffman walked back to St Anne deep in thought. Whatever protection Fuller had, surely this was one issue that could not be ignored. He wondered who he should speak to. Hoffman's SS friend, Captain Jürgen Heyden, was too close to the Gestapo man Erich Kratz. Hoffman didn't like Kratz. He felt vaguely threatened by him; certainly he would not confide in him as Heyden did. Walking slowly back to his office he calmed a little. He would have to think very carefully about what he should do. Nobody yet knew what he had discovered so he had a little time. He needed that to make sure that he did precisely the right thing.

Erich Kratz was suffering something of the same frustration. The disappearance of the SS Sergeant Gerhard Holmeir worried him considerably and it could not be concealed for much longer. If it was reported he would be exposed to charges of trying to implicate Fuller who enjoyed the Führer's protection. Yet if he continued to ignore it he could see Captain Heyden being forced to make out a report which would undoubtedly involve him. Heyden would set out to save himself. It was true that the German army issue radio found at Fuller's house was sufficient, normally, to have the doctor shot, but this fact could not be used yet. It was strange, though, that enquiries had produced no reports of a missing radio, so where had the doctor obtained one?

When the news of the death of the Swede, Ardense, reached Kratz he immediately became interested. Fuller had lost no patients on whom he had operated; now he had lost a VIP. Instinct told Kratz that a solution to his problem was imminent; he could not explain why but the net was closing on Fuller. He would wait a little longer. As soon as he knew it to be right he would pounce.

Fuller personally took his reports to Wendel's quarters. He was shown up to Wendel's room and an orderly was sent to find Walter Schellenberg. Wendel had no intention of solely accepting responsibility; Schellenberg must be involved whether he liked it or not. By the time Schellenberg arrived, Wendel had read the two versions of Fuller's report.

Fuller had not been invited to sit down and he was standing by the window when the Standartenführer arrived. Wendel handed over the two foolscap sheets of well-spaced careful handwriting. 'I've read them both and I must congratulate the doctor on his translation. You will presumably find the German version easier to read.'

Schellenberg ignored the barb and sat down to read in silence. He studied both sheets while the others watched. Some minutes passed before he handed the sheets back to Wendel. He eyed Fuller thoughtfully. 'You've been very generous, Doctor. There are points there you need not have elaborated.'

'That's because I fully understand your position. I am not a hypocrite. I don't like what either of you stand for, but it's important to me that there's no misunderstanding over Lord Arden's death. It is purely a medical matter.' Fuller turned to Wendel. 'You have probably had time to reflect that it was lucky that I performed the operation and not one of your own surgeons. I can assure you the result would have been no different.'

Wendel did not reply. His mission was in danger of failure. He had not exaggerated when he had told Schellenberg that he was dreading putting in his report to Hitler. He held the sheets in his hands, gazing reflectively at them. It was all that was left of a dream. It was vitally important to get a report back to Berlin at once, well in advance of his own return. Perhaps Hitler's rage might by then have abated.

He glanced down again. Fuller had claimed in the report that both Wendel and Schellenberg had made every effort to ensure that Fuller was not baulked and that every help was given for a speedy operation from first to last. He could not have hoped for more.

It was still important to keep from English ears the fact that he and Schellenberg had come to confer with Arden: generously, their presence had been omitted from the English version. He looked at Fuller with fleeting compassion, feeling almost sorry for him. 'All right, Doctor. Get back to your duties.'

After Fuller had left, Wendel rose and checked the door. He

still held the bilingual reports and he waved them at Schellenberg before sitting down again. 'I have Lord Arden's personal items. His documents are, of course made out in his pseudonym. It will confirm to whoever issued them that he was here. We want no mystery about it, no repercussions. It's important Lord Arden's friends know what happened to him at the earliest possible opportunity. It will then be up to them to make contact. If we move now we may salvage the situation, and get it moving again before the Führer explodes.'

'We can't delay informing the Führer.'

'Of course not.' Wendel paused thoughtfully. 'I believe that the handwriting of the report in German is clear enough for it not to be typed. I don't like the idea of someone else here reading it.'

Schellenberg agreed. 'It gives it authenticity. We'll add our own notes, of course.'

After both men had carefully written and cross-checked their own observations on the back of Fuller's report, Wendel said, 'I'd better see Helke.'

Wendel left the room and went straight to the office of the island commandant. He demanded two long envelopes into one of which he inserted the English copy of Fuller's report and into the other the German copy which he addressed to Hitler. He handed the letter to the colonel.

'This must be flown to the Führer today. It will be taken by an officer who will hand it over personally. I want a sturdy packet to take this second envelope and these small documents.' Wendel pulled Arden's false papers from his pocket. 'These are to be dropped over central London by parachute before dusk.'

'They will need a container for weight. A small parachute will be needed. It will be difficult, Herr Wendel, to get a plane off today. I'll have to contact the Luftwaffe in Cherbourg.'

'I don't care who you contact, Obersturmbannführer. Just see that it's done. You have an airstrip here. Clear it and use it.'

'It is kept cluttered on the Führer's orders,' Helke said pointedly.

'It was cleared for us. Clear it again. Get a plane in from Cherbourg and get it over London. Use my authority but signal now.'

'Yes, sir. A high-altitude plane if it's not to be shot down. And high speed. Stripped of everything but fuel.'

'Just get it there. And don't drop the damned thing in the Thames. Daylight. I want it to be seen. The container is to be addressed clearly to Mr Winston Churchill.' Colonel Helke hastily reached for his telephone. He was wondering why the canister wasn't being sent more safely via a neutral country but he wasn't going to argue the point. Perhaps it would take too long. He was convinced he was dealing with a panicking fool.

Fuller waited for Claudie to go out with Blanco before he lit the fire. When it blazed up he dropped the X-ray plate on top of it, jumping back at the sudden burst of flame. It was late afternoon when he heard a plane droning in. Claudie came back just after. 'We're leaving this evening,' he said as soon as the door was closed.

'Are you first going to tell me what's happened to you. You've changed and I do not recognise you.'

'It might destroy us if I do. Claudie, I can barely think.'

'Can't you see that you're destroying us if you don't?'

As they held each other fiercely Blanco leaped jealously up at them. Over her head he said, 'Lord Arden's dead.' He felt her stiffen in his arms. 'I killed him.'

It was some time before she broke away. 'You think I am shocked? Yes, of course I am. But I know what it must have cost you to do such a terrible thing. The man was a traitor. And traitors deserve to die.'

'Not the way I did it. I've betrayed every trust given me.'

'Do you think he didn't?'

Fuller tenderly stroked her hair. 'You were always able to surprise me. I thought it might break us up.'

'You fool. Nothing could do that, George, nothing. Do they know?'

'Not yet. We go to the cellar at dusk.' He was uneasy then burst out. 'We'll have to put Blanco down. It will be impossible to take him with us.'

Claudie did not flinch. 'Blanco comes with us or I don't go. We cannot take away a life we saved.'

Fuller bent down and stroked the tail-wagging terrier. What did it matter, anyway? What difference could it make? He heard a plane again and ran outside but in spite of the clear sky he could see nothing. With a sinking feeling he realised that it was probably a second plane landing and not the first one taking off. He went back in, disappointed.

Claudie said perceptively, 'There's something else on your mind.'

'I must see Joachim Brocker again.'

'He's in danger and you're going to warn him?'

'I've already done that. I think he deserves the same chance as the rest of us.'

Claudie tilted her head coquettishly. It was a pose he knew so well; she was about to challenge him.

'And what chance is that? To be caught in the cellar instead of here?'

'At least I must put it to him.'

'It will not be fair to the others. He might find it prudent to inform if you tell him where it is.'

Fuller had considered the possibility. 'Claudie, he stuck his neck out for me. I couldn't have stopped Arden if Joachim hadn't helped.' Seeing her look of doubt he added: 'There's nothing that can save him; informing won't help. He might prefer to die in our company than on his own. They'll trump up something and put him before a firing squad.'

'Only you can decide whether you can trust him so far.'

'I have to be honest to myself. In view of what's happened I can't run out on him. I'd be as bad as Arden.'

Claudie shrugged. 'Have I ever tried to stop you doing something you believe in?'

'Repeatedly.' He smiled at her and thanked God for her.

He cycled over to Brocker's quarters and they walked the short distance out of St Anne to the tree where they had talked before.

There was no point now in diplomacy and there was no time for it. Claudie had placed a doubt in Fuller's mind but even so he realised there was nothing else he could do. He could not betray Brocker even if the reverse became true.

'Claudie and I are leaving shortly,' he said bluntly. 'We're going underground. I think you should come with us.'

Brocker had a cheroot halfway to his mouth and it stayed an inch from his lips. 'Underground? On *Alderney?*'

'I know a place. I told you you were in danger the moment I'd served my purpose. Now that Arden is dead that danger is very real right now.'

Brocker lowered the cheroot. 'What went wrong with Arden? He must have been far gone for you not to have saved him.'

'I killed him.'

'You *what*?'

'On the operating table. Deliberately.'

The cheroot snapped in Brocker's fingers. He threw it away, shocked and confused. 'You used me to get him there. You *lied* to me.'

'No. The powder did no more than I said it would. I wasn't sure what I'd do until I had him there.'

Brocker was too stunned to reply.

Fuller said, 'What I did doesn't alter anything except perhaps the method they'll use to execute us. And only then if they find out. From the beginning they knew they would have to seal it up tight as if nothing had ever happened. It's the big cover-up, Joachim. And we know much more than they think we know.'

Brocker recovered a little, and paced as if searching the ground. He stopped. 'This is unbelievable. You're such a patriot that you would cold-bloodedly kill a compatriot? I learn something new about you every day.'

'He was selling us out. Betraying his lifelong friend, Churchill.'

Brocker blew out his cheeks and raised his gaze to Fuller's. It was still difficult for him to believe what Fuller had told him. 'I could save myself by handing you over.'

'They'd still kill you. And you know it. Anyway, I've no doubt that whatever you do you'll do it for the right reasons. If you decide to join us I'll tell you where a guide will meet you to take you the rest of the way.'

'I've repeatedly warned you, George, that a day would come when our paths might separate. This is the day.'

'I've got to live with my conscience: I hope you can do the same. I'll still give you the meeting place.'

'Don't trust me with it.'

'I owe it to you. I owe you a great deal. I can't stop you bringing the troops with you, but I'd lose more than my life if you did that.'

'Don't rely on me. It's the fairest warning I can give.'

Fuller told him where to go and suggested a suitable time.

Brocker had regained his composure but he looked very tired as he said, 'Wherever you go underground on this island they'll find you. You know that.'

'But I don't intend to stay on it, Joachim.'

Wendel raged while the Luftwaffe major stood rigidly to attention in front of him. 'You are telling me you can't do it in daylight? What sort of pilot are you?'

Behind the pilot stood the navigator, equally rigid. Neither had expected this blistering attack. The major had encountered laymen in positions of power before but was stunned by the extent of Wendel's ignorance. He controlled his feelings and tried to explain.

'There are two possibilities, sir. An ME 109 can fly in at zero feet below the English radar screen. The weather has to be perfect and we understand that over England at the moment it is not. This is a single seater used for speed, but a pilot on his own would have navigational problems. It is extremely unlikely that he would reach London before being shot down. The alternative is what we intend to do. A twin-engined ME 110 with pilot and navigator to go in at night above the flak and drop the package down the flare shute over London. It is safer, more reliable.'

'But you won't know where the parachute will land?' Wendel tried to control his rage.

'No, sir. There could be quite a lot of drift. The flak will be about 26,000 feet. We would go in safely at 30,000. But the chute will land. Surely someone will find it?'

'Why can't you go in during daylight at high altitude?'

The major considered he had already explained. He said patiently, 'Because the radar would pick us up and the RAF would be able to see us to shoot us down. A single plane would not survive in daylight.'

'The canister could land anywhere. Can you be sure of a drop on London?'

'Of course. We will drop it centrally. I have one of the finest navigators with me.'

Wendel couldn't argue further. He had to settle for a guaranteed arrival at night somewhere against an extremely unlikely arrival by day. What also irked him was the way that Schellenberg had detached himself from the detail. The ME 110 took off just before complete darkness closed in. Clouds were already rolling across the island in south-westerly gusts.

The Messerschmitt had been airborne for perhaps thirty minutes when Major Carl Hoffman sought out Schellenberg as the man nearest to Hitler. It had taken him longer to reach a decision than he had anticipated but he was dealing with highly classified information in a situation in which he could now only lose. He saluted very correctly and quietly insisted that he spoke to Schellenberg privately.

In the Standartenführer's room Major Hoffman told his story and Schellenberg sank to a chair, grim-faced. The implications hit him one by one. His first reaction was to attempt to get the plane back but he quickly saw the advantages of letting it go. He sent for Wendel and when the diplomat arrived made Hoffman relate his story once more.

In the major's presence the discussion was limited. Wendel said to Hoffman, 'Find Fuller and bring him in. Get a list of everyone he's friendly with or has been seeing alone. And *get* the X-ray plate.'

Alone with Schellenberg Wendel said, 'Now we know why Lord Arden died. God, it's a nightmare. We'd better get our surgeons over at once to do an autopsy and to examine the X-ray. We must kill anyone he's contacted, anyone he might have told.'

Schellenberg was shaken to the core. Wendel was as well but he showed it less. The two men had found a common bond at last. Fear.

When the news reached Erich Kratz, the Gestapo chief could barely contain himself. He sent for Captain Heyden and they quickly discussed plans. It was no time for petty division. Major Hoffman made contact with them shortly after seeing the island commandant. The whole garrison had been placed at their disposal should they need it. None of the three had believed that they would.

For once in complete unison, the three men departed for Fuller's house with a detail of SS. They motored up in an open car. Their day of revenge had arrived.

17

Fuller and Claudie left their house as soon as it was dark. Their main problem was to keep Blanco quiet on the lead but Claudie was capable of exercising remarkable control over the terrier.

Kremple was on duty outside the safe house when they arrived. He stepped silently from his hiding place to acknowledge his presence; whoever was on duty carried one of the modern MP-38s. He followed them down the ladder. There was a high-spirited atmosphere in the cellar, as if everyone knew this might be their last night of relative safety. The very presence of Fuller and Claudie together indicated the strong possibility of trouble.

None of the others knew what had happened above ground. Fuller had to go through the agony of explaining about Arden again. And then he told them about Brocker. This met with an uncomfortable silence; he could not expect them to understand when even Claudie had difficulty to do so. Schroder said uneasily, 'Are you sure about this guy?'

'I've had better opportunity to get to know him than I have any of you.'

Schroder smiled, 'You don't mince words, do you? Okay, Doc, we're in no position to complain. You've made all the right moves so far. And I admire you for what you did to Arden; the bastard deserved it.'

Fuller took time to reply. 'I'll take care of Brocker. I'll meet him. If I'm wrong about him I'll be the first to know and I'll deal with him.'

Kremple had loaded the MP-18s they had stolen. The remainder of the 9mm ammunition was divided among them so that the box now contained only fuse wire, detonators and explosive.

Half an hour before Brocker was due they climbed up the ladder, each taking a machine pistol. Claudie stayed with Blanco in the cellar. Schroder took over the disposition of the defence and spread the meagre and strangely mixed force as widely as he dared. He had learned of every undulation, every possible point of cover around the farmhouse. He had been on the island only a short time yet he felt he had known no way of life other than that of being under constant threat.

This might be their one and only stand. It depended on Brocker, and only the doctor knew him. Kremple, Jacqui and Gorkov had kept their counsel over Fuller's action with Brocker; the doctor had done too much for them to complain, but they were secretly appalled, particularly the German and the Russian. Jacqui kept as near to Schroder as she could as if in him lay her best protection.

The half an hour of uncertainty was protracted as each one of them waited nervously, listening, watching. The night was still cloudy, the wind fresh and rifling through grass and gorse. And it was chilly. They heard a movement at exactly 8.45.

Fuller recognised Brocker's faint silhouette. Even in outline the German captain appeared quite relaxed, what little light there was picking out the polished peak of his cap. Fuller waited. Five machine pistols were pointed at Brocker; his posture gave no indication that he sensed it. Still Fuller waited. All of them were listening for the faintest sound. Had Brocker brought anyone with him?

After standing still for almost five minutes, Brocker turned round slowly. He faced the direction of the farmhouse, out of sight of his position. His loud whisper cut the air as effectively as a warning siren. 'George, if you're out there you'd better show yourself damned quick. The whole garrison is searching for you.'

Fuller came scuttling down the rise. Brocker wheeled and once he had recognised Fuller's shape said, 'If you have a place to hide we'd better get there now.'

Fuller waved his gun high and the faint movement was seen by the others who came from every direction. Brocker was startled at seeing strangers, one of them a slip of a girl.

'Follow me.' Fuller led the way. The others fanned out.

In the cellar Gorkov lighted the lamp and Brocker said, 'I think you'd better put that out. The island will soon be crawling. The alarm's gone up. Schellenberg has given instructions to Major Hoffman to arrest you, George. And me. And your outlying patients. The poor devils stand little chance.

Hoffman, Kratz and Heyden have been waiting to get you for a long time. They could only just have missed you. Make no mistake, they will have the island combed.' Before the light was extinguished, he tried to see who was there. The escapee from Sylt was obvious, but the girl and the two men, one of whom was in a German officer's uniform came as a big surprise.

'There's not a lot they can do at night; they can't use lamps,' Fuller observed.

'Don't be so sure. They'll do everything they can and dawn will bring out every soldier on the island. Sylt will be closed until we are found.'

'I'm glad you came, Joachim. I thought you would. I'll introduce you to the others. You'll have to work on voices.'

After the introductions, bizarre in the blacked-out cellar, Brocker said, 'It's perhaps better that I don't know your reasons for deserting, Sergeant Kremple. As for Oberleutnant Schroder, I don't know what to say except that you speak colloquial German faultlessly.' And then to Fuller, 'You've been up to far more than I realised but I suppose I should not be surprised. I must confess that this is a most unlikely resistance group.'

Kremple nervously handed Brocker a machine pistol; everyone now had one.

There were footsteps overhead less than half an hour later, and the group were silent. Suddenly Claudie panicked because she could not find Blanco who was unusually quiet, except for a suspicion of a whimper. Gorkov whispered. 'I have him. Don't worry.' Where the ceiling had burned slivers of flashlight penetrated cracks in the floorboards. Footsteps raced up the stairs above them, voices called, arms clattered. That torches were being used so freely showed the measure of alarm.

Sounds of the house being searched were clear but when the shed was entered the thump of jackboots was almost deafening. Seven submachine pistols aimed at the trapdoor. The first soldier through would be riddled.

It did not happen. The crate nailed to the trapdoor formed an effective screen. Noise of the search gradually faded. The last footstep receded. The silence was painful then, for no one in the cellar was willing to speak too soon. Eventually Claudie said in a breathless whisper, 'I'll take Blanco now.'

They could hear Gorkov rustling but he said nothing and there was no sound from Blanco. Worried, Claudie said, 'What is happening? Curse this darkness. Blanco, where are you?'

The terrible, strained voice of Gorkov came like a lament, 'Madam, he does not move.'

'What are you saying?' Claudie scrambled across the floor towards the Russian. '*What* are you saying?'

Gorkov pushed the terrier out to her. 'He is here.'

Claudie groped, touched the fur, took hold gently and pulled Blanco to her chest. No one could see what was happening but after a few moments her sobs filled the cellar.

'Get the light on.' It was Fuller, concerned for Claudie.

'No. They may have left someone upstairs.'

'They would have heard us by now.' Fuller struck a match, lit the lamp. In the dim light Claudie, on her knees, clutched the dead terrier to her, rocking to and fro. Fuller turned to Gorkov and immediately bit back what he was about to say. The Russian was almost as distraught as Claudie. 'I held a blanket over it. I had to, the dog was whimpering. It was just to muffle him, no more. I swear to you, madam.'

Claudie did not reply. She had her face buried in Blanco's small body. Fuller realised, with horror, that the wheels had gone full circle. He had deliberately tried to smother Blanco when they had first found him; now the unfortunate Gorkov had finished the job accidentally.

Everyone was silent, upset over Claudie's distress. Brocker said gently to her, 'Terrible as it is, my dear, it is for the best. We could not have survived with Blanco; he would have been a constant risk. Be brave, Claudie. I feel as you do. George, all of us do. We know what he meant to you.' It took all his strength to keep the catch from his voice; then was the moment when those still suspicious of him accepted him.

Fuller moved over and cradled Claudie. She would not let go of Blanco. He wiped her eyes and face. 'Joachim's right. Claudie. We really are at war now. We had better get used to it. I loved him too.'

Progress was painfully slow. They had to keep close to the coastline to head south-west to avoid the three main central gun sites. Their nocturnal excursions had always been silent and skilful but now they were forced to stop frequently for the island was alive with sound. They could hear distant voices, see the glow of torches. In the frenzy of the search blackout precautions were being ignored.

They had set off at 10.00, reckoning that the whole farmhouse area had been cleared. Kremple had donned one of the spare uniforms, so that now three of them were in uniform. There were resistance nests and light-flak emplacements between the coast and the major sites. Schroder still had his compass.

Between them they probably knew every established pitfall. To avoid some of these they had to go nearer to the airport than was safe; there was grave danger of arousing the dogs at Sylt. The wind was luckily in their favour. Fuller, after his many excursions and medical rounds over the last two years or so knew virtually every out-of-town dwelling. Instinct prodded memory to warn him as they approached them. With luck and skill they could cope with these hazards, but there was no way they could anticipate the pattern of the increasingly massive search.

Major Carl Hoffman, Erich Kratz and Captain Heyden had combined under a common need to quarter the island systematically. The emergency had placed all sections of the forces on duty. Beds lay empty that night. Fuller and his party were hoping to pass through an area before or after it had been searched. While they were still on the south coast they were forced to climb down a cleft on the upper slopes of a cliff and cling to the gorse face-down with the rocks and sea below them, to avoid a string of soldiers advancing like beaters in a shoot.

Patience and caution were their common denominator. Their ears and eyes were attuned to night activity and they had in their favour the cunning of the hunted.

They started to cut across the island north of the airport and now had to travel slightly north-west in order to avoid the massive naval batteries being built in front of the small peninsular of Fort Clonque; the west coast was their destination. During one of their many pauses Brocker estimated that there were nine emplacements of various kinds which would either flank or obstruct their progress. And they would still have to half-circle the naval battery after that.

The two women were superb. Claudie had thrown herself into the long night walk as the only way to put out of her mind the little dog she had just lost. Heartbroken, she still responded to the others; she would not pull them down because of her grief. Jacqui felt that she still had much to make up for her past behaviour to Schroder on whom she was becoming so dependent; she would not let him down again. The weakest member of the party was Gorkov. He made no complaint, but it was a miracle that he kept going. Perhaps suffering had become so much a part of his life that he remembered nothing else. He simply kept moving when the others did. Fuller, Schroder, Brocker and Kremple showed no distress. Their determination was a force on its own, keenly felt by the others and probably Gorkov's main support.

After four hours of tortuous movement, much of it on all fours, of flattening and rising, hiding and waiting, of dodging patrols, of sometimes impudently and with incredible nerve following them, of superb fieldcraft, they reached Fort Clonque. They were exhausted but quietly excited at getting so far.

They rested above the most southerly of the twin quarter-moon beaches. From there they could just see the distant shape of the old fort at the end of the peninsular. The problem now was how to approach along the narrow strip of road before it spread out to the fort area. They knew that the beaches were mined. But they believed they had breathing space in which to work things out. It was their first mistake.

They were trapped by an infantry force approaching the fort from behind them. Voices, flashlights, the broken footsteps, were all too familiar. They had nowhere to go except into the arms of the fort garrison.

Perhaps the relief of reaching the fort, of outwitting the searchers, had lulled them at a critical time. It did not matter; they were caught off guard. A beach lay below them but they couldn't reach the doubtful refuge of the sea through a minefield. The small peninsular, its waist like a squeezed balloon, stuck out to the left flanked by rocks. A strong obnoxious smell drifted with the wind from the base of the rocks. Fuller recognised it all too well.

The line of searchers drew nearer. There were sentries at the fort and a contingent inside it. Fuller saw only one chance. He signalled the others and worked his way down the slope to the end of the small bluff above the beach near the fort road. The smell was stronger as he lowered himself on to the rocks and down as near to the restless sea as he dared. He crawled over dead bodies. He reached behind to grasp Claudie's hand, stumbling as the number of corpses increased. They were cast-offs from the naval site, dumped or fallen in various states of decomposition. When he had created enough room for the others he stopped and began to bury himself in the misery of human flesh, keeping his gun under him. One by one the others did the same, knowing it was their only chance. They lay there shielded by the stinking dead.

The line of searchers came up slowly, ringing the ground above the beach. Flashlights covered the coast, swung along the peninsular, over the rocks. Footsteps pounded along the peninsular road, and voices called to the sentry.

The little group lay prone in increasing horror. A body at the side of Fuller moved. The poor sod isn't dead, he thought. He had an arm round it yet dared not take it away. But it was far worse than that. They were all being covered by slithering creatures they could not shake off. Slimy tentacles gripped legs, and wet bodies passed over side-turned faces. Pincers dug deep into flesh and the two women had to bite their lips to avoid screaming; the place was crawling. *They were being eaten alive.*

Fuller realised what was happening but it was not the moment to explain to the others. The gradual and persistent pile-up of corpses had attracted a huge colony of octopus, crab and lobster who were feeding off them as they lay there. Jacqui vomited but somehow clung on without moving in spite of the added infliction of her own sick. Gorkov survived the terrifying experience best. They could do nothing but wait and suffer, to bite their lips to stifle pain and horror and to stay absolutely still while the lights passed over them. Brocker, Kremple and Schroder, because of their uniforms, had been forced to bury into the putrid mess more deeply than the others. They had to resist the mad urge to jump up and break free from the mass of sea-scavengers – until, eventually, the troops finally departed. It had taken a lifetime.

Schroder moved first. He came up behind Fuller who was

just rising. They tried to shake off the creatures still clinging to them. The others now rose, plucking frantically, kicking out in revulsion, the women half-sobbing. Schroder found Kremple and whispered in his ear; he then asked Fuller to keep the others quiet. Schroder and Kremple climbed over corpses and slime to reach the rocks along the side of the fort. They cleaned themselves down as best they could but the smell of putrescence clung to them. Schroder peered round the corner of the fort wall. The sentry was standing some hundred feet back in front of the big double gates.

Schroder gave a nod and the two men stepped on to the road. They marched loudly towards the gates in step, Kremple slightly behind Schroder. The sentry, at first wary, saw the outline of two uniformed figures and brought his rifle up to an on guard position. He made his challenge and then saw that the nearest figure was an officer.

Schroder sensed the sentry's uncertainty but reasoned that he would stick to routine.

'Halt! Who goes there?'

'Stand to attention, you fool. There's an emergency on.' Schroder's command was like a whiplash; the sentry was well aware there was an emergency on; only recently practically the whole fort garrison had been turned out.

The sentry sprang to attention as Schroder drew nearer. The light was bad but good enough for him to pick out Kremple slightly behind and to one side of the officer. Where could they have been, the smell from them was terrible? His suspicions were just rising when Schroder and Kremple rushed him.

Schroder grabbed his throat two-handed while Kremple stopped the gun from coming up, then eased behind the sentry, hooked a leg round the sentry's shins to stop him kicking and clung to his arms while Schroder strangled him.

They lowered the dead soldier carefully, removed two stick grenades from his belt and then heaved the body on to the rocks to join the mass already there. Kremple flung the rifle after him.

Getting the inflatable rubber dinghies from their protected niche in the forecourt was relatively simple.

Ideally, the dinghies would be better launched from the beach, but that was impossible. The men callously arranged a string of corpses to form a cushion on the rocks so as to prevent the rubber being pierced and for everyone to climb over more easily. They inflated the dinghies, and with difficulty, cast off. The tide tried to take them straight back, but with Schroder, Kremple and Jacqui in one with the ammunition chest, Fuller, Brocker, Gorkov and Claudie in the other, they gradually pulled away, the noise of oars covered by the constant stirring of the sea against rocks and shore. They had about six miles to go to reach Casquettes Lighthouse. On so treacherous a sea and in such heavily laden dinghies even that distance could be too great. But whatever happened to them now would be better than staying on the island. Brocker had already warned them that the lighthouse was manned by an infantry unit.

Baling soon became essential; they used hands as scoops to keep the water level down. They were already close to the sealine but their weight gave some stability. The currents were dangerous, but they were lucky the wind was moderate.

But luck was relative. The dinghies pitched and tossed, swayed and yawed, slid down waves at a sickening angle. There was no time for sea sickness, no time for anything but to keep at the oars, bale, balance and sometimes to gaze up at a wave and wait for the crash. Schroder periodically tried to read the compass. If they didn't reach the lighthouse the dinghies would not hold out for long.

They clung, each battling against the waves to keep the dinghies from capsizing. They were soaked and exhausted but somehow kept afloat. The immense relief of being off the island sustained them; once it had all seemed so impossible. Occasionally, they caught a flash of light from land and they knew the search was continuing. Time and distance became meaningless but the currents started to help them. They struggled on with flagging strength. All they knew was that it was still very dark and dawn was some way off. They were swept past the lighthouse and they saw the dark long shape of the rocks and the froth swirling around them; the towers loomed higher up. They had a wild sense of freedom as they came in towards the ghostly smudge of the landing stage.

There was still no respite as they fought to hold the dinghies on course. Then luck ran out for them again. The nervous infantry unit were geared to the possibility of a British commando raid. Isolated as they were, they had long accepted that they could be a tempting target. The lighthouse had become the least popular of island duties. A light came sweeping down and picked up Fuller's dinghy almost at once, the huge beam breaking across the whitecaps.

The blinding light took the group by surprise. Fuller's dinghy was isolated, the other some distance to starboard. The reaction of all four was the same; arms shot up to cover eyes. Brocker, quick to think, rose shakily, hoping his uniform would save then and he waved wildly. The bluff had no chance of succeeding. Schroder was also quick to react in the other dinghy but he did so quite differently. He rose, legs spread for balance, gun tucked under his arm. He fired in a wide sweep, knowing that his aim was unsteady. The beam disappeared in spectacular fashion with the whine of bullets and the crash of broken glass.

The flash of Schroder's gun pinpointed his position and Fuller's was already known. Both crews realised it and strained at the oars like madmen. Machine gun fire came bursting at them but the darkness and the awkward angle of fire upset the aim and the dinghies were now out of sight and seeking the shelter of the rock base.

The dinghies were compartmentalised; if one section was punctured another would keep afloat, but with the amount of fire power still pumping out at them they could not keep up for long.

The currents helped to land them. They crashed in. It no longer mattered if the dinghies were holed. The men grabbed at rock and held steady while the women got ashore, crouched, getting what cover they could against the continuing hail of bullets spraying out from the gunners above. Another light came on, sweeping the sea where they'd been, not finding them, pulling in towards the base but finally defeated by the steep angle as the beams could dip no further. Reflection from the light cast protective shadows. The men clambered up the rocks to join the women.

Gunners in the upper windows started firing down with the more flexible machine pistols. Again the steep angle and the difficulty of aiming from a height helped Fuller's party. They dispersed round the base to make themselves difficult to hit. It was an advantage that could not last. If the groups were to survive they had to capture the lighthouse; staying outside meant being picked off at leisure. They had lost the element of surprise which had been essential to success and there were signs now that the soldiers were becoming more co-ordinated after their early panic.

As the group spread out round the base an infantry unit burst from an annexe to the main tower. Gorkov was the first to be cut down. He died instantly, falling back over the rocks, a skeleton sliding into the sea to a death he had known would come. From the other side, Schroder saw them come out and, before Gorkov hit the water, he was spraying bullets in a cold rage.

Schroder accounted for a good number before he was hit himself. He sank to his knees as Kremple took over Gorkov's place and the infantry were caught in their crossfire and at first confused by another German uniform. Schroder kept firing until he was hit again and finally fell back against the wall, still on his knees, the gun in his hand while he tried to raise his head. Kremple was firing in controlled bursts before he took a volley in the chest and fell back on to the rocks. Fuller and Brocker split up and took over from Schroder and Kremple, who between them had done such a magnificent job that what was left of the infantry was totally demoralised. Two more were shot down and the remaining three held up their arms in surrender.

Out of twenty infantry, thirteen were dead and four wounded. Fuller and Brocker forced the three fit men to drag the wounded back into the building. They switched on the light, and at gunpoint demanded that all arms be thrown out. By this time a highly nervous, but armed Claudie had joined them. Fuller demanded the key and locked them in.

With the intervention of the main unit, fire from above had stopped and Fuller and Brocker made the most of the time of confusion, slinging the captured guns into the sea. Keeping close to the wall they found Jacqui with her arms round Schroder. She wasn't crying but cradling him, his bloodied body against hers. They were not sure whether he was dead and they were afraid to ask her.

Brocker crept round to find the ammunition box and was inspired to bawl loudly in German, 'We have casualities but we killed most of them. The others are captured. Open the main door.'

He was partially successful. Those in the lighthouse weren't sure so held their fire. It could last for only so long. Brocker fumbled in the ammunition box, produced the ammonal, gun cotton, fuses, wire and fuse matches. With Fuller's help he laid charges against the solid main door. Because explosive takes the least line of resistance they dragged dead soldiers to pack them over the charges. Brocker lit the fuse. They ran back, warned Claudie and Jacqui. The garrison must have guessed something was happening; they started firing again, but it was sporadic and blind.

The door blew off with an enormous flash and explosion. Dead soldiers were blasted to bits and hurled into the sea. Fuller squeezed Jacqui's arm gently. From the way she responded he knew that Schroder was dead. She unhooked the two stick grenades from Schroder, kissed his forehead with great tenderness, stroked his face as if they had been passionate lovers, then, before anyone could move, raced round to the door and was inside before they could stop her.

She stood in the hall, composed and white-faced. She pulled a pin out with great calmness, listening to the clack of boots on the stairs, and the voices from the room facing her. As the door opened she tossed a grenade underhand. She was helped by the complete surprise of the two soldiers who first appeared; they could not believe what they saw and were blown to bits a fraction after.

The blast blew Jacqui back into Fuller and Brocker, who had just come dashing in, and the three were thrown off balance; Claudie, just behind, missed this. Jacqui, her face streaming blood from a shrapnel gash, coolly rose, stepped forward and tossed the second grenade at the group racing round the curve of the stairs. She took the full impact with them and fell for the last time, with the dead and wounded tumbling in an untidy, screaming heap down the stairs towards her.

Fuller and Brocker crawled forward as they landed. Another group came round the bend and opened fire. Brocker crumbled as a leg caught a bullet and Fuller fell back with a shot in the stomach. Claudie stood over Jacqui, then, seemingly adopting her spirit she stepped through to finish off the three still coming down the stairs.

The noise of firing stopped as she lowered her gun but the

screaming continued. She looked down at the carnage, at the slight, unrecognisable Jacqui, then at the soldier still screaming and holding on to what had been his stomach. She put him out of his misery with a short burst and the silence was unbearable.

Claudie looked for Fuller and found him lying against the wall. He too was holding his stomach but he was not ready to be put out of his misery. She went to him, stepping over the dead, undid his clothes, heard a noise and spun round, gun in hand, ready to shoot. It was Brocker, dragging himself across the floor, pushing bodies away with his good leg. He propped himself up beside Fuller, kept a hand on his gun and an eye on the stairs. With his free hand he cut away at the bloody patch of his trousers.

Claudie's hands trembled as she ripped off Fuller's shirt.

'Don't die on me, cheri. Not now.'

Without looking up, Brocker said, 'Don't make him talk, Claudie. He's too tough to die on you, and far too obstinate. He will stay alive to spite everyone.' He looked up then. 'When you've plugged his holes will you give me a hand with this?'

When they were roughly patched up the shock hit Claudie. She gazed around in disbelief. The floor was a patchwork of bodies and blood. On the bottom stairs two men lay sprawled. She couldn't raise her eyes to the higher level where the grenade had taken its worst toll; or to the open door of the room at the back. It was all too horrible to face. She wanted to get away, to be privately sick, but she wouldn't leave Fuller or Brocker, and neither could move. Through the open main door the sea splashed and sucked at the rocks and the light streamed out into the night. What did it matter? Who cared now? She said, 'Do you think there are more upstairs?'

Brocker shook his head wearily. 'Who knows?' His hand crept back to his gun. Fuller, his stomach burning, had barely spoken, to conserve energy and to avoid more pain, but now he said, 'Tell her the truth, Joachim.'

Brocker held out a hand to take one of Claudie's as she squatted in front of them. Loud enough for Fuller to hear, he said, 'Don't let him see I'm holding your hand. He's a difficult man.' She wasn't taken in by the forced lightness. She knew what to expect then. 'It makes little difference whether there are men upstairs or not. If we'd taken the place by surprise we could have got away with it. We could have held out for a while. It didn't turn out that way. Whether they will have heard the firing on Alderney I don't know. I would expect the sentries on the Fort Clonque ramparts to have heard the explosions at least. In any event someone would have sent a signal. At dawn they'll send out troops from Guernsey. The Luftwaffe will come, and the navy from Cherbourg. We are two wounded men and one woman. What can we do, Claudie? What can we do?'

She raised his hand, kissed it and then released it gently. 'Poor Jacqui.' She shuddered. 'Rod, Max, Vassily. Oh my God. What had they done?' She turned to Fuller. Without being dramatic she said, 'It might have been better if we had gone with them, we are as good as dead now.'

18

Colonel Helke should have organised the search himself but Schellenberg and Wendel had taken over from him. They had also taken his office and before them now were the men whom they considered mattered most. Major Carl Hoffman, Captain Jürgen Heyden and Erich Kratz. Schellenberg fed upon the hungry look on the faces of these three men. They wanted Fuller more than anyone.

Schellenberg stood behind the desk and glanced at a signal slip in his hand. 'Casquettes has been raided and there are many killed. A sentry and two dinghies are reported missing from Fort Clonque. The doctor and the traitor Brocker must be involved.' He glanced at the slip again. 'It is clear that there were several in the raid, so the doctor has help.' He glared at the men in front of him. 'How can that happen on an island this size *under your very eyes?*'

Hoffman said uncomfortably, 'We weren't allowed to interfere with the doctor in any way, Standartenführer.'

'You mean you couldn't watch him without interfering? You useless fools.' Schellenberg snarled. 'Get as big a force as you need and get out to that lighthouse now. I want the doctor and whoever is with him. Tonight.'

Colonel Helke, who had been standing in the background, stepped forward. 'With respect, sir, we must wait till dawn. We haven't the right kind of craft here and the currents are treacherous. I will raise Guernsey and have them ready and contact the Luftwaffe also. We can be ready to move at first light.'

Schellenberg could hardly contain himself and Helke added quickly, 'We don't know how many of our own people are still alive there. But even if the doctor has survived where could he possibly go? If we want to avoid another fracas let's go in at dawn.'

Schellenberg did not like being reminded that there had already been a fracas. He glanced at Wendel who was only too

247

glad to leave everything to Schellenberg and was secretly delighted to see the cracks appear in the man of iron. Schellenberg glared icily, 'You'd better get them. My God, you had better.'

The parachute container dropped by the Luftwaffe major landed on the flat roof of a building near the Duke of York's barracks in Chelsea. The noise of the landing behind him gave the soldier on roof duty a shock and he fell flat on his face, instinctively waiting for the blast.

When he was satisfied with the time lapse he went forward, found the parachute spread out and caught up in pipes running across the roof. Seeing the container he thought it was some kind of incendiary. They had all heard the solitary plane droning overhead and the night fighters trying to track it. He went down and made a report to his officer. The building was evacuated and the bomb squad called in.

It took them a little time to decide it was not some new form of booby trap. They had, of course, noticed that the container was boldly addressed to Winston Churchill but the Germans were apt to scrawl that on any bomb. When they had examined the contents an officer decided that they should be sent by hand to the Prime Minister.

He received them at 11.0 p.m. that night, only a few hours from the time the canister had been dropped.

He read the carefully worded and self-incriminating medical report. It came as a shock to discover that an old friend had died but the whereabouts surprised him. He sent for George Fuller's father, and for Major General Sir Stewart Menzies who would be the most likely to know what Lord Arden was doing on the captured British island of Alderney. Later, Fuller senior confirmed that it was his son's handwriting, though much neater than usual, but it was Menzies who insisted that the report be placed with a cryptographer; his men had picked up the transmissions to Canaris and the Luftwaffe and, with the German code broken, had quickly wondered what had happened on the island.

It took less than an hour for the expert to find the real message written in milk, and it was startling.

'The medical report is rubbish. I killed Arden because he was arranging a peace deal with the Nazis. Hitler intends to use Alderney as a base HQ for an invasion of Britain the moment the Americans have left our shores and while our troops are scattered in Africa and the Far East. If you need to know more we are attempting to reach Casquettes Lighthouse tonight.'

Menzies had not known what to expect, but certainly not such a massive betrayal as this. He knew that the Prime Minister would find the attempt to sell him and the country out exceedingly hard to take. But he had to be told.

Fuller, Claudie and Brocker were picked up by a strong British commando force shortly after 5.0 a.m. The two men had lost a good deal of blood but Claudie had followed Fuller's instructions on what to do to stem the flow. They were dozing uncomfortably when the commandos raced in, silently and heavily armed. They reached for their guns in a reflex action but were stopped by a cheerful cockney voice saying, 'Touch them and we'll blow your bleedin' 'eads off.' Brocker was the first to respond; he was in uniform. Fuller managed, 'Welcome, Sergeant. The German officer is with us.'

The sergeant looked at the carnage about him. There was respect in his voice as he said, 'If you took care of this lot and those outside, you did well, guv.'

'Our friends took care of them and *they* didn't do so well. Get us off this bloody rock, Sergeant. Get us home. The Germans will be here any moment.'

Fuller never understood why there were always two sentries outside the door of the private hospital ward; he did not believe his life to be in danger. Since the operation, which his father had refused to perform on account of emotional ties, Fuller had received a succession of visitors. One of them was a clergyman who performed the wedding ceremony for Claudie and himself. Brocker had received special dispensation to be best man from the confines of a wheelchair, and, with Fuller still in bed, the ceremony had not been without humour. The small room had been crammed.

Once Fuller was fit enough to endure interrogation, intelligence men came and went asking the same questions over and over. One of them was a dignified American who wanted to know about Schroder. There were times when Fuller found questions emotionally difficult to answer.

He learned that the Hon. James Arden had now inherited his father's title but had been interned on the Isle of Man with other British doubtfuls. He had one visit from Winston Churchill who neither thanked him nor condemned him for what he had done, but Fuller strongly suspected that it was with some difficulty that the Prime Minister hid his distress over the treachery of a family friend. Claudie, of course, was a daily visitor.

The news of Lord Arden's death could not be kept secret. A short piece appeared in the 'national' press to the effect that he had died of natural causes while in the service of his country. It was better to avoid scandal at a time of low morale, and there was little fear of contradiction from Fuller or James Arden. Fuller was, in fact, asked for his word that the tragic events on Alderney, would never be publicised by him and he signed a document which was a completely false and innocuous account of what had happened there.

After the wedding Joachim Brocker was returned to the PoW camp near Aylesbury where Claudie was able to visit him once or twice when he was able to use crutches. Fuller intended to go with her as soon as he was fit again. He never had the opportunity.

Joachim Brocker was killed in the camp by several blows on the back of his head. It was alleged that a fellow officer had murdered him but the officer was never identified nor the weapon found.

When Fuller was told, he was shattered that Brocker had escaped to be slaughtered in this way. And he suffered a deep loss for a true friend. Yet, distraught as he was, he began to ask searching questions. It was suggested to him that word had been secreted from Germany to a dedicated group of fanatical Nazis imprisoned at Aylesbury but Fuller would not accept the premise. It was too soon. From the beginning he had fought in vain to keep Brocker out of a PoW camp but he had not believed that his friend stood the risk of being murdered in one; not by other prisoners, unless word had been deliberately leaked to them that Brocker had deserted the German army and had killed a few compatriots on the way.

Fuller and Claudie could not be consoled, and they did not believe. Fuller became deeply bitter; his word was his bond and it always had been. The same was true of Brocker, a trait both men had identified in each other. The last betrayal had been performed. Fuller was in no doubt as to who had closed Brocker's mouth forever and his disillusion was total. Brocker need not have died and there were moments when Fuller was sorry that he had not died with him. It was left to Claudie to hold him together at such times as she had done throughout all their troubles.

Epilogue

The course of the war began to change in the middle of October with the battle of El Alamein and the holding of Stalingrad, and it swung in favour of the Allies as it gathered momentum into 1943.

The work on the Alderney fortifications continued throughout the war as though Hitler could not accept that he would never use it. The slave labour increased and so did the atrocities and deaths.

The bunker was destroyed on the 2nd June 1944 but traces of the tunnel still remain today.

Major Carl Hoffman was hanged in front of forty thousand Russians at Kiev in the Autumn of 1945.

Admiral Canaris was hanged at Flossenburg prison in April 1945. General Oster died alongside him.

Walter Schellenberg died of cancer on 31st of March 1952 at the Clinica Fornaca, Turin.

Klaus Wendel was killed in an air accident in the spring of 1943 at a time when he was much out of favour with Hitler.

Eric Kratz was imprisoned for fifteen years for war crimes during the Nuremberg Trials. He died in 1958.

No records can be found of SS Captain Heyden.

Claudie and George Fuller returned to France immediately after the war and still live there. George Fuller never performed another operation or revisited Britain.

Lord James Arden is still alive and as self-effacing as his father before him. He lives in England with his wife and they have two sons and a daughter, all of whom are married.